INTENDED BY THE ROSE

This is a work of fiction. Similarities to real people, places, or events are entirely coincidental.

INTENDED BY THE ROSE

First edition. October 2, 2022.

Copyright © 2022 Abby McCarthy.

Written by Abby McCarthy.

To Kayla, you're beautiful inside and out.

Note to Reader

Dear Reader,

Thank you so much for being right here in these pages. This book picks up exactly where Fated Under the Moon, Book One in the Destined by the Fates Series, ends. You should read that book before exploring this story. Please enjoy.

Prologue Ryker

I'd gone to bed without making love to my mate. My dreams were fitful. I tossed and turned. Something wasn't quite right, but I couldn't quite pull myself out of the dazed sleepiness.

She was close. I felt her heat.

Then she wasn't.

"Ariel!" I roared her name in my sleep, feeling her loss but unable to get to her.

I couldn't wake. My mind was a haze of going in and out from complete darkness to hearing a conversation around me. I struggled to listen in hopes I could find out what was happening. It was all too jumbled.

Was I dreaming?

"Why isn't he waking?" Reece asked. This wasn't the first time I heard my family arguing.

"My guess is *she* did this to him." Bitterness and disrespect coated Grey's words, and I didn't like it. I couldn't do a damn thing to defend my mate.

"You all read the letter. She didn't mean to do it, and I'm sure she has no idea Ryker's still sleeping," Mindy spoke in a low tone, trying to diffuse Grey.

"I like her as much as you do, Mindy. But I still can't help but wonder if she was right. She is better off learning about herself away from us," Micah added.

"First off, I like her just fine, but he's our brother—our leader. If he doesn't wake, then what? Secondly, they're mates. He's asleep, and she's off doing Lord knows what. Ryker is going to lose his mind. And lastly, if the other pack members find out ... We're in some serious trouble. Raymon will jump at the opportunity to take over as pack leader. This stays with us. Not a single word," Reece ordered.

"Brogan should know," Grey said.

"I'll tell Dad," Mindy replied. "But Reece is right. If anyone finds out he's asleep, it could disrupt the entire pack.

"What about the games?" Micah asked.

"Everything should go on as planned," Reece replied.

"How were things last night with the bar, Grey?" Mindy questioned.

"It was fine. They closed early as we planned. The rain helped make it seem like no big deal."

"Make sure you stay on top of it," Reece ordered.

"I will."

"I'll work on the games," Micah added.

"Why don't you guys get started? I'll sit with Ryker for a bit and set up some stones, then I'll talk to Dad."

"Sounds good, sis," Reece said, his voice drifting off.

"Are you sure you're feeling all right today?" Grey asked Mindy.

"I feel fine. Seriously, it's not her fault."

"If you say so, love."

"Go. Seriously. I'm fine."

A few minutes of silence passed, then a calmness settled. I was at peace. Finally, I could rest. Everything I just heard slipped away as fast as I heard it. Then, the thought of Ariel filled me with panic. Ariel.

Ariel.

Even her name was fleeting as I drifted into nothingness.

Chapter One

"No!" Ryker's voice called out in my head. Swirls of color flashed around me, then I stepped onto the sand. Father Archibald followed closely behind. The sun overhead was hot, and I had the strangest sensation between my shoulder blades, like a string being pulled before the tension was released.

"Where are we?" I asked the father, who stepped beside me.

"We are in a small town east of Bethlehem."

I gasped. "Bethlehem! Like where Jesus was born?"

Father Archibald chuckled, "Is there another Bethlehem?"

I looked at him like *I don't know, you tell me.* "We could have at least brought water bottles or something. I wish I was prepared. I have sand in my shoes."

"Patience. Our destination is just over this peak."

It looked like a never-ending desert. I had a hard time believing anything but sand would be over the peak, but I'd trusted him this far. I'd better trust him more.

"Before we go any further, can you make me a promise?"

"Of course. Anything for you, Elle."

"Can you bring me back whenever I want?"

"I can do that."

"Promise?"

"I promise."

"Vow it," I ordered, and I had no idea where that came from. I'd never vowed anything before in my life, let alone asked someone else to.

His step faltered, and he stumbled over his words, then said, "I vow it."

We walked for about ten more minutes up the sandy hill, and a breeze blew away our footprints as we walked. It seemed strange, though, because it was hotter than hell, and I didn't feel a breeze.

If I thought Ohio was hot, this was its unique hellish heat.

We cleared the peak, and that's when I saw it—an ancient building carved into the side of the mountain built right into the stone.

There were huge turrets reminiscent of a Roman church with no windows. Nothing but a single, large entryway. As we drew closer, I stopped focusing so much on the church-like structure and realized there were guards at the front and off to the side. As we approached, several other people stopped what they were doing to stare at us.

Each step was another step closer on this unknown journey. It wasn't the same as when I neared Ryker's town. This was different—an unknown, and I felt uneasy about it. I had no real idea about what I was walking into.

"Wait," I grabbed the father's arm, halting him.

"What is it, Elle?"

"You said I'm different from other Rosi, and they don't know how special my sect is. How can they train me if they don't know? Surely someone knows. Who are you taking me to, and what do I tell them? Will you be near? What can I expect?"

If I'd given this whole "leaving with Father Archibald" more time, I would've already asked these questions. But I'd jumped the gun. I was wildly unprepared for this. The man standing next to me had answers, and I needed them.

"We will tell them who your father is, and it will be clear to those who need to know who you are. To everyone else, you will simply be a student. I would advise against telling them about your back."

"Ya!" A male called out. "Ya! Ya!' He approached on a horse, kicking dust in his wake as he sped towards us.

"Be strong, Elle. It will be okay," the father assured me.

The man drew closer, and I felt on edge. With Ryker, I felt grounded, and without him, I now felt adrift.

The horse came to a sudden halt, pulling back on the reins once he was in front of us. "Who are you? What business do you have?" he asked. He was of middle eastern descent with tan skin, and dark hair swept over his forehead. He had an athletic build, nothing like Ryker's large build, but still attractive. His eyes were dark with a subtle roundness to the apple of his cheeks, and his lips peaked higher than most men.

"You must be Cain, son of Abbas. You are a mere spitting image of him. Please let your father know Father Archibald is here with the daughter of John Katz."

Father Archibald was speaking strangely. I'd never heard him talk that way before. Then again, the father had just walked us through a portal. There was a lot I didn't know about him, and I needed to remember that. As much as I have considered him a longtime family friend, maybe there was more to him than I realized.

Cain's eyes widened, and he lifted his chin to the father as a show of respect.

"Follow me." He turned his horse and trotted toward the large entrance. We passed several people milling about. They either looked down or away as we passed them. We walked through the large sandstone entrance into a tunnel.

I had no idea what to expect, but I didn't expect it to open into a large courtyard with hundreds of people. Large, old trees grew from the sand with partially-exposed roots curving around buildings and huts. There were stands with vendors all selling various goods. Some sold material and sarongs, and I could see how that would be useful in this heat.

We passed a vendor selling books. I wished I could stop and browse.

Another man with a boa around his shoulders kept a captive audience enthralled as the snake slithered up his arms and through his shirt.

A little girl squealed as a boy chased her, laughing.

"Come taste my wine," another man cried, beckoning me over. I ignored him and carried on.

We passed a group of beautiful, enchanting belly dancers. I wanted to stop and watch them.

"Come, dear," Father said.

"What is this place?"

"It's Zoar,"

"It's so green and alive. Where did all of these people come from?"

"This is an ancient city cut off from the rest of the world. Most do not leave. It's unique in that technology hasn't evolved in the same way here."

"What do you mean, like no one has cell phones?"

"Dear, most have no idea what a cell phone is."

"How is that possible?"

"Elle, you should've learned by now anything is possible."

As we followed Cain, I took in the houses on the outskirts of the bustling, ancient city. They were all single-story homes made from stone. There were no yards, just house after house, with narrow roads, and I could tell they went on like that for a while. We approached a tall, wide set of stairs leading into a mountainside. A feeling of dread passed through me like an oil coating my skin.

Cain swung off his horse and handed the reins to a waiting boy. "This way," he said sharply.

We followed him up the stairs, which put those stairs in Philly that Rocky climbed to shame. I was a runner, so I could do going the distance, but poor Father Archibald needed water. Sweat dripped off his brow, and he panted a little more with each passing step.

We finally reached the top, where two armed guards with huge staffs stood on each side of what appeared to be palace doors. The structure was glass and dome-shaped in front of it with huge, rounded towers. On further inspection, I saw the outline of plants. Beyond the glass, I could also make out a traditional structure made from sandstone and cut into the earth.

A guard opened the door, and as we stepped inside, I noted it was a greenhouse. Huge plants grew the likes of which I'd never seen before. I immediately spotted tomatoes and grapes growing among the plants then my eyes took in their water source, moving through an ancient turbine. The air held a thick scent of jasmine and something citrusy that I couldn't quite put my finger on. There were birds everywhere. The entire space was a cacophony of many species of birds singing. I must've stopped to figure it out when the father called, "Elle."

Looking away from the interesting plants and water setup, I spotted Father Archibald several yards ahead. Cain glared at me impatiently. He seemed *real* nice.

I hurriedly caught up as Cain opened another set of doors with several stationed guards. This led down another passageway with several large wooden doors arched at the top.

Finally coming to a stop, he knocked once, then the huge doors swung open.

We walked into a large room with rows of seats filled by patrons while a man paced back and forth, lecturing in a language I didn't understand. Beyond him was another man who obviously held rank. He didn't have a crown or anything, but I knew that man was Abbas. He looked like an older version of Cain and had an authority about him that you could tell others cowed to.

"Stay here," Cain ordered, then walked around the seated patrons and whispered into his father's ear. Abbas's eyes dart to me and then to the man speaking. "That's enough for today, Seth."

The man abruptly stopped his lecture. Several people in the crowd clapped, and others put away paper and pencils for their notetaking.

"You're free to go for the day," Seth told the room in English—thank God. I could barely understand Hebrew, which is what he was speaking. My dad attempted to get me to understand it. Languages came easily for some people, but not for me.

"Father Archibald, old friend!" Abbas called out. "What have you brought me?"

The room wasn't completely empty yet, and several people looked up with squinty eyes and raised brows in odd curiosity.

I also didn't miss that Abbas asked "what," not "who," and that didn't make me feel all warm and fuzzy inside.

We walked up a center aisle towards Abbas. Father Archibald attempted to stand straighter, squaring his shoulders. At five-ten, there was no standing straighter for me.

We finally stood before him. He was averagely dressed, wearing linen pants and a light blue button-up rolled at his sleeves. Cain took his place to the right, and side-by-side, their resemblance was uncanny. If not for the creases at Abbas's eyes and the slightly more angular chin, one could almost think they were brothers.

"Who's this?" he asked good-naturedly.

"May I present Ariel Katz, daughter of John Katz, a senior Rosi." Father Archibald took a small bow, and I had no clue what I was supposed to do. It felt like there was a protocol I was supposed to be following, and someone forgot the handbook. I shot Father Archibald a look that shared my feelings of ineptness.

"Hello, nice to meet you. I go by Elle if you don't mind." I smiled and stuck out my hand.

"Elle, no," Father Archibald attempted to lower my hand with his.

"It's all right. Elle, step forward, and let me take a look at you." I wanted to tell him that sounded creepy as hell, and there wasn't anything for him to see. He stood from his chair that, on second thought, might've had some throne-like qualities.

I didn't want to take a step forward. So, I didn't. Instead, Father Archibald took a step back to make up for my disobedience. Abbas appraised me the way one might purchase cattle at a livestock auction. He looked at me from different angles slowly.

I turned to Father, gave him a look, and mouthed, "What the hell?"

I felt my ring warm against my finger. I had a feeling it was changing color again, and for some reason, my gut told me to hide it from Abbas. Tucking my hand in my shorts' pocket, I turned as Abbas walked behind me.

"Nothing to see back there," I said.

"She's very tall," Abbas said to Father Archibald.

"I am tall, yes, and I *am* right here. Please stop perusing me. You're making me uncomfortable."

Abbas laughed. "You have about as much tact as your father did. It's a shame. He was a good man. She has his spirit, that's for sure," he said to Father Archibald like I wasn't right there.

"Son, she is pretty, isn't she?"

"*She* is mated," I said smugly.

"You're what?" Cain asked.

"Mated, as in I found my one."

"Father, how can that be?" Cain asked, irately and slightly whiny.

"I am not sure, son, but do not fret. You have a mate, do you? Where are they? Why do you refer to him as such? Most would say "spouse" or "boyfriend," "husband" even, but mate? What an interesting choice of words."

I didn't want to tell them Ryker was a werewolf. "Father, maybe coming here was a mistake," I said straight out. I wasn't one to beat around the bush or hide my distaste, and this situation was putting me off. Surely, there had to be another way to learn my skills.

"Nonsense, dear." I again shot daggers at Father Archibald. "We are here because ..."

"I know why you are here. My son will show you to your quarters. Dinner will be in one hour. Miss Katz, someone will be in to help you dress more appropriately. I expect you will mind your manners in the presence of company. Tomorrow, we will get started on your purpose for being here. Now, is there anything else?" His question was directed at Father Archibald. I wanted to say, *"Damn straight there is something else,"* but was there anything else? I wasn't sure I needed someone to help me dress, but if it was a fancy dinner, I could see why my attire might not be appropriate. My shorts were on the shorter side, and my tank was on the tighter side, but it was hot outside.

This made me wonder. "Why isn't it hot in here?"

Abbas narrowed his eyes at me. "We are in the Earth. This place is built into the mountain. There are no windows because the Earth cools us."

I nodded. That made sense.

"Now, if there are no other questions."

I was about to ask about this dinner, but Father Archibald placed his hand on my back. "No, no more questions."

Abbas gave a quick nod of his head and said, "So mote it be." Then he turned his back on us like we were dismissed.

"This way," Cain said, looking at me strangely.

He led us through a different set of doors than the ones we came in through, down a long hallway, through another door, another hallway, down a flight of stairs, then stopped outside a plain-looking door. "This is your room," Cain told Father Archibald.

"Thank you. Elle, I will see you shortly. He does always put on quite extravagant dinners. It is an honor to be invited. Please try to stay positive. These people are our friends."

I returned his words with a tight-lipped smile, and he returned that with a disappointed head tilt.

We left Father Archibald, and I followed Cain down the hallway and up a short flight of stairs. Down another hallway, he finally stopped outside a large wooden door, different from Father Archibald's door. It was more elaborate and larger, and it wasn't lost on me that there was a rose carved into the front of it.

He opened the door and inhaled as I moved past him to step inside. What the F? Was he smelling me? It was beyond strange. Did I smell bad? It was nine million degrees outside, so there was that.

I walked into the room and immediately noticed how grand it was. A large bed was in the center of the room with a huge wooden canopy. Dark red sheets covered the bed. There weren't windows, so overall, it was dark, but tall pillar candles were lit along the bed, leading to a wooden divider that I could make out a tub behind. A large wardrobe was against the wall, and next to that were several mirrors. The way they were positioned made me think it was to get different angles of the wardrobe.

"So, this is nice. Whose room is this?"

Cain tilted his head at me curiously, "It's yours."

"But it looks so lived in. How are candles burning already?"

"My father sent someone as soon as you announced who you were."

The candles looked like they'd been burning longer than that, but who was I to argue?

"All right, so ... bye?"

I didn't want to be rude, but apparently, I needed to dress for dinner.

Cain looked at me for a few more beats, then finally said, "Your hair is blonde."

"Uh, yeah."

He squinted his eyes at me. "And you are very tall."

And the award for Captain Obvious goes to ... "Mmhmm," I agreed.

"Your lady's maid will be in shortly to help you dress. Please take a minute to refresh." He turned and walked away, closing me in.

Once he was gone, I walked around the room inspecting the craftsmanship of the wood, which only made me miss Ryker. I rubbed my chest. The longing I felt for him was a dull, physical ache. Had he woken already? And how pissed was he? I hoped he understood why I left. Was Mindy okay? Had I made a mistake?

Please, God, let them forgive me. I sent a silent prayer up, hoping they would indeed forgive me. I reminded myself I was doing this to protect and keep them safe. I hoped they saw it that way.

I inspected my ring. It was no longer a dark shade of red and didn't feel nearly as vibrant as it did when I was with Ryker. Maybe that was my imagination, and I was projecting perfection onto my short time with him. That would make sense.

Never in my world had I felt anything like what I'd experienced with him.

I opened the wardrobe to check out my clothing selections and was surprised to find clothes unlike any I'd ever seen before. The colors were rich, and the style was similar to what you might find an Indian bride wearing. I imagined the tops would be a midriff when I tried them on, and the skirts were wide and flowy but made from a lightweight material for the hot sun. Still, I wouldn't want to run in a skirt. I failed to find shorts or pants. How would I conceal my dagger? There was no way I was leaving it behind.

With a knock on the door, a beautiful woman with raven dark hair and amber eyes opened it enough to poke her head in. Once she was content with whatever she was checking, she entered and gave me a quick curtsy.

"Hello, Miss. I am Esmerelda. I will be assisting you with dressing this evening." She had an accent as she spoke, and I could tell English wasn't her first language. Her "S" had a Z sound to them.

She wore a linen top with a simple skirt and sandals on her feet. I was more interested in dressing like her than getting all done up for a dinner I didn't feel all too excited about.

"Oh wee. These are beautiful." She moved to the wardrobe and sifted through the clothes. "What should we pick? Oh, dear, you are quite tall. I will have to see what can accommodate your height." She quickly looked at each garment, and several were dismissed right away. She then grabbed a fuchsia gown and held it up to me. I groaned. Fuschia was not my jam. I moved to look at the gowns with her.

"I like black. Are any of them black?"

"Black is so boring. With your skin and your eyes, you should have color."

I moved to the black dresses and pulled the simplest I could find. "Here, this one will work."

"That is like dressing you for the dead. We cannot dress you for dinner in that. They will think you mourn."

I shrugged. "They can think I'm an alien for all I care."

She gasped at my words, then pleadingly looked at me. "Please, it is an honor to dress you. They will not let me see to you if this is what you come out in. We do not have much time."

I sighed. Playing dress-up was not what I had in mind when I left. If I had to do it, it really didn't matter what I wore. So long as I could move and conceal my dagger, I should be fine. "I'm sorry. You know what I'm walking into far better than I. Pink and fuchsia are not my thing, so how about we try something else?"

She sifted through and grabbed a dark blue dress and also a red one. "What do you think of these?"

Red suited me, but it would make me stand out more than I already did, and I didn't need that. I wanted to learn what I could and get back to Ryker as quickly as possible. I didn't want to be the center of attention and wearing. Wearing the red with small jewels all over the front of the top and along the hem was sure to bring attention to me.

The blue was so dark that it could almost be described as black, however, as it moved, you could see the blue threads weaved throughout the fabric. The top was a midriff halter. Instead of jewels, there was thick corded braided material from the hem connected at the back, moving up the spine to clasp around my neck. The skirt had that same braided material around the waist, then multiple layers of fabric overlapped and swung loosely, making it seem like it would be easy to move in it.

"I think this one will do."

She held it up to me. "With this high neck, your hair should be up. We don't have enough time to wash it, but let's get you in the tub." She stepped forward and reached for the button on my shorts.

"Hold on, sister." I put my hands up and backed away. "I can shower on my own."

"Shower?"

"You don't know what a shower is? God, where in the world did Father Archibald bring me?" I asked, looking up for answers, and obviously, I got no response.

"You speak to the heavens? Oh, dear." She made the sign of the cross. I had no idea what to do with her.

"No. I mean, I guess. Not like that. We're not having a conversation or anything."

"Listen. I'll throw my hair up in a ponytail and bathe. I can bathe, right?"

"Of course. I should help you change, no?"

"No, I'm capable. Thank you." I walked past her to the other side of the wooden divider. There was a low-set tub with water in it already. I ran my fingers through it, feeling its warmth. I figured they must've warmed it when they lit the candles. It all seemed odd and contrived.

I quickly stripped and stepped into the bath, which could probably fit several people inside it. It reminded me more of a hot tub than a bath. "Is there soap or a washcloth?" I asked.

She came in and looked at me strangely, then motioned to a pile of oversized green leaves sitting on the side of the tub. "Uh, what are these?"

She tilted her head and looked at me as if I was a child. "These are fig leaves with lavender oil and orange extract. The bath also has goat milk added to it. Use the leaf on your body. You will smell divine, trust me."

Great, I was bathing in goat milk and wiping with figs. Definitely not the oddest thing to happen to me today, though.

I grabbed the leaf, and she left me to it. It was strange, but my skin felt soft, and I enjoyed the scent.

"Time is ticking. Are you about done?"

"Sure, do you have a towel?"

She again looked at me strangely and walked to me with a robe. It was not made of terry cloth. Instead, it was silk and would stick to my body and not dry me the way one would hope. She held it open for me and looked at me expectantly. Apparently, I would just get out naked in front of her.

I stood, and immediately, the robe stuck to me. She then handed me a tan piece of leather, and I assumed I could use that to dry myself? So, I did, and again, she looked at me strangely. We walked back towards the bed, where she had a pair of black underwear that looked remarkably comfortable. I set about putting those on. She handed me the skirt, which was easy enough to put on. While I did this, she unbraided the back of the halter top part of the dress. It would seem that it had to be braided to be worn.

I was waiting for the top with one arm pressed over my boobs, hiding my nips, when the door opened suddenly, and Cain was standing there.

I turned immediately. "Excuse me. Do you not have the decency to knock?"

He cleared his throat. "Dinner is in fifteen minutes."

"Esmerelda, see to it that you hurry her along. I came to escort her, but apparently, she is not ready yet. I will return shortly."

The door closed. "Is there a lock?" I immediately asked.

She again looked at me curiously. I was agitated. Who walked into a woman's room when they knew they were getting ready without knocking? Ryker would be beyond pissed. He would probably eat Cain. That mental image made me smile.

We hurriedly got the top on me. I fixed sandals to my feet and found a long ribbon with the hair things to tie the dagger to my thigh with, securing it in place. I wore my ring and decided there wasn't anywhere I could safely keep the medallion on me.

"Will my things be kept safe while we eat?" I asked Esmerelda.

"Yes, of course." She asked while braiding my hair, and quicker than I ever would've imagined, she was pinning the braid around my head. Staring at myself in the mirrors, I was in awe. In such a short time, I felt like Esmerelda transformed me. I didn't feel like myself. I both liked it and didn't. Sure, I looked beautiful, but I liked myself. I was confident in my skin and didn't feel like I needed to be done up for anyone. Well, except for one person, but he wasn't here. Guilt tore through me along with that familiar pang of longing. I wondered again how Ryker was. I was so lost in my thoughts about what he was doing that I didn't hear the door.

Chapter Two

A throat cleared behind us, and I turned. Of course, I should've guessed it was Cain, the no-knock-ass.

"Wow, you ... You did well, Esmerelda."

I gave him a tight-lipped smile. I didn't like that he came and went as he pleased, and I didn't want another man to be looking me over with eyes that seemed hungrier by the second. It felt like a bigger betrayal to Ryker than I'd already done. And although Ryker and I had never explicitly outlined the details of our relationship, I would have his balls if he looked at another woman, and it was the same for him.

I stepped away from Esmerelda and towards Cain. His eyes roamed over my body. "Hey, Buddy. Eyes up here."

He met my eyes and squinted his response. "I'll look where I please."

He infuriated me.

I shook my head in annoyance. "Let's just go."

"Yes, let's go."

I turned to look back at Esmeralda. "Thank you again for all of your help."

She shrugged, "It's my job and my pleasure."

I smiled and took another step more tentatively towards Cain. "Let's get this show on the road."

He looked at me strangely. "What road?"

"It's a figurative road ... Never mind."

We left the bedroom and continued down a bunch of dark hallways that looked identical. I was sure it was done this way by design. You could easily get lost.

Finally, we came to a set of flush double doors that you would've had to know to look for. Cain banged once, and both sides opened wide. Inside was a large table, maybe twenty-five feet or so in length. Abbas was seated and down the table from him was Father Archibald. A few other people sat at the table, all equally sitting far apart. I didn't have much time to take in any more of the room because Abbas spoke.

"Nice of you to finally join us, Miss Katz."

I wanted to roll my eyes at his tone. I didn't care for these people and was regretting my decision by the hour.

"Elle, please sit, dear," Father Archibald said, trying to diffuse the tension. "You look lovely."

"Thank you," I replied and went to move to an open seat, but Cain grabbed my elbow and walked me toward the seat he wanted.

"I got it," I said through gritted teeth.

He let go of my elbow and pulled out the chair. I sat, more annoyed than ever.

Abbas clapped twice, and a group of scantily dressed women wearing skirts that barely covered their butts came forward. They looked more like erotic belly dancers than waitresses. Each wore a top resembling a bra but was made of sheer material. I could even make out an areola or two. *And he had the nerve to comment on my short shorts and tank.*

In unison, they set down bowls of soup. I was immediately reminded of Lillian and how I felt she'd done something to my soup. I became incredibly wary about eating it. Father Archibald watched me curiously as several people at the table sipped their broth.

"Is it not to your liking?" Cain sneered.

I squinted my eyes at him and got the urge to punch him. Maybe I could mind control him to shut up. No, I needed to keep that close to me as well. That was going to be a secret I didn't let others in on.

"I recently had a soup that didn't agree with me. Father," I asked. "Would you mind switching your soup with my own?"

He looked at me curiously. "But it's the same ..."

I met his eyes with a tight-lipped smile.

"But of course," he responded, then motioned for a waitress to switch our bowls.

"Odd behavior from such a girl," Abbas spoke to Father Archibald. "She dines with us. She has come to us for help. However, she does not trust us, and she does not hide it either."

"I'm thinking, Father, that you should have warned her *she* wouldn't be directly spoken to. I think *she* made a rash decision, and *she* isn't that hungry. *She* also didn't appreciate *him*," I looked pointedly at Cain, "walking into her room while *she* was changing. Trust is earned, and where I'm from, you earn trust by speaking to someone and giving them common courtesy, like knocking."

Abbas put his spoon down, and everyone followed suit. He looked pointedly at me. "She would be wise to learn when to speak and when not to."

That felt like a threat. I felt my ring warm, and if I could look at it without anyone knowing, I would've most likely noticed the color change. Instead, I ran my hand along my thigh, feeling for the dagger. If I needed to defend myself, I'd do it.

I felt a searing pain in my head and immediately clutched it. "Ariel," Ryker growled in my head, and it felt like a vice had a grip on my skull. I couldn't help it—I gasped.

"Elle, are you alright?" Father asked.

I squeezed my eyes shut, waited a minute, then felt the pain recede. I opened my eyes. "I apologize, Abbas. I do not know your customs. I didn't even know of your existence until a few days ago. I need to learn as much as possible and return to my mate. I can feel him, and every moment I'm away from him isn't easy. I'd like to learn what I can and take that with me. If this is not something you can help me with, I understand. My father explained the Rosi were truth-seekers, which is why I'm here, to seek information. I do not have time to sit and eat. I'm sorry if I come off ungrateful. This is a beautiful dress, and I appreciate your hospitality, but truly, I'd like to have a little knowledge, and I'll be out of your hair."

"Women do not generally address me."

"Again, I apologize. Where I'm from, that's misogynistic. Women are equal to men." The women serving us gasped.

"I do not know that word," Abbas looked at me suspiciously.

"I'm certain you do not."

There was a collective gasp from both men and women.

Abbas smiled at me as if he found me amusing, and his smile only irritated me. So I smiled back as I straightened my shoulders and then took a sip of Father Archibald's soup.

Abbas took a sip of his then everyone else resumed eating.

"So, you have a mate, you say?" Abbas asked.

I felt like I scored one for the sisterhood because at least now he was speaking to me instead of talking about me. "We're fated."

I didn't know if I should tell him this or not, but I'd already called him my mate. Knowing I was a fated mate, I hoped Cain would behave and Abbas would understand my urgency to leave.

"That's impossible," Cain gritted out beside me. "Father, you said you would bring her here, not that she belonged to another."

Guilt flashed throughout Father Archibald's features, and I got the distinct impression he was betraying me. My heart beat furiously in my chest, and I again rubbed the dagger, wondering if I would use it this evening.

"I did not know of her mate until I was there." Father Archibald didn't look at me as he spoke, and I thought it prudent to sit and observe instead of strangling him from across the table like I wanted to.

"Tell me, how do you know he is your mate?" Abbas asked, taking the attention off of Father Archibald and Cain.

"If you had a mate, you'd understand. It's not just that we're mates, but we're fated to one another. Because of this, we've both experienced some changes. We also have an urge to be with each other. If we're not, it physically affects us if. So you see, it's not just that we are mated, but the fates have deemed us one."

"Cain, calm your temper," Abbas ordered.

Cain's jaw was tense, and he was gripping his cutlery.

Abbas clapped, and the servers brought forward plates with roasted meat and vegetables. "Miss Katz, since you do not trust us, please choose any plate to switch with yours."

I chose a plate from a man who had yet to be introduced to me. I nodded a thank you to Abbas.

"Tell me about your mate. Is he a good man? A wise man?" Abbas inquired.

That searing pain went through my skull again, and I gripped my forehead. This time I heard Ryker's voice as if he were sitting next to me. "Ariel."

"Are you all right?" Abbas asked.

I blew out a breath, trying to get through the pain. "He's a strong man."

"Is it him? Is he somehow hurting you?" Cain asked, and for the first time, I saw something more than contempt from the man. He seemed genuinely concerned.

"He'd never hurt me. It's the bond. I think I came in haste. Perhaps I shouldn't be here."

"That leads me to a very interesting question," Abbas spoke, "Why did you come? What is it you hoped to gain? And if you truly are fated, which I'm not certain I believe, how could you leave your mate?"

I paused and tried to eat my food while thinking of what I could say and couldn't. I didn't want to tell him they were wolves or that I had changed Mindy. I came here for answers about what I was, but now that I was here, I didn't trust anyone. Somehow Father Archibald lied to get me here, and I needed to be back with Ryker. I made a mistake. I was sure of it.

Pain lanced through my skull again, bringing tears to my eyes. A whimper left my lips.

"I'm sorry. I'm in a great deal of pain. Would you mind if I lied down?"

Abbas looked irritated but nodded his head.

"I'll escort you," Cain said.

He was the last person I wanted escorting me anywhere, but I'd never find my way back. I stood, and more pain shot through me, making me unsteady on my feet.

Cain grabbed my arm to steady me. I wanted to knock his hand away, but the pain in my head caused my vision to blur.

"Father," I tried to speak. My voice felt faint. I was going to tell him I wanted to go back, but I didn't get the chance. My vision went dark, and I passed out again.

Chapter Three

Blackness surrounded me. I could see myself and nothing else. I was wearing the shorts and tank I had on the day before. Had it only been a day? Ryker's voice soothed my racing worries.

Ariel, come back to me!

I'm in the dark. I can't.

No, I'm in the dark. You, my love, are Gods knows where.

What do you mean, you're in the dark?

This is where I'm at, Ariel. It's something you did. You need to come back to me, and you need to wake me. I'm not eating or getting fluids. I need you. Wherever you are, come back to me. I'm not mad at you. You had your reason for doing this, but I need you to return. Do it fast. The pain, Oh, Gods, the pain.

He roared out in agony.

What had I done?

I'm sorry. I didn't know. I left to find answers so I wouldn't do what I did to Mindy again, but I somehow hurt you. I'll come back. I'll do whatever I can to get back to you.

Promise you'll hurry.

I'll hurry, I promise. I should've told you before, but there's something I wish I had said to you. To think you're hurting now because of me. I...

I was going to say, "I love you," but he cut me off.

No, I need to hear it from your lips the first time you say it. I need to be there to look into your eyes and tell you I feel the same when you admit it. Not like this. Not when I'm in darkness. Starved. Pissed. Feeling the worst pain of my life because you're not with me. Come back to me. His voice faded.

Don't go. Don't leave me. I'm sorry.

Come to me, Ariel. I need you. Come...

His voice trailed off, and I slowly opened my eyes, taking in my surroundings. I was in bed. Candlelight flickered and bounced off the dimly lit room. I wanted to close my eyes and speak with Ryker again. I wanted to call out to him to wake him.

I tried to sit, but my head hurt. Plus, it was better to lie here and keep my eyes closed to eavesdrop on the two males speaking.

"Why did this happen to her? I want to know everything there is to know about Ariel Katz."

"You know she is special. She's the only female to be born into the line. You need to calm yourself, son."

"How can I calm myself when she is destined to be mine and yet is so tied to another that she passes out?"

"This is only your interpretation of the scrolls. You do not know that it means what you think it does."

"Something is not right with her. Did you see her eyes? I swear they shone a blue light right before she passed out."

Fucking-fuckity-fuck. My eyes did the thing again.

"Something is different about her, all right. I will not have you going half-cocked and scaring her away before we find out all there is to know about Ms. Katz. You need to calm yourself, son."

"I've waited."

"And patience is a virtue you will continue to hold onto."

"We must find her so-called mate and discover why she thinks she is fated."

"Agreed."

I couldn't believe what I was hearing. Cain believed I was destined to be his because of some scroll? Abbas had more sense than Cain did. Still, the entire conversation seemed bazaar. I had to find Father Archibald and get home.

A wet cloth brushed over my temple. "There you are," Esmerelda, my lady's maid cooed. "You had everyone worried."

She must've known I was awake and gave me a second before announcing it to the room. I wanted to know what scrolls he was talking about, but I also didn't care what he thought. I needed to get back to Ryker.

I moaned at the pain in my temple. Two sets of male eyes hit me a second later. Cain and Abbas.

Cain rushed to my side and grabbed my hand. "Are you well?"

I pulled away and stuttered, "Don't touch me." Regaining my voice, I asked, "I need Father Archibald."

"I'm so sorry, dear. The Father has been sent on an assignment for us," Abbas said.

"He... he left me?" Rage burned behind my eyes, and I worried they'd go all blue again.

"Nonsense. You came here of your own free will. He works with us, and since you've been sleeping for over a day, we needed him to do something."

I sat, fighting against how much pain it caused me. I knew what would cure me, and I stupidly left him behind in Ohio. Now we were both suffering, and without Father Archibald here, I couldn't get back there as quickly.

"I need to use your portal. I have to return home."

"You'll do no such thing," Cain argued.

I shot Cain a look that said try to stop me, then turned to Abbas. "May we speak candidly for a minute? Just the two of us?"

"Of course not. Anything you say in front of my father—"

"Yes," Abbas spoke, cutting Cain off.

Cain gritted his teeth and moved away from me. I was grateful to not have his watchful eyes.

"Esmerelda." Abbas nodded his head in her direction, signaling her dismissal.

She left the room first, and Cain reluctantly followed, looking at me with a longing I did not like.

Abbas leaned against the wooden canopy bed frame and waited for me to speak.

I steeled my nerves and spoke frankly, "Your scrolls are wrong. I'm already fated. I'm in pain because of the distance between my mate and me. He's also in pain. I can feel it. I need to get back to him, or I'm afraid of what will happen to us. I don't know what I expected in coming here. I'm different. There is something unique about me, and since you saw the blue in my eyes, you already know this. I was hoping you might have answers as to what was happening and if there was a way to control it. However, I did not expect the harm my being here would cause my mate or me. I need to return, and if you have another portal, I would appreciate it. Otherwise, a lift to the nearest airport is also appreciated."

There. That came out well. I said enough without going into too much detail.

Abbas watched me intently, and long seconds passed before he spoke. I got the impression that it was intentional. He wanted to make me squirm. "What is it about your eyes? What do you think makes you special?"

I inhaled, hoping for patience because I was quickly learning Abbas wanted to be the one to ask questions. Rarely had he answered any of mine. It felt like a game, and I was unaware of the rules.

"My lineage," I answered. "Father Archibald said I was the only female to be born of the Katz line. And our line is unique within the Rosi, so I hoped you could tell me. Why were my eyes blue?"

He again was quiet and eventually answered, "I do not know."

"Do you have any information, any texts, that speak of my line? Can you answer my question about sending me back home?"

"We have an extensive library. You are welcome to look through it. However, nothing is to leave the library. If you want to research, then you will have to stay here to do so."

"You would have me stay, even when I tell you it's physically hurting my mate and me?" I asked incredulously.

"Tell me again about this so-called mate?"

I gritted my teeth. It didn't feel like it was his to know.

"He is not so-called. Ryker is very much mine, and I am his."

"Then how could you so easily leave him? That doesn't quite add up, young Ariel."

He added the young part to belittle me.

"Something happened with my eyes, and I was afraid my lack of knowledge might hurt him. I left to protect him, but in doing so, I'm afraid I've hurt him even more. I need to get back to him."

"What happened to your eyes?"

"I don't know, all right!" I snapped.

"Tell me what you do know!" he snapped back.

It was the first time he lost his patience with me. I took a deep breath, attempting to keep from screaming at him at the top of my lungs. "I thought you'd have answers because my dad worked for you. I thought you'd be able to help me, but instead, after blacking out again—might I add—all you're doing is interrogating me. Your son somehow thinks he is prophesied to be with me, but yuck, no. No offense, but he's an ass, and Father Archibald, who promised to bring me home when I asked, is no longer here. Yes, I might not be freely giving up information, but I thought the Rosi were supposed to be protectors of the truth. Whatever you're trying to accomplish with me doesn't feel like it's protection. It feels more like an inquisition."

He ignored everything and pressed on. "You showed up here, Ariel. If I am to help you understand more about yourself, then perhaps you can let me know more about what's been happening. You are a stubborn girl. But you're holding your cards too tightly. Coming here is something you should've done decades ago. Your father should've brought you to us, but he didn't. Why is that? What is it about you that he didn't want us to know? So, you see, we are curious and have questions. There is much to learn, and as you know, we are seekers of truth. I intend to learn all there is to know about you, Miss Katz," he said the last part with finality. Then he strode out of the room, and if he had a cape, it would've flown high and mighty behind him.

***

I was in the library, dressed in another ridiculously unfunctional dress. This one was a light blue halter top with a light, flowy skirt. It was pretty, but I didn't feel it was sensible to spend so much time getting ready.

Once Abbas left, I lay in bed and thought about Ryker. I tried to send him thoughts to wake. I was oceans away from him, though. I hoped he would feel me through our link and something would happen. I had no idea if it would or not.

I kept thinking about Father Archibald, whether he intentionally left, and what nefarious role he might be playing. I'd known him my entire life, and I couldn't help but feel betrayed by him. I didn't even understand how he betrayed me; however, I knew he was.

I wasn't sure what I was supposed to be looking for. It would be nice if there was a book titled: "The Katz Family Line," but there wasn't. Instead, I searched for books about ancient priests. I also searched for books regarding the Arc of the Covenant and the Pharaohs. If there was a place that might mention the Katz line, it might be there. The problem was that many texts were not in English, and after several hours, I was agitated. Without guidance, it was like looking for a needle in a haystack.

I sighed, feeling fed up and kicking myself for not trusting Ryker and staying with him. I should've relied on his family to help me figure out what was happening. Guilt poured through me, reminding me of what I did to Mindy and how I unintentionally left Ryker asleep.

A door creaked, taking me out of my thoughts. It was none other than the supreme asshole, Cain. He stalked towards me, determined to say whatever was on his mind. Once he reached me, I noticed his nose was slightly turned up, even though I was sitting. He reeked of arrogance.

"Cain," I greeted.

"Elle. It looks like you're feeling better."

"I'm fine, thank you." I semi-lied. I still had a persistent headache.

"Have you found anything of help to you?"

My lips thinned. "I haven't found much in English, so there is a language barrier. I suppose I should be on my way now if you can't help me," I said hopefully.

"Why did you come all this way for answers but are so quick to dismiss any we have for you?"

"Abbas sent me on a fool's run."

"How would he know that not only did your father fail to bring you forth, but he also failed to teach you languages. How can you be a Rosi and seek the truth without knowing how to read the information you seek?"

"Apparently, he didn't want me to be a Rosi."

"And yet you came here anyway."

"I made a mistake, and I'd like to leave."

"Now, now. Don't be so precipitous. I've found someone who knows about your blue eyes. Do you want to leave before you find out what they mean?"

I wanted to unearth the truth, but Ryker needed me. I was torn.

"Is this person here?"

"No, but I've summoned them. You must wait. In the meantime, would you enjoy a lecture with the rest of the students?"

"How long will it take for the person to arrive? I need to be with my mate."

He grabbed my wrist painfully, and I fought my natural reaction to put him flat on his ass. I couldn't give away my cards yet.

"You will not speak of him." His grip tightened as if he was making a point.

"What a weak man you are, grabbing me. If you do not remove your hand this instant, I will make you regret it."

He maintained his hold. We were in a stare-down. A beat passed, then another. Fire blazed within me. I was so close to dropping him. Still, instinctually, I felt like I shouldn't expose everything I could do—not yet, maybe not ever.

He released my wrist, leaving a red, bruising mark. I pulled my wrist toward me and shot daggers at him.

"I'm leaving," I declared, sidestepping him. He moved to block my path.

"You're not going anywhere."

"Am I your prisoner?"

"You're whatever I say you are."

I had to think fast. Either I stuck around and waited for his guest, or I used my powers and got the heck out of dodge, and this whole trip would have been for naught.

I could use my powers of the Earth and make him nap or move out of my way. Either worked for me. I closed my eyes and called on my inner strength. I thought about the land and the Earth and what I wanted to happen to Cain. An idea clicked. *Pretend I don't exist.*

I couldn't put him to sleep and risk him not waking. This way, he would leave me alone, and I would be free to go home and hopefully put this entire thing behind me.

Chapter Four

"What are you doing?" Cain asked.

I opened my eyes to find he very much knew I still existed. It didn't work. *Why didn't it work?* That was my get-out-of-jail-free card I'd been holding onto. My ace in the hole. My ... You get the picture. It should've worked. I was counting on it to work. What in the what was going on?

"Nothing," I lied.

He narrowed his eyes at me.

I took a step back. If my Jedi mind trick didn't work, then I wasn't sure I could defend myself the way I thought I could. Fear was settling. I was drowning in a sea of unknown and swimming among sharks. I was the prey. I knew it, the way I knew I'd miscalculated coming here. Maybe miscalculated wasn't a strong enough word. Maybe it was a fatal mistake that would cost me more than I'd be willing to give.

"I'll go to a lecture," I blurted. Anything to get away from Cain.

He clapped once. "Wonderful." Then he smiled brightly as if he was proud of himself for putting his hands on me and getting me to do what he wanted. I'd learned from a good man that only weak, inferior men, put their hands on women. If he was willing to grab me, I had no doubt he would be willing to do more. I hated him.

I hated him. Hate was a strong emotion for me. I wasn't sure if I ever truly hated anyone. However, there was something about him, even if he hadn't put his hands on me, but especially now that he had, which made hate an inherent feeling.

He walked, expecting me to follow like the obedient woman he thought I had decided to be. But following behind him gave me time to think. These men obviously didn't hold women as their equals, so no matter what they thought they were seekers of, it was obvious they lacked seeking the most obvious truth: all men and women were created equal. Cataloging that information and learning how to play it against them was something I would do. I could pretend I was obedient until I got what I wanted or saw my opening. I needed to do it quickly because my mate's life was in jeopardy.

He led me to the same hall I was originally brought to. There was another lecture, and the room was filled with maybe thirty men and women, although there were definitely more men than women. I went to sit in the back, but of course, the arrogant ass grabbed my elbow and led me to the front, where there was a chair, seemingly left open for me.

I sat, feeling many eyes on me. A few quietly whispered but quickly shut up when Cain's eyes hit them. Cain walked to the lecturer, stopped them from talking, and said something quietly into their ear. His eyes widened as he looked at me. I then noticed him make eye contact with several guards at the exits and entrances.

Cain left without saying another word, and I finally let out the breath I'd been holding.

"Right, class, we have a new student who will join us today, and since she is not versed in languages, we will be doing the remainder of today's lecture in English." I studied the man in front of me. He was shorter than the average man, and I was sure I'd tower over him. He also was mostly balding on the top but had hair on his sides. His small nose with his narrow jawline made him appear almost misshapen. I took a second to sit back and look at my peers around me. Most were younger than I was. Some might've been as young as twelve or thirteen, but most were around eighteen. It was too hard to tell.

The lecturer, who I found out was referred to as Parsons by a few of the students, spoke at great length about the rise and fall of the Roman empire. I'd been through similar classes during my academic career, so I yawned, feeling bored. It also didn't help that Parsons had a monotone voice that could easily put the Discovery Channel's narrator to shame.

"Am I boring you?" he asked.

Uh-oh. I drew attention to myself.

"By all means, please don't mind me. I apologize," I said, not understanding why he needed to stop his class because I yawned.

"Well, if you think you can do it better ..." he trailed off. I was so sick of the men's attitude around here, so I stood. Probably not the wisest thing to do or the best way to stay under the radar.

"Where were you? Right, discussing the rule of Tiberius and the torturing and killing of Christians, including Jesus Christ. Hundreds of years passed, and the persecution for one's faith remained a stronghold of the Roman Empire. It wasn't until Constantine was in power in 313AD that all religions, including Christianity, were tolerated. Now, we could discuss if the fall of the Roman Empire had to do with bigotry. I could see that; people were resistant to accepting others, and perhaps that's why many fled to the east. Or we could discuss the traditional response on how exports in the east were greater than in the west and the inequity within the empire ultimately led to its demise." I was proud of myself. My Elle Woods moment was complete.

"There is no 'perhaps' about it. That is exactly why it failed," Parsons argued.

"Is it? Is it really? Do you not think religion and being open to others' religion played a larger role in the demise than you're letting on? I mean, come on, look at what part of the world we're in. To this day, they are still fighting about Christianity. The closed-mindedness and inability to accept everyone as equals ultimately leads to most nations' demise.

"And look around this room. Even in this modern age, it's filled mostly with men. Not once since I've been here have I seen an evolved culture that understands equality is key to a growing society. So, it's probably safe to say you will also eventually fall. Some young women are looking at me right now with their jaws wide open because they've yet to find their voice, and I'm getting the impression this is the first time they've seen a woman have one."

"That is quite enough," Abbas spoke, coming from the shadows. I had no idea he was here, witnessing my tirade. "It is one thing to come into our home unannounced, but to pass judgments so quickly without even spending a full day here is also closed-minded. Young Jomana comes from a line of women who, indeed, are very strong. They just use their strength to raise strong families of both men and women. Jomana was the first to break from her family's wishes and join the school, and we welcomed her with open arms. If they are looking at you, it might be because you are the tallest woman most of them have ever seen. And I do not think most have even seen your shade of hair color. Do not presume that we would not gladly take a female and teach her the ways. That is your arrogance. Many families here cling to their cultures. They do not want change. They do not like it, so yes, I suppose you are right. People are creatures of habit, and we can offer them an alternative, but do you not think most cultures, including Rome, could have fallen after trying to force a different way of life on its citizens?"

I opened my mouth to speak, then closed it again. I wasn't sure what I wanted to say and needed to ponder my thoughts.

"Miss Katz, please sit. Parsons, perhaps you can share something not written in a textbook with the class. Something new to Miss Katz and our class. I think that will go a long way in teaching her what the Rosi can do."

I sat and listened avidly to stories of the Dead Sea Scrolls that I'd never heard before. I found that once Parsons changed his story to more fascinating topics, he became more animated. I witnessed the girls in the class actively participating, and perhaps I was judging them too quickly.

After a while, we were dismissed for lunch. I followed a group of students who grabbed a small lunch satchel from an awaiting cart, then made their way through several long corridors that eventually led to a set of glass doors. Light poured through the glass from a courtyard, filled with an abundance of life, making me feel at peace for the first time since I arrived here.

The courtyard had a single tree whose trunk was wide, twisty, and at least fifteen feet in diameter. Its branches spread wide overhead, providing shade from the intense heat. Various flat boulders were spread out, and students were grouped in different sections.

"New girl, that takes guts speaking up to Parsons and Abbas like that," an older teenage boy spoke. He had light brown hair and hazel eyes, making him one of the more fair-colored people I had run across.

"What are you even doing here?" Jomana asked. She didn't seem pleased with me.

"Hey," —I ran my hand through my hair— "sorry about earlier."

She lifted her chin, made a harrumphed noise, then walked away.

I nearly gasped as I felt the tree. There was a gentle hum below the surface, and I seriously needed to hug the tree. Totally weird. Me, a tree hugger? Who would've thought?

Walking around the tree and strumming my fingers along the trunk, I ignored the looks of other students. The energy hummed the loudest at one spot, so I sat against it and closed my eyes.

"What is she doing?"

"I don't know. What was she going on about in the lecture hall? Equality?"

"It was weird. Who is she anyway?"

"Why does she look like that?"

"Is she smelling the tree?"

"Who smells trees?"

I blocked out the questioning voices and moved into that special place inside me.

"Ryker, can you hear me? I need you to wake up. Wake Up!" I shouted inside my freaking head. *"I made a mistake. I shouldn't have trusted Father Archibald. I'm sorry. I'm with the Rosi in some secluded town in the middle of the Middle East. I don't think they're going to let me leave here. If you can hear me. I fucked up. I'm sorry. I need you to wake up."*

Silence.

I squeezed my eyes tighter, sent an outpouring of love through the link, and prayed he would wake.

After a few moments of silence, I opened my eyes, and there was a different vibe from all the students. They were dead quiet—so quiet, were they breathing? Every pair of eyes were on me, and when I looked up, I saw what they saw. The tree that was so twisty and beautiful and finally gave me some peace had bloomed beautiful light pink flowers.

Drats, I did it again.

***

Soft murmurs flowed through the lecture hall, and every pair of eyes followed me. Parsons caught on quickly that something had happened, "Jomana, what's happened?"

Her eyes grew wide. "Was this a test to see if we were worthy?"

"Whatever do you mean, child? Speak up and stop talking nonsense."

"It was her," another student called.

A few fingers pointed at me, and I didn't think I could sink any lower into my seat. So much for keeping my powers secret.

The young guy who sat next to me earlier dropped to his knees in front of me. "Blessed be. Dear Lord, blessed be." I had no idea what he was talking about. He prayed, and at least I understood that.

I may have heard a Wayne's World "We're not worthy" thrown in there, or at least I was pretending in my head it wasn't as heavy as it seemingly *was*.

"Someone explain to me this instant what the big deal is?" He looked pointedly at me. "Miss Katz?"

I shrugged my shoulders. There was no way I was fessing up to that!

A teenage girl spoke, "It was a miracle. She must be blessed by the Gods, or one herself."

"A miracle," others mumbled.

Could my seat swallow me whole?

"She made the terebinth tree bloom."

"But that's impossible. It hasn't bloomed for centuries."

"Look!" another shouted.

The class, including the guards, who also seemed beyond curious, made their way, mumbling about the tree. I slunk into my chair, hoping no one would notice I didn't follow.

Alone, at last, I looked around the room and wondered if there was any way to escape this place. I couldn't leave from the door they had just exited. Instead, I slowly made my way toward the door at the back of the room, the one I remembered first coming through. I wasn't sure I could remember how to get out of here, but I had to try.

Chapter Five

I made it to the greenhouse. I wasn't exactly sure how I didn't run into a zillion guards on my way here, but I made it. Those double doors would be my way out, but even if I made it through the greenhouse, there would surely be guards on the other side.

A thought occurred to me. I was finally surrounded by nature. I found a quiet place, hiding behind a huge tomato plant, and leaned into them. I closed my eyes, unsure why, and asked the plants for help. I requested strength and prayed I'd find my way out of this place.

Feeling a renewed energy, I opened my eyes and walked toward the door. In my head, I requested the guards open the doors and not see me.

In a flash, the doors opened, and I walked past the guards without even a blink in my direction.

I felt alive with my spidey senses. When people looked in my direction, I sent them a message that simply said, *"pretend I'm not here."*

The further I moved away from the greenery and into the desert, the more eyes were on me. The bustle of people surrounded me, so in a way, they weren't paying as much attention to me. The only difference was that they didn't look away from me, either. My clothes were fancier than most. Was there anything I could do about it? I needed to blend in, not stick out.

I walked through the various stands selling their wares and finally settled on a woman selling clothes.

"Excuse me," I queried, hoping she spoke English.

She didn't. She looked at me questioningly.

"Trade?" I said, showing her my clothes and pointing to a tan tunic she had folded.

She spoke rapidly in a language I didn't understand.

"English?" I tried and again moved my hand between garments, hoping she would take the hint.

"English," she repeated brokenly, then held up a finger and returned minutes later with a boy.

"I speak English," the boy offered.

Thank Heavens.

"Can you ask her if she would be willing to trade my dress for a tunic and a leather water flask?"

The boy nodded and translated. "She said that is too much. The dress is worth far more than a tunic. Take something else, please."

I didn't need anything else, but I took a few seconds to peruse her store anyway, and in doing so, I stumbled upon some shiny rocks. One looked like the stones Mindy had shown me how to use, but I wasn't one hundred percent certain.

The merchant spoke, and the boy translated again, "She says if you like the stones, she has a special pack used for healing she would part with."

I nodded and asked the boy to ask her if I could change. She moved a curtain and tilted her head to the side, indicating I should change there. I thanked the boy and left him to change.

The tunic was tan and lacked shape; however, it was airy, and I fit in more. My blonde hair and height would still make me stick out. I was glad the boy was still waiting when I stepped out. "Can you ask her if she has anything that will cover my hair? I can trade her shoes."

He did his thing, and she nodded, then grabbed a long, dark piece of material that she tied so tightly around my head that I'd have no idea how to take it off. She measured my feet with another pair of shoes and found a pair more comfortable than the pair I currently wore. It was clear the quality wasn't the same, but in this heat, I'd take comfort over quality any day.

Nothing I could do about my height, so I had to try and blend in as much as possible.

I thanked them again, took my stones and my water satchel, and, as inconspicuous as I could, made it toward the exit. There was a commotion ahead, and I stopped someone I overheard speaking English to ask, "What's happening?"

"I'm not sure. There are whispers from the students of a miracle." A search was going on, and they undoubtedly had figured out I had left. Considering my height, I did what I could to not be seen. I tried to call on nature, but it didn't feel as close to the surface since I wasn't near a tree or greenery.

A horse galloped my way with Cain on its back. I dove behind a clothes rack, nearly getting caught.

"Have you seen a woman with hair spun like the sun?" he asked a man. I was eternally grateful for the wrap covering my head.

"No," the man responded.

"Hey, Miss, what are you doing?" the boy who helped translate for me crouched beside me.

"I'm playing a game with a friend. Have you ever played hide and seek? It's like that, only we use disguises as well. Can you help me find a really good spot?"

He grinned. "Follow me." I followed him and stayed low. He was swift in his movements, and I assumed I'd be noticed several times. Somehow, he moved so he wasn't seen, and in turn, neither was I.

We moved away from the market and in-between houses. They all looked so similar. I wasn't sure how anyone could decipher one over the next. "Come this way," he ushered me into a small home, and I followed.

A door slammed behind me, and suddenly thick arms circled me.

"What have you brought me, boy?" A man stood before me while another, larger man, restrained me from behind. The man I was looking at was around my height and maybe ten years older. The sun aged his skin, and under his dark eyes was a noticeable scar down his face. Chills ran down my spine.

"They're all looking for her. There's a search party going on right now. I'm unsure what she can do, but she must be very valuable."

"Let me go!" I struggled. "He's right. They're looking for me. I'm a special guest of the Rosi, and they'll be displeased if I'm harmed."

The man ignored me, opened a satchel, took several coins from it, and was about to place them in the boy's outreached hand when he paused and asked, "Were you followed?"

"N-no, Sir," he stuttered. "I did like you taught me, and I circled back."

"Good." He dropped the coins into his hand, and the boy took off without glancing at me.

"Who are you? What do you want with me?" I questioned.

"I'm not sure that is the correct question. The question is: who, dear, are you?"

"If you let me go, perhaps we can have more proper introductions," I gritted out, continuing to struggle. "Let me go!" I demanded again.

He ignored me, then moved to a black box he had sitting on a small wooden table and opened it. As the lid sprang free, dread assaulted me like oil coating my skin. His eyes turned black, and he repeated several words in a language I didn't know. Fear racketed my body.

He opened a jar, stuck his fingers into a black paste, walked to me, repeated more words I'd never heard before, and rubbed the paste against my forehead.

Ice coated my veins, and I was reminded of the cold, strange sensation when I was drowning in the swimming hole. The man gasped. I tried to struggle but began to feel worn out and limp in a way I imagined someone who was slipped a mickey felt.

"I can't believe it!" the man said. "You're remarkable."

That was the last thing I heard before I completely went black.

Chapter Six

I was surrounded by blackness. "Keeper," the voice called. "Keeper, wake, child."

I looked around, seeing nothing but blackness. There was no glowing blue orb like last time. I was in the same void as before.

"What's happening? What did that man do?"

"Keeper, you are in the den of a viper. His venom shows him who you truly are. You need to dig deep within yourself to wake and flee. Do you understand? Dig deep, Keeper. The flame will guide you." The voice trailed off, leaving me alone with my thoughts. Was the voice being literal? Was I about to be eaten by an actual viper? I didn't have time to question what it meant. I suppose, either way, figuratively or literally, I needed to get my ass up. But how?

The flame. I conjured an image of it in my mind, like I did nature and let it flow through me. It was different than the calmness of the trees. There was a power inside me I'd yet to even broach. Maybe I always knew it was there under the surface, and I never wanted to admit it because once I focused on it, a strange surge pulsed through me.

I felt whole. I grasped onto that power within myself and commanded myself to wake.

My eyes snapped open, and I was so grateful they did because I was being tied to a board. One ankle was already secured, and the big man holding me before was about to grab the other to tie that down. I kicked out, connecting with the middle of his chest, and he flew backward, crashing into the wall.

Holy shit!

I did that!

I didn't have much time to marvel at my strength because the other man was coming toward me. I pulled at the rope, somehow snapping it. He had more of the black paste on his hand, trying to put it on me.

"You shouldn't be awake," he accused dumbfoundedly.

I scrambled backward off the table. He held his hands up placatingly. "I'm not going to hurt you."

"Lies."

"No, you misunderstand. I only wanted to find out what you are and what an interesting creature it turns out I found, indeed." His big oaf stirred.

He was trying to distract me until his *muscle* recuperated. I wasn't going to take any chances, but I did want to hear what he thought I was.

"Oh, yeah, and what's that?" I asked.

"Why, you're an angel, of course, and something else ... I just haven't had enough time to figure that out yet. If you lay back down, I can finish my—"

Nope, not going to happen.

Two things happened simultaneously: the big guy stood and lunged for me, and I did a back handspring right over the man in front, landing on the table where I threw my palm against the big one's head. He immediately fell backward, getting knocked out (Tyson would be proud), then I spun on the table and lunged for the man.

"No, please don't hurt me. I didn't mean you any harm, I promise."

"Lies, lies, lies," I tsked, then pounced. I grabbed his throat and commanded, "Sleep." He began falling to the ground. So, I caught him so he didn't hit his head, then quickly secured him to the table. I looked at the big guy and secured him, just in case. It wasn't hard to find the rope. In fact, there was so much of it ... how frequently did they tie people up?

With both men secure, I looked around since he was the kind of man who valued information. I spied a bookshelf right away and ran my fingertips over the edges. I had no idea why, but a book sang to me. It made my fingers twitch, and my belly flip with excitement. I grabbed it and, at first glance, was bummed because the words were in a script. Then, I blinked, and suddenly I could read the script! The title of the book read *Angels of the Light*.

***

Hours passed, and I was invigorated with the knowledge. It spoke of ancient angels and what they could do. Different angels were more in tune with different things, and low and behold, Ariel was the angel of nature. It explained so much. But I struggled with the idea I was that angel. What happened to her? Shouldn't she be in heaven?

The next passage made my heart beat wildly.

The universe, in its divine nature, has always required a balance. For there to be evil, there shall be good. For there to be death, there shall be life. Finality is only a state of being. Thus, when an action is taken, a reaction follows.

Lucifer, having fallen from grace, desperate for life, fed from mortals, creating vampirism.

To counter the dark, the body of light was placed on earth. This powerful entity, as long as it exists, shall counter the darkness Lucifer casts. It shall not only stop vampirism from spreading if touched directly, but it can also counter the effects.

Such a force should be guarded, as with all light, its power can be limitless.

The man strapped to the table stirred, and I snapped the book shut, found a leather satchel, and placed it inside. I secured the satchel around me. It was time to ask him questions. "Wakey, wakey, sleepyhead," I nearly purred, confident in a way I'd only begun to understand. The big guy on the ground was still out cold.

The man on the table stirred and then struggled against the ropes. "What ... What did you do to me?"

"Why did you have the boy take me?" I asked, ignoring his question.

He didn't answer.

"Who are you?" I asked another.

"If you don't want to answer me, I can knock you out again and leave you tied up permanently. No one would find you for days. Or you can tell me what I need to know, and I can let you go."

"He'll come for me. Then he'll come for you."

"Who?" His eyes flashed black. He was some of the evil the book spoke of.

"Better yet, maybe I'll alert the Rosi to your presence," I said, taking a risk, hoping the Rosi had no idea he was here.

He paled and struggled against the ropes even harder. "No, you have no idea what they're capable of. Maybe once they were pure, but not anymore, not since Cain started to grasp for power."

"What has Cain done?"

"What hasn't he done? Please, if you untie me, I will tell you anything you want about Cain."

I thought about this for a second. I wanted to know how he acquired the book and who he thought would come for me, but I also wanted to know about Cain and the Rosi.

"If you try anything at all, nighty-night you go. Do you understand?"

He nodded, and before I walked over to untie him, I checked within myself to ensure my energy was still at the surface. The moment I did, it sparked to life. He couldn't hurt me. I untied him and felt a small amount of guilt as he rubbed his wrist. I shouldn't feel that way. He was going to do Lord knows what to me.

He sat, and I backed away, feeling skeptical. He walked to the bookshelf and ran his fingertips along the spines of the books, then turned and smiled knowing which book I had taken.

"The time to start talking is now. Tell me what you know."

"I am a man who collects information. There is a lot I know."

I unsheathed my dagger from the inside of my thigh and quickly brought it against his throat. "Do not play with me!" All right, I felt bad about that too, but I needed answers, and I felt like to get them, I had to at least pretend to be a badass.

He eyed the dagger. "Where ... where did you get that?" his voice quivered, relaying his fear.

"It was my father's. Now, answer the question."

"Wait, your father was John? You're Ariel Katz? How can that be?"

I immediately dropped my blade from his throat, completely taken aback that he knew my name and who my dad was. "How do you know my dad?"

He blew out a puff of air, sat in an armchair, and motioned to me. "Please, Ariel, sit. There is much for us to discuss."

After sitting, I tilted my head to prompt him to talk and talk is exactly what he did.

"I met your father years ago. He didn't like the shift within the Rosi. Most Rosi have no idea a shift even happened. However, Abbas is getting older, and he has been prepping Cain for some time to take his place."

"Neither of them looks all that old. Cain doesn't look much older than me."

"He has at least fifteen years on you."

"No way!"

He nodded his head and smiled at my enthusiasm. "Abbas is also your father's senior."

That was hard to believe as well.

"Your father didn't like the changes he saw, and he significantly pulled back from the Rosi. He gave me the book you were reading and told me if anything should befall him, the book should land in your hands. I always thought it was such a strange word choice. Not that I should find you and give it to you, but that it should land there, and it appears that is exactly what fate had in mind."

"You know, I've heard much about fate in the last few weeks."

"I'm sure you have. Nothing is a coincidence."

I looked at him skeptically. "I'm not sure if I believe that."

"It doesn't matter what you believe. What will be, will be."

"Very Gandhi of you."

"I'm nothing like him!"

"Surely you couldn't know Gandhi. He died ages ago."

"You must know by now nothing is exactly how it seems."

"Clearly," I replied, deadpanned.

"Wait, I always thought my father died in an accident. Do you think the Rosi had something to do with it?" My heart beat wildly in my chest. He wrote me a note, so maybe he always thought it would be inevitable.

"I am not sure. It's never been the Rosi's way to be violent. However, I've seen Cain do things." He shook his head. "Things that if Abbas knew, he would not be pleased."

"Then why doesn't someone tell Abbas?"

The man sighed. "Parents can be blinded by their love for their children."

I nodded. Parents needed to see the best in their children.

"What more can you tell me about my dad? How did you meet?"

"I am different."

"I saw the whole evil eye thing you have going on. You're not telling me anything I don't already know."

His eyes grew wide, and he pushed back as if struck, "You ... You know there were always rumors your line held angelic blood. Your father wasn't an angel, though. Why do the Gods choose now to bestow his line on you?" He said the last part almost like he was spitting it. And his nice-guy facade was slowly slipping.

"I'm not sure. Who do you work for? Who else would be interested in me?"

He smiled wickedly. "Everyone will be interested in you, dear."

Outside, I heard a commotion, and I sprang from my chair to gently pull back the curtains and peek out the window. The Rosi were going from house to house. They were looking for me, I was sure of it. I needed to hide, and I needed to do it quickly.

"They're coming for you," he surmised.

"They are, and sorry to do this to you again, but it won't do me much good if they find you and talk to you." I closed my eyes briefly, thought, "sleep," and then opened them. I'd knocked him out.

Panic rose inside me as I frantically looked for a place to hide. I didn't have much time. Their voices grew closer. There was a small crawl space under the stairs, and I cursed my tall frame. It would be a tight fit. I was just pulling an old box in front of the space to hopefully make it so they wouldn't look there when someone pounded on the door.

Chapter Seven

Feet shuffled into the house, then a whistle blew, and boots pounded into the tiny space, getting louder and louder. I closed my eyes, sensing how many men were there, and mentally felt twelve, not counting the additional knocked-out two. Then, like a slick oil coating my skin, I felt Cain's presence.

"What do we have here?" Cain asked the room.

"Don't let them find me," I silently prayed.

Another man spoke to Cain, but I couldn't make out what he said. There were too many of them talking over one another.

"She's got to be here somewhere. Find her," he ordered before speaking loudly, assumingly for me to hear. "I have something you want. Why don't you make it easy on both of us and come out now? We may have gotten off on the wrong foot, but if you come out, you'll see I can be generous. If you come out, I'll even let him live."

My heart thundered in my chest. *Who could he have? Certainly not Ryker.*

"That little errand I had Father Archibald run? Well, he brought back someone you will be interested in seeing again. Come out, Ariel, don't make this harder than it needs to be. I'll even give you a hint. He howls at the moon."

My stomach dropped. He had Ryker. I didn't hesitate to come out from my hiding spot. I pushed the box back and immediately crawled out. When I turned, no one was looking. They were all standing around, waiting for me to come out.

Cain clapped. "Very good. Look at how well you follow directions." He approached, causing me to flinch. It was far too intimate of a gesture.

"Where is he?" I growled. I had it in me to take on the entire room. I wasn't sure I was capable of winning, but I could try. Except what if attacking meant Ryker would be hurt? I had to remain calm.

"Relax, I'll show you to him soon enough. Tell me what happened here?" His eyebrow quirked curiously at the two unconscious men.

"I don't know what you mean."

"Don't play coy with me."

"They were like this when I got here," I lied.

His eyes squinted on me, then Cain ordered, "Amon, take her to the Eastern wing. Bring her through the back. Make sure she is not seen."

A man close to Ryker's height but double his width stepped forward with a grunt. I wanted to put him on his ass so badly. Something in me told me I could do it, but what if they hurt Ryker because of my rashness? No, I had to go willingly and see for myself that Ryker was safe.

Amon placed a black silk cloth over my head. "Is this necessary?" I seethed.

"Until you can be trusted, my bride, I'm afraid so," Cain retorted.

Now, what in the what did that mean?

"I'm not your bride."

"Oh, it's just a matter of time."

I couldn't see him leave, but the strong evil grip lessen a little. But another strong evil held on to my arms before throwing me over his shoulder and marching out. I was jostled back and forth and walking so long with my head upside down that I grew light-headed. The nausea was hard to control, and it took everything in me not to throw up. Throwing up with a bag over my head sounded worse than being waterboarded. Not that I knew what that was like, but I was sure it wasn't pleasant.

I tried to close my eyes, feel for Ryker and send my thoughts to him, but given my current predicament, that was easier said than done.

I wasn't sure how long we moved, but eventually, I was placed upright, and the hood was taken off, which was good because as soon as I was upright, I couldn't hold it another second. "Going to be sick," I muttered, then spotted a latrine in the corner of the room. I immediately ran to it and emptied the contents of my stomach. I was a crier when I threw up. I could never stop the tears from forming when I got sick. So not only was I throwing up, but I was also silently crying. I was sure whatever makeup I had on earlier in the day was a mess all over my face. I only cared because I didn't want Ryker to be scared half to death once I finally saw him again. Who was I kidding? He was probably beyond furious with me.

When I was finished, I sat and took in my surroundings. At some point, while getting sick, the room cleared out, and I was all alone. Gone was the lush room I'd originally been placed in. This looked more like a dungeon. I tried the steel door and immediately realized it was locked. I wasn't surprised.

The room was dark, but somehow, I could see more than I normally could, as if even in the darkness, my eyes adjusted. Weird, did I get that from my mother or father?

There was a cot that had seen better days along one wall, the latrine against the opposite wall, and that was it. I sat on the bed, conjuring an image of Ryker in my head.

"Ryker, it's me. I'm here. Can you hear me?"

He didn't respond, so I tried again.

"My love. I'm sorry. If you're near, please respond. I need you."

Nothing.

I focused on all the inner energy deep within myself and tried again.

"My wolf!"

That's when I felt it—confusion at first, then something different.

"Ariel?"

"Yes, my wolf! I am here. I'm so sorry. I've gotten us into a bit of a situation."

"I'm in the dark. Where are you? I've been in darkness for so long."

"What do you mean? Does he have a hood over your head, too?"

"Who is he? What are you talking about? Are you hooded? I need to get to you, but I can't find my way out of the damn darkness! Ariel, what is happening?"

"How long have you been in the dark? What's the last thing you remember?"

"Stop answering questions with a question, Ariel! Tell me what's happening!"

"Well, my moody wolf, if you'd tell me what's the last thing you remember, we can go from there!"

"You're so difficult, woman. Fine. Mindy was sleeping after changing. I feel like I had a dream a few times where I sensed your loss, then lots of pain. So much pain. I heard from my family too, but that's fuzzy now."

I squeezed my eyes tight. A sob tore through my chest. What had I done?

"Ariel, I can feel your pain. What's happening? Are you all right? I need to get to you. Tell me!"

I had to tell him. But the pain of my betrayal from leaving him cut deep. Not knowing where he was or his situation, I had to do it, even though it'd hurt him.

"Forgive me, my love."

"Your love?" he questioned like that was the most important thing I said there, but if he hadn't read my letter, he wouldn't truly know I love him. He must not recall when he was in my head before. Could that have been a dream?

"Yes, I love you. I don't know when exactly it happened, and I'm sorry I'm not in front of you to tell you, but I love you. Please forgive me."

"I love you. I can't tell you how long I've waited to hear those words. Centuries ... And I'm so lucky to have you."

"Ryker, I need to tell you what I've done. The night Mindy wouldn't change, and I hurt her, my magic was too out of control—I was too out of control and would undoubtedly hurt you or your family. I was unpredictable, and I needed training. I didn't think you would ever in a million years let me leave, so I wrote you a letter and told you to sleep, then I left with Father Archibald."

"You what!" His angry voice vibrated in my head. *"How could you do that?"*

"I'm sorry! I knew it was a mistake almost immediately."

"Ariel!"

His frustration was like a vice grip on my shoulders, shaking me.

"I screwed up! Okay! Do you want to hear what happened and where I am, or do you want to pummel me with your feelings?"

He was trying to calm himself—trying to tame his inner beast. After a few tense moments, his anger pulled back, and I continued.

"He brought me through a portal, and we were in an ancient city near Bethlehem. At first, it seemed like a school, but then Abbas, who runs the Rosi, wouldn't tell me anything. And his son! His son, Cain, apparently, is set to take over for Abbas, and he is not right. He thinks some prophecy says I'm going to be his wife, and I'm currently in a dungeon! Oh, and I ran away but came back when they told me they had you. When I ran away, I found this ancient book. I'm pretty sure I'm a descendant, or I am—I'm not sure—Ariel, the Archangel of nature. How cool is that! But then Cain showed up again, and I have the book hidden. He didn't take it. I have my dagger, too. I'm sure I could leave if I wanted to. I kicked some serious ass. But I need to make sure you're okay. I need to make sure you're not hurt. Can you wake? Can you tell me, are you okay?"

There was a beat of silence, then another.

"Ryker? Are you there?"

"I'm here. I'm trying not to hurt you with my anger right now, but I've barely got a grip. Did this Cain ... did he ... touch you?"

"I'm fine. I let his goon drag me back here, so I could be closer to you. Ryk, I messed up. I should've trusted we'd find answers together. I couldn't stand the thought of hurting you or anyone else. I can be impulsive. I just left, and now ... You've been asleep. Forgive me."

Calm washed through me along with overwhelming love and devotion.

"I could not stay mad at you. I understand how you could've thought you were doing the right thing. I must remember you are young and guided by your heart. The angel of nature? The Gods have fated me with a nurturer of life. I may be dreaming, but I'm blessed to have you."

"I..." I snapped my mouth shut, unsure of what to say, then finding anything else insufficient, I responded, "*I love you. I'm in love with you.*"

He sent me an overwhelming feeling of love that wrapped me up and made me feel safe, even though we were anything but.

"*I want to try to wake you, okay?*"

"Do it."

Chapter Eight

Squeezing my eyes shut, I focused on the light, then pushed my inner power out, ordering Ryker to change. Then, I prayed silently, begging it was fully when he did.

His pain slammed into me, making me clutch my stomach and double over. *"Ryker?"*

No answer.

"Ryker! Tell me you're okay."

Another lance of pain shot through my gut, and then there was a roar and a rumble through my chest as the force of Ryker's rage vibrated the room.

The pain stopped, and I checked our link. What was happening? I hated being blind.

I paced the dark dungeon, increasingly apprehensive. Where was he? Was he hurt?

The door flew open, revealing Cain surrounded by armored guards. "Seize her," he commanded. "He'll cooperate when he sees what he has to lose."

I froze, my instincts screaming to fight back, but my logical side needed more information. I struggled against the men as they grabbed my arms, holding me tight.

"Ryker!" I yelled in my head. *"They're taking me to you. I could fight them, but I need to see you. I need to be sure you're safe."* I hoped he heard me, and I continued to struggle.

"What are you going to do to me?" I questioned. "Where's Ryker? What have you done to him?"

Cain didn't answer, but I noticed a small pool of blood at the corner of his mouth and I just knew Ryker had something to do with it.

I fought against them for show. I was afraid, but I had a renewed sense of empowerment. I was undoubtedly angelic and somehow a vampire, both of which I was beginning to wrap my head around.

"No, Ariel. Fight," Ryker responded in my head.

I wished I had listened, but they dragged me from the room and down a dark hallway. It all happened so quickly that I wasn't prepared for what came next. Several men lay dead on the floor. Ryker had attacked them. There was a smashed chair, and ten men held Ryker back, pinning him against the wall.

It was dark, but even through the darkness, I could make out blood pouring from Ryker's temple. "No!" I shouted. "Let him go."

Cain stepped forward with all the arrogance of a pompous douche. The giant brute of a man who'd carried me to the dungeon stood between Ryker, Cain, and myself.

"Now, why would I do something like that?" Cain sneered.

"I swear to God, if you don't, you'll pay."

Cain laughed at me. "You? What could *you* do to *me*?"

"Ariel, do it!" Ryker yelled. "Whatever it is, you do it, now!"

A man punched Ryker in the gut, and I physically felt his pain. He'd taken on a lot of hits, and dread and guilt formed in my stomach.

"Ariel!" he gritted out.

"Isn't this cute?" Cain mocked. "The wolf thinks his woman can save him."

I conjured the entire well of light within me to the surface, muttering a quick prayer, asking to be strong enough and capable of doing what I needed to do. I flung my arms backward and shook the two men off me. Surprised, they reached out and tried to grab me again. I could fight them, but I didn't think that was what I should do at that moment. There were too many of them. Acting on instinct alone, I dropped to the ground and sensed everyone's energy but Ryker's and ordered them to sleep.

It took so much more energy to hold this many people down, but it worked! They crumpled, and I rushed to Ryker, who slumped forward once all the men had fallen. I flung my arms around him, and felt a wholeness filling my chest that I'd been missing, at the same time I felt his rage and physical pain rise.

"My wolf," I pleaded into his throat. I wanted to cry with relief that he was there.

"Ariel," he said painstakingly. "We have to go."

He was right. I knew it. He stood and shook off the passed-out bodies. I could feel his pain. "You're hurt."

"Not now," he gritted out.

"Then let's go."

He grabbed my hand, and we began to move toward the door, but I paused because Father Archibald was slumped on the ground. I couldn't tell if he was alive or not, but one thing I was certain of was he had betrayed me.

Pain lanced through me as Ryker urged, "Come on."

Hand in hand, we moved down the hallway and past the room I was being kept in.

Each step we took told me a story of the pain Ryker had endured. How long had they hurt him before I finally woke him? Painful guilt settled deep in my gut.

We came to an alcove leading up a set of stairs, and my hold on all the sleepers felt as though it might snap.

"Ryker, we have to get out of here. I'm holding them down, but it's taking everything in me too."

He squeezed my hand, and we ascended the stairs. "We need to hurry but still be conscientious of our surroundings." There was a door leading outside with a sleeping guard next to it. Ryker bent, took his keys, and unlocked the door.

We were on the backside of the building, facing the barns but away from the main entrance. It was odd we didn't hear the bustle of the town.

"Let's see if there are any horses and get the hell out of here," Ryker rushed out, grabbing my hand and moving us as quickly as his aching body would allow. I was trying not to panic or show him how afraid I was. But he was covered in bruises, and dried blood ran down his cheek. He had taken a beating and for Lord knows how long.

Upon entering the barn, we passed two more sleeping forms. Ryker led us to an already saddled horse. "Why don't you just shift?" I asked.

"My ribs are broken. I'm not sure how my wolf will do with a passenger with broken ribs."

"I'm ..." I wanted to say how sorry I was again, but if I muttered the words, I might break. I was already having a hard enough time holding myself together. It wouldn't take much for the dam to break, and the small amount of control I had left on every sleeping person would slip.

"Get on, Ariel."

The horse whinnied as I mounted it, and I dug even deeper into my well of energy, asking him to calm down and get us out of here quickly. Ryker got on behind me, pulled the rope securing the horse, then yelled, "Ya!" at the horse. He took off at full speed with remarkable grace and swiftness.

We passed the townspeople in a blur, but they were all asleep. I hadn't just put the room to sleep, but every single person except for Ryker. I held on as we rode faster and faster. As Ryker approached the main entrance to the city, I noticed that the tall doors were closed. He climbed off the horse. Witnessing his painful movements as he dismounted made the ache in my chest spread.

I had to hold it together for a bit longer. He turned a crank, and the door slowly drew open. I wanted to get down and help him, but I'd be in the way. Once it was open enough, he remounted the horse behind me, grunting as he did so.

Then we took off, riding for a while. With the sun beating on us, I wasn't sure how much time had passed because I became increasingly exhausted with each passing minute. "Ryker," I whispered.

He grunted a response. "I'm not sure how much longer I can hold them. It's ..." I yawned, not finishing what I was going to say. Then, like releasing two strings on a bow, the light that held an entire town asleep snapped. Immediately, I slumped forward and passed the heck out.

Chapter Nine

"Ariel, my love. Wake up," Ryker pleaded.

My eyes blinked open to a small fire glowing in front of me. The tiny sparks weren't enough to keep me warm, and my teeth rattled from the cold. "It's freezing," I murmured. "How long have I been out?"

"It's been hours. It's cold out here. I don't know how much longer the horse can move, and I worry a search party will be after us."

I felt within myself for any hold on anyone and I knew that I did not. I sat, feeling dizzy, looking at Ryker, who sat across from me.

"Why are you not sitting with me?"

"I'm trying not to throttle you for getting us into this situation."

My teeth still rattled. "I'm s-sorry."

"Dammit," Ryker cursed, then sat behind me. His legs pressed against mine, and his arms wrapped around me. He began to say something but stopped. He shook his head, and I was glad I didn't have to look into his disappointed eyes. "Why the fuck did you leave, Ariel?"

His heat helped warm me. "Do you remember us talking while you were sleeping?"

"It's like a dream, just bits and pieces. Start at the beginning and explain to me everything that has happened."

"I'd love to do that, I really would, but you're hurt, and you need rest. Are you sure we are far enough away that no one would find us?"

"Link with me. It will be faster that way." He was talking about when I showed him all of the images of my past very quickly. I grabbed hold of his fingers and tried to send him images, thinking about all that happened and hoping he got it all. Then I yawned, feeling like that took all my energy.

"It was blurry, but I got some of it." My head fell back as I was lulled to sleep.

"Christ but that took even more out of you. I'm sorry."

The next time I awoke, I was back on the horse, and the sun was rising. "Where are we?"

"We've been heading west. Any idea where we are in the world?"

"Father Archibald brought me through some type of a portal. He had said we were somewhere east of Bethlehem in an ancient city cut off from the rest of the world. Do you have any recollection of how you got here?" I asked, knowing he was probably knocked out because of me.

"No, I didn't wake until I was in that dungeon, and they'd already beat me. If you didn't wake me when you did, I'm not sure what would've happened."

There went that guilty feeling again.

Our horse whinnied, needing water. His steps were slowing, and I was afraid he would fall if he didn't get something soon. "Ryker, our horse is thirsty. It needs water."

"I haven't seen anything living for some time."

"Then I need to try and find a water source. We should stop the horse."

"No, you expended too much energy."

"I can't let the horse fall. We have to get down, Ryker."

He reluctantly slowed the horse, wincing when he hopped off with a bigger wince when he helped me down. "How badly are you hurt?"

"I've been worse than this."

"That doesn't answer my question."

"Shifting would help me heal faster, but I won't do that right now."

"Why?"

"First, I'll spook the horse. Second, I'll need water as well. And third, but most importantly, I need to be with you, like this, as a man." He grabbed my hand reassuringly.

We walked on, and I could tell the horse felt relief without us on its back. "How much did you get when I tried to show you what happened last night?"

"I got enough to know that if I ever see Cain again, he's a dead man." He brushed his thumb over my wrist, and I got the impression he saw Cain grab me in the library. I looked at my wrist and noticed that indeed a bruise had formed. Was that a day ago? Two? I couldn't seem to keep track of how much time had passed.

We continued walking, and with each passing step, I sensed the horse growing more and more tired. An idea occurred to me, and I bent, placing my hands on the sand, asking it to show me water. A faint breeze drifted over my neck, and the most remarkable thing began to happen ... It began to rain.

I didn't know much about the desert, but I didn't think rain was supposed to happen—as in ever! A puddle formed almost instantaneously in front of us and the horse bent low to drink it.

"You did this. You're amazing," Ryker said, gripping my hand.

We looked up at the heavens, opened our mouths, and let the rain wash down our throats, all the while, I silently thanked God for the generosity.

After several seconds of getting our fill, I asked Ryker, "Do you have anything we can collect it in?"

"I don't. What about your headwrap?" I'd forgotten about the wrap I traded for in the market. It hadn't even crossed my mind that it was still on. Then, I took stock for the first time since I was with Ryker. I still had the satchel with the water flask. I had the stones, the book, my dagger, ring, and medallion. How had they not taken these things from me?

"Oh, I got it!" I opened the satchel and handed him the flask.

He shook his head. "This would've come in handy already." He opened it and then grabbed a nearby piece of wood that was small enough to funnel rainwater into the flask.

"I forgot I had it."

"What else do you have in there?"

I showed him the items and mentally sent him a picture of the book and what I read. "I think I can heal you," I said after I sent him the images, not giving us time to address what he saw. Digging through the satchel, I found the small bag of healing stones and poured them into my hand. He continued to collect the rainwater still pouring over us. Looking over his shoulder, he noticed the stones.

"Do you think you can use them? Mindy only worked with you one time."

"It's worth a shot. I mean, it's raining, so anything is possible, right?"

The satchel was almost full, and the horse appeared to have perked up. The thud of the rain against the sand slowed. Ryker capped the satchel and I took his hand. We sat on the ground, facing each other.

The stones warmed beneath my fingertips then I reached around us and placed them in a circle on each side of us.

"I don't know the words Mindy spoke, so I'm going to go with my feelings, okay? It seems to be working for me thus far."

"Do it."

I touched the earth, and the rain abruptly stopped. My eyes flew open, and Ryker spoke to me in my head. *"You're remarkable. Do it. Try."*

I nodded back, shocked by what I could do, but strangely coming to terms with the fact that I wasn't normal. Who wanted to be normal, anyway, right?

I closed my eyes and felt the Earth and the way the water reacted with the sand, as a foreign entity, making itself known. I suppose the sand reacted that way to me as well. There was barely any life here, and here we were, asking it to live.

Focusing all my energy on the stones, I thought, *Heal* Ryker. *Heal.* I didn't know any of those fancy words Mindy used. I only knew to put my thoughts into his healing. Or at least I hoped he would. After several long moments, I opened my eyes and glanced at Ryker. He was staring at me, grinning.

"Did it work?"

"Yeah, it worked. Look around."

The horse was bouncing around like a foal trying out new legs. I sensed him and could tell immediately his body was renewed. Then I spotted a cactus with flowers blooming on it that had most definitely not been there before.

"Do you truly feel better?"

"I do, thanks to you."

Feeling slightly insecure by his praise, I gathered the stones and stood.

"So what now?" I asked with my eyes averted.

"No, don't shield yourself from me."

I met his eyes. "I'm sorry for everything. I'm sorry for leaving. I just thought … I would find all the answers. Gah! I wish my dad's note gave me more than a bunch of mysterious clues. I found this book, though, and this guy told him my dad said I'd find it. I'm so thrown on this destiny thing, you know? And then there's you—you physically took a beating because of me. Now we are in the middle of the desert. No food. No shelter. Lord knows who is after us and why! And how about what I did to your sister? I thought

I was going to get training here, I'm so flipping, sorry." I babbled. I was a jumbled-up mess.

"Shh. Come here," Ryker demanded. He waited for me to make the small steps into his waiting open arms. Once there, my entire being felt complete again. He pulled me close, his chest was snug against mine. His salt and pepper beard tickled the top of my head. My heart soared, feeling like it was finally home.

"Mate." I met his eyes. Hearing him call me that sent pleasure through me. "You acted impetuously. You made choices that hurt us both. Am I angry? Yes, but not at you. I'm angry that there are those who wish to hurt you. I'm angry that the place your father implied would help, didn't. I'm angry Cain thinks what's mine is his. You're not his. You're mine. You always have and always will be. You're meant for me. I'm angry that you're feeling lost. I want to take that from you. I want to bring you back home to the safety of the pack and let whatever is happening with you happen organically. We can't force nature to happen at our will. There is much to be discovered still, but we will have to wait. Mostly though, I need you to know the most important truth, the thing that is more valuable than anything else ... I love you. I love you so incredibly much that my heart hurt knowing you were in danger, and I had no way to get to you. You amaze me. You—"

I cut him off. I couldn't take another second of his declarations. I kissed him hard and deep and unrelenting. I put every bit of pent-up emotion into the kiss, all of my remorse, my pain of being unsure of my identity, then finally, and most importantly, my love.

Finally, I broke the kiss. Our lips were swollen from the intensity of it. "I love you. I'm in love with you. So stinking in love with you."

He kissed me again, then pulled back and placed his forehead against mine. "I'd love nothing more than to be with you right now, but we need to move. I'm not sure how far we've traveled, but the further away from those people, the better." I nodded and took a step back, even though every fiber of my being wanted what he wanted. I needed him inside of me but now wasn't the time. The cost would be too high.

Chapter Ten

Relief rushed through me as we spotted a small village emerging in the distance. We'd finished our water supply some time ago and were exhausted from the beating sun. My lips were chapped and I was beyond exhausted.

"We need rest." I said what we were both thinking.

"We will rest. Not much longer. I'll find us food and shelter, okay? Hang on just a little longer."

I nodded, trusting he would do exactly as he said.

We shuffled on in silence, too exhausted to speak. I had no idea how many miles we had covered today, only that the soles of my leather shoes were worn from the hot sand. And the sun that had peeked now slowly descended the sky. Night was upon us again, and with that came the cold. I'd always associated the desert with heat and never given the coldness much thought until now.

The closer we got to the village, the first sign of modern life flashed as headlights from a passing car. Thanks to the darkness, we had no idea a road was even there. *Welp that would've come in handy,* but I was too exhausted to add my sarcastic quip out loud.

Small farmhouses emerged. A sheep baaa'd in the distance, and life slowly revealed itself. The houses grew closer, and the scent of cumin and other rich spices hung in the air from nearby open windows. I let Ryker lead the way. With his years of knowledge, I had to trust he would take care of us.

We came to a stable where a young boy, maybe around nine or ten years old, was carrying a bucket of water into the stalls. I could've easily taken the horses' trough and drank the entire thing. I was that parched.

Ryker called out to the boy in a different language.

"What language was that?" I whispered.

The boy said something back, and Ryker sniffed the air, handed the boy our horse, then grabbed my hand and led me around the barn.

"Ryker, what's happening? Where are we going?"

"There's a wolf. I can smell him."

"Wha—what?" I stammered.

He squeezed my hand reassuringly and requested my silence.

I silently followed him behind buildings, passing several streets as we went. Finally, we stopped at a door, and Ryker's face lit up. He didn't need to knock because, as if sensing his presence, the door flew open.

A man with dark hair who stood a few inches shorter than Ryker, but was equally as wide, if not wider, opened the door. His head swung back, and he laughed with great hilarity, making his stomach shake as he did.

"This is rich! You show up on my doorstep after what ... How long's it been? Fifty years? Seventy-five?"

"Too long, Brother. Too long." Ryker slapped him on his back, and they hugged the way two friends who hadn't seen each other in fifty years would. "Ledger, you old man, how have you been?"

"I'm good. I see age hasn't made you any better looking."

"You're one to talk!" Ryker chuckled, releasing him. "Are you going to keep us on your doorstep all night, or are you going to invite us in?"

As if on cue, the moment Ryker mentioned us, it was as if Ledger only then noticed I was there. His eyes widened, and he sniffed the air. "You've found your one."

"I've found my one," Ryker confirmed. They shared a look that was both tender and intense. Ledger closed his eyes for a brief second, then opened them. "I'm happy for you, Brother."

His door opened wide, and we entered the modest space. There was a small lamp sitting on an end table. It didn't give off a ton of light, but enough to see a futon next to it. On one side of the house, there was a small countertop, a sink, and a miniature refrigerator. Across from that was a modest table with two chairs. There were two closed doors; I assumed one was a bedroom and the other a bathroom.

"We've been traveling some distance. We need food and water."

"Yes, yes, of course. Where are my manners? Please have a seat." He moved into the kitchen, and I plopped onto the futon, too tired to say much. He took out a few glasses, grabbed a jug of water from the fridge, and poured our drinks. He handed the glass to Ryker, then handed one to me and said, "Well, Ryk, are you going to introduce us, or what?"

Ryker gulped his water, poured himself some more, then cleared his throat, "Sorry, this is Ariel."

"Elle, I go by Elle," I corrected, sipping my water, afraid that if I drank it too quickly, it would make me sick.

"Ariel, Ledger and I have known each other since we were basically pups," Ryker informed me.

"So, what brought you all the way out here then?" I asked, curious about why we randomly ran into a wolf Ryker knew in the middle of the Middle East.

"Ah, I never could stay in one place for very long. The better question is, what brings the both of you way out here?"

Ryker cleared his throat, and Ledger's attention shifted from me to him.

"How about we eat and rest first?" Ryker said, sitting next to me.

"I'm a shit cook. I have a can of beans in there. If you want, I can see what I can scrounge up in town."

Ryker gave him a chin lift, and the two shared a look like they were having a wordless conversation.

A few seconds passed, and Ledger eventually left. I found it hard to keep my eyes open, but Ryker insisted I drink water and stay awake. Maybe fifteen or so minutes had passed by the time Ledger returned. I jumped as the door opened, fearful they had somehow found us.

"It's just Ledger. It's okay."

I didn't feel okay. I was exhausted and nervous about being stationary. Ryker put his arm around me and squeezed, leaving me a little lighter from his touch.

"It's late. I got what I could. Some bread and freekeh, which is a fancy word for soup."

He poured the soup into bowls and handed them to us. I reached out to Ryker and spoke into his head.

"Do you trust him?"

"I do."

"You don't think it's strange he's out here by the Rosi?"

"When you've lived as long as I have, you know there are wolves all over the world."

I nodded as Ledger took a seat at the small kitchen table, giving us space. The soup was good, and I slowly sipped it as Ledger cleared his throat, looking for answers.

"Not to try and rush you or anything, but it's been a long time."

"I know. You need answers as to why we're showing up on your doorstep in the middle of the night."

"I do."

Ryker nodded, and I watched the exchange with avid fascination. "Have you ever heard of the Rosi?"

Ledger's demeanor changed, and he nodded once.

"Have you ever had any dealings with them?"

"A time or two, yes," Ledger said, his jaw ticking as he spoke.

"They convinced Ariel to leave with them, then basically kidnapped me, and when I woke, they were beating me half to death."

"Christ. But why? And I know you ... How in the world could anyone kidnap you while you're sleeping?"

"It's a long story, but let's just say magic put me to sleep."

"Magic." He shook his head as if everything Ryker was saying was bizarre. "The Rosi was good. They were truth seekers. They have always hunted for ancient knowledge. But lately, there's been talk of corruption."

"This is the same thing the guy who grabbed me in the house said," I added, then asked, "What do you know about Cain?"

Anger emanated from Ledger as if it was a physical force.

"Watch yourself, Ledger. She can feel that."

Ledger closed his eyes and took a second to collect his thoughts. When he opened them again, his temper had calmed. "I know he's next in line to take over as the head Rosi, but he's no truth seeker. He's as corrupt as they come."

"He's who we're running from," I shared.

Ledger walked through a door that had been closed and returned with a huge black trunk adorned with small copper beveled nails along the sides, then popped the latches. Inside was an arsenal of weapons. He pulled a crossbow out and set it on the table, then sword after sword came next. Fear coursed through me and the images of a war played out in my mind, filling me with dread.

I looked down at my ring, which I'd nearly forgotten I was wearing. It was bright red. I didn't have anything to fear, so I swallowed back my emotions and looked at all the weapons with interest. The swords all looked ancient, with intricately carved handles. Ryker reached for one with a carved wooden handle. He tossed it back and forth between his hands. "I can't believe you still have this!"

"Of course I do. It's some of the finest craftsmanship I've ever seen."

I inspected the sword, recognizing Ryker had made the handle.

"Does he know you're here?" Ryker asked Ledger. "Will he think to look for us?"

"They don't know I'm here. Still, we should be cautious. Why don't you two try to get sleep, and I'll keep watch? You can take my bed."

"A bed sounds nice," I said, yawning.

Ryker helped me up, and we entered the small bedroom. It didn't matter that the bed was a twin. I'd make us fit, even if I had to sleep on top of him.

Ryker led me to the bed and pulled back a blanket. "Get in, my love. Rest. You've created miracles today. I know you're dead on your feet. I'm going to talk with Ledger. I'll be in shortly."

I didn't have it in me to argue. I was exhausted. So I did as he said and crawled into the blankets. He kissed me and it was soft and sweet. I wished for more, but he was right, I could barely keep my eyes open.

"Sleep. I'll be back," he whispered, then a moment later, the latch on the door clicked shut, and I immediately passed out.

***

"Keeper. Keeper," a voice singsonged. Blackness surrounded me. I wasn't afraid. I'd been here before. I conjured the blue light within myself. I didn't even have to think about it. I just felt for it and; it was there.

"Keeper. Keeper," the voice sang again.

I could see myself with the blue light but nothing else except blackness.

"Who are you?" I asked.

"We forgot. You do not remember." The voice felt layered, as if it was actually multiple voices. "You've come far in your journey, yet have much more to learn."

I wanted to ask so many more questions, but then it dawned on me who the voices were. They were —the Fates. I had no idea how I knew, but I did.

"She's remembering."

As if something clicked inside me, I blurted, "I'm an anomaly."

"You are that, but so much more."

"I'm a guardian angel. That's why I'm the Keeper. I protect the flame."

"Yes! Go on."

"I protect nature and life."

"Yes."

"But this time is different. This time, I love."

"It is a gift."

"It is." I knew innately I'd done it alone every time I'd been the Keeper. I'd been here many times before, but this time was different.

"To give you love, you needed a balance. Without evil, there can be no good. You are here to balance out the good and bad. You are both guardian and fallen. You will choose your destiny and your path. But we have faith in you, that you will choose wisely."

"But you're the Fates. Isn't my destiny already written in the stars?"

"We can pair you with your perfect match. We can set things in motion, but God has given you free will. It will be your choices that ultimately determine your fate."

I wanted to ask what I'd have in store for me. I wanted a clue as to what I should do, but instead, as if pulled from my dreams, my eyes shot open, and a different warmth surrounded me.

Chapter Eleven

Ryker was all around me. His bare chest and thick arms enveloped me. The reality of my dream faded as I inhaled his scent. A switch was immediately flipped, and my body reacted how it had longed to since we'd reunited. Wetness pooled between my legs, and even in the darkness, I saw his wolf flash in his eyes.

I felt his hard length through his jeans and mewled.

"That's right, purr for me," he coaxed, running his fingers inside my top and along my body. Chills broke out across my skin.

"Open your mind to me," he ordered.

I closed my eyes and immediately did what he wanted. I felt the outpouring of love, want, and need.

"I missed you."

"You have no idea."

He sat and peeled my shirt from my head.

"Will he hear us?"

"I don't care."

Suddenly, his mouth was on my breast, his tongue flicked my hard bud. My back arched and I whimpered, drawing his body closer to me.

"I need you," I pleaded.

"Not yet."

I licked his throat and sensed his pulse. The heavy thrum made me wild.

"Then touch me, please."

"Good, I need you to beg. Sometimes, I'm unsure whether to throttle you or take you over my knee."

The thought of him taking me over his knee made my clit throb.

"Definitely over the knee."

He shook his head. "*You left me.*"

My body stiffened. "*Are you mad at me?*"

He closed his eyes and then hugged me. *"Just don't ever leave me. Promise?"* Guilt coursed through me. *"No, my love. Don't feel guilty. I understand why you left. It's just—I need you to promise."*

Suddenly, I needed him to open his eyes and look at me. I didn't like this subtle game we were playing. Making sure our link was completely open, I poured love, remorse, and an infinite feeling of connection through it.

"*I promise.*"

His eyes opened, and stared into mine. I felt the brevity of the moment and our souls sang to each other. I was complete in an indescribable way, and he needed our connection the same way I did.

I undid his jeans, licking my lips in anticipation as he guided them off his hips, making quick work of discarding them. Shifting my leg from my clothes so that I was open to him, I straddled his lap, needing to be closer. His heat lay across my core, and I needed him inside.

As if knowing how badly I yearned for him, he entered me with one deep thrust.

"*Yes!*" I cried, my nails digging into his back. I rode him like my life depended on it. I wanted him to see and feel every ounce of desire I had for him. I wanted him to know I knew I'd made a mistake. I wouldn't leave him. We were connected eternally.

His fingers dug into my ass as he pumped vigorously.

"*Ariel,*" he worshiped my name.

His fingers moved between us, circling my clit. Pleasure shot through me, and I helplessly called out his name. "Ryker!"

We were no longer in our heads. The world could burn around us, and it was just the two of us connected in perfect synchronization. I licked his skin and nibbled at his throat while he rolled my clit and simultaneously pinched my nipple.

My legs wrapped around his waist, and I kissed him. His tongue mingled with mine, and that's when it happened. The intensity of the moment blasted us apart. His thick shaft pulsed as he released his seed. My body spasmed against his, and everything was right in the world.

***

A knock at the door broke us apart. "I think I smell something," Ledger said through the door.

I looked at Ryker curiously. *"He has the best sense of smell of any wolf I've ever met. We need to dress quickly."*

I hurriedly did as Ryker suggested, ensuring I had my ring and dagger. Something told me to hide my satchel. I didn't want anyone to find the book. I had no idea why, but I searched the room and noticed an old bookshelf that looked like it hadn't been touched in years. I placed the book in the space behind the books and hoped whatever Ledger smelled wouldn't hurt us.

"Grab a weapon. Take her. I'll distract whoever it is while you keep her safe."

Ryker nodded once, then grabbed the sword he'd made. *"Are you ready?"*

"I'm ready."

"Be safe," he said to Ledger.

"You too. I'll find you."

The sun crept back into the sky as we stepped outside. I could see more modern-day amenities than the night before. I didn't have a chance to take much in because Ryker quickly pulled me away. I chanced one last look at the house, knowing I'd need to return one day for the book, and as I did, a large black wolf nearly the same size as Ryker stepped out. He had a fierceness to him as he stalked in the opposite direction from us.

Ryker prowled through the streets, darting his head back and forth. Although he wasn't in wolf form, his jerky head movements reminded me of it. We came to a break between buildings. Ryker made a right, circling back toward the house.

"Why are we headed back?"

"Instinct."

I couldn't argue with that.

We moved through alleyways and in between houses. The streets were narrow, and the homes were close together. Sand kicked up under our feet as we scurried along. Ryker's arm shot out and stopped me from proceeding. *"I hear something."*

I tried to listen to see if I could hear it as well, but heard nothing. I felt for our link; somehow, instinctually, once I did, it was like I could hear what he did—soft footfalls surrounding the house. How I knew that it was the house we'd been in, I wasn't sure, but I just knew. Fear washed through me. They'd found us. Was Ledger okay? Would we be okay?

He pulled us to the left, away from the house. It was easy to follow him with our minds linked. There was a succinctness to our movements that made them effortless. We reached the back of a house, and several garbage cans were stacked next to one another.

He climbed on top, then hauled himself onto the roof before reaching for my hand. I followed his lead and climbed, my fingers meeting his as he pulled me beside him. I was afraid but was also filled with a sense of exhilaration. We crept slowly over the roof and found we were close enough to the building next to us to climb atop. We did this for several buildings creeping over one to the next until we were on the rooftop next to Ledger's house.

Once there, I spotted Ledger several rooftops over and being linked with Ryker, I was keenly aware of Ledger's wolf. He instinctively looked at the men surrounding his house. I felt a deep-rooted hate pulsing toward them. It wasn't my feelings; it was feeling Ledger's wolf. Violence surrounded him. What was the full story behind the Rosi and his feelings?

Ledger's wolf made eye contact with me, and I shuddered at the violence behind his eyes. Ryker pushed out a calming feeling toward him, which immediately made him change. I looked at Ryker questioningly.

"It's the alpha in me."

We watched the house for several minutes. People went in and out. Eventually, I saw Cain, making my blood turn cold.

"They're not here. Find them. I want them brought to me, and I want him to suffer," Cain ordered.

Anger permeated off Ryker. His control was close to snapping. He wanted to shift, and he wanted to end Cain. I placed my hand on his arm, hoping to calm him.

"You're mine. I'll never let him take you," he said.

"Nor I."

His men knocked on every door near the house we stayed in. It was early, and you could tell how annoyed each household was, even from above. People were brusque with his guards, attempting to slam the door in their faces. It made me smirk until I witnessed them shove an elderly lady to the ground. That was not okay. I made a move to defend her, but Ryker held me back.

"Not now."

Something deep inside me felt the heinousness of this. *It's wrong.*

Ledger's wolf felt my anger, and I sensed the moment he decided to do something about it. Springing from the rooftop to the ground, his wolf grabbed ahold of the man and threw him to the side. The old woman shrieked, and the guards' attention shifted in Ledger's direction. Another man headed toward him. I wanted to shout for him to look out, but as if sensing my panic, he turned at the last second and threw that man to the side as well.

He sprung over another man. Having been seen, it seemed all of Cain's men were now after him. *"We have to help him,"* I pleaded with Ryker, still holding my arm in place, communicating he didn't want me to move.

"He's strong and fast. There's not a single man there who can catch him."

I needed to trust what Ryker was saying, but it was hard.

"They're distracted. We need to go."

"Go? What if he's hurt?"

"He'll find us."

I don't know how or why I did it, but I sent an image of Ledger's wolf to him, showing him finding us, and hoped I portrayed what I wanted.

He momentarily paused, and guilt coursed through me. I distracted him. I knew I did. I spotted a man a few yards ahead with a spear. I sent the image to Ledger, hoping he would see it.

"Come on!" Ryker said, grabbing my arm. I couldn't see what happened to Ledger, but I had to hope he was okay. He put himself on the line for us. I didn't feel right leaving him, but surely Ryker would know if he could handle himself.

I followed Ryker in the opposite direction as we swiftly moved away from where Ledger was headed. We moved from building to building. A few jumps seemed hard, but Ryker mentally assured me I could do them. And each time I jumped, he was right. I could do it, far easier than I would've ever imagined. Our speed was quicker than ever, and I noticed I was losing Ryker once we got moving. How far had we moved? Fifteen, twenty houses away?

We were at the end, I could no longer hear Cain's men, and there wasn't another house for us to jump across. We waited several long minutes, making sure the coast was clear for us.

"I don't see a way down for you. I'm going to shift. I want you on my back."

I nodded and watched with quick appreciation as Ryker stripped, then, within seconds, shifted.

His wolf was magnificent. I didn't waste time marveling at him how I would've liked. Instead, I quickly grabbed his clothes and sword, ensured my dagger was secured, then mounted his back as he leaped from the building.

He was moving swiftly, taking us away from the village. We found a barn on the outskirts of town that I was pretty certain we had passed the night before. Once inside, he quickly shifted back, and I handed him his clothes to redress. We both took a minute to gain our breath and collect our bearings.

"Do you think we're safe?" I finally asked out loud, looking around the old barn and scrunching up my nose from the scent of dirty stalls.

"As long as we're in this part of the world, we'll never be safe. We need to figure out his fascination with you and what he knows about your existence."

"Do you think those answers could lie more with my family than anything we might learn out here?"

"I'm not sure. We haven't even talked about the book. What you showed me ... That's heavy stuff."

"I had another dream!" I shouted, remembering I'd yet to tell him about it. "Oh, my God. Oh, my God. Oh, my God!" I repeated.

"What is it?"

I began to tell him, but his head jerked to the barn opening. He shoved me behind him as Ledger appeared as a man, bleeding from his side.

Chapter Twelve

"Brother," Ryker said, rushing to Ledger's side.

"You're hurt!" I cried out, overwhelmed by my anger, guilt, and frustration. "You were helping us, and you're hurt! We shouldn't have left him."

Ledger coughed. "It's just a scratch."

I ignored his nakedness and looked at his wound. It was jagged and deep. Without medical care, this could turn ugly real fast.

"We need a hospital," I urged.

"Were you followed?" Ryker asked.

"Would I be here if I had a tail? You know me better than that," he coughed out again.

"We have to do something, Ryker. He's hurt."

Ryker ignored me and questioned Ledger, which outraged me.

"What happened?"

"They all had spears, and were ready to use them. They came prepared. I dodged a dozen or so, then one of them ... Eh, I wasn't so lucky," he coughed out.

"Ryker. We need the stones. They're in the satchel with the book."

"What stones? What book?" Ledger asked.

"I have stones I might be able to heal you with. I left them at your place for safekeeping. We have to go back."

"He'll heal," Ryker replied.

"We're not going to sit here, waiting for the other shoe to drop."

"He's right. I'll heal. You can leave me here, and—"

I cut him off realizing since we'd been linked in his wolf form, I now felt a kinship toward him.

"We're not leaving you! That is the dumbest plan. What if they find him, torture him ... Lord knows what else to him. He helped us get away back there. We're not leaving him."

Ryker closed his eyes as if he was searching for patience. "You're right, Mate. We won't leave him. I only wish to keep you safe. I will retrieve the stones."

"No!" I shouted. "I'll go."

"Over my dead body."

My anger was rising again, and I tried to keep it in check. "They won't touch me. I'll put them all to sleep or something."

"Wait, you can put them to sleep?" Ledger asked, but we ignored him.

"And if you do that, how will you have enough energy to heal him?" He looked at me questioningly.

Shit, and fuck, he had a point. *"I'm afraid something will happen to you." "I'll be safe, my love."*

"What's happening between you two? It's like I can feel it," Ledger asked. *"I thought only your pack could feel it."*

"You're magnificent. How you connected with him in wolf form makes him feel like part of the pack. You know how long I wanted him to be a part of my pack? He's always been a lone wolf."

"Seriously," Ledger coughed, "This is getting weird."

His coughing had me pulling back. He was hurt, and we were silently communicating.

"I know all of this might seem strange. But, Ledger, Ariel's special."

"Special, how?"

"Did you feel her connecting with you in wolf form?"

Ledger looked confused for a moment, winced in pain, then nodded his head once. "I wasn't sure ... I never felt ..."

"Connected?" Ryker finished for him.

Ledger nodded. "How did you know?"

"Since you moved around so often, I always thought maybe you didn't feel as connected to the earth as the rest of us. Linking with me and, thus, Ariel, made you finally feel what it was like to be a part of a pack."

"This is neat and all, you guys, but Ledger's bleeding out here."

"I can't let you go," Ledger said. "I'll heal. But feeling what belonging to a pack feels like, even if only for a second, is something ..." his voice trailed off as if it was too much to cope with. "I can't let you do anything that might harm either of you."

Ryker nodded once as if he was reserved to go along with Ledger.

"What? No! You can't just go along with him. He's obviously hurt. And you guys want to what? Just wait around and sit here, hope he heals and we can get out of here without them finding us?"

"Calm down," Ryker pleaded. He wrapped his arms around me, attempting to calm me, but all I saw was Ledger lying there bleeding from something that felt inexcusably my fault. Instinctually, I dropped to my knees beside Ledger and placed a hand over his bloody wound and my other hand to the earth. Finding that well deep within me, I let it grow. Seconds passed, and all I imagined was the light, the earth, and the power from it all expanding.

"Ariel," Ryker shouted, but I ignored him and let the energy come. *Heal him, I pleaded. He deserves our strength. Heal him. Earth that we walk upon, that provides us with a steady place to keep our footing, heal him. Please, heal him.*

Energy surged through me, and I didn't have a chance to see if it worked. My vision felt fuzzy, and I saw blue. I knew what would happen next. It had happened so often already. This time, I was prepared for it, though. I saw the fear blazing in Ryker's eyes, followed by his immense love.

"Don't fear it. I love you."

Then, like every other time this happened, I passed out.

***

My eyes stung as I opened them. I remembered the pain from the first time I'd passed out, but this was nowhere near as severe. Darkness surrounded me. I was alone but somehow innately knew Ryker, and even Ledger were nearby. Silky sheets covered me, and the air smelled of curry, making my stomach rumble.

The room momentarily spun as I sat up. I was no longer wearing the blood-covered tunic but now wore a simple linen dress. My hair lay perfectly flat, and I could tell it had been brushed. My skin was clean as if I'd bathed while out, making me wonder how long I'd been passed out.

I swung my legs off the side of the bed. They were jelly-like and wobbly as I did. The pain I momentarily felt when I opened my eyes quickly faded. The floorboard creaked as it bore my weight.

I took another step, a little surer of my footing. The door swung open, and hallway light flooded into the room. There was Ledger. The sight of him took me off guard and made me lose my balance. I fell back toward the bed.

"Whoa there," he said, closing the small distance between us. "She's up."

"You're okay?"

"Thanks to you, I'm as good as new." He took a bite of an apple and casually leaned against the wall. "Sleeping Beauty, if I'd known your saving my butt would put you out for days, I might've waited to heal."

"Days! I've been out for days."

Ryker's feet pounded down the hallway, and he came into the room in a huge rush.

"Ariel." My name was rushed out with a sigh of relief as if he were thanking the Fates I was awake. Then I was in his arms. His mouth was on mine, and I couldn't stop my burning need for my wolf.

"Out!" Ryker ordered Ledger, breaking our connection momentarily.

Ledger chuckled as he left the room and closed the door reservedly. And something about that caused more fear to run through my heart than knowing I'd passed out again..

"I did it to save Ledger's life."

"And I told you that he'd heal. It was an unnecessary risk."

"What if we were ambushed while waiting for him to heal?" I shot back.

"What if we were ambushed while waiting on you!"

All right, so he had a point, and again I might've acted a little preemptively. "I hadn't thought about that. I just saw him bleeding out, and I knew I had to do something because it was my fault! All of this. I caused it all, and I'm so stinking sick of my actions hurting others. Do you think I'm the type of person who learns I can heal people and sit there and not do it because it might cause a consequence for me? A consequence, might I add, that I knew I would wake from."

"How? How did you know you would wake? Because you did before? What if this time was different?"

"It's not. Here I am."

"Do you even know where you are or what we had to do to get here?"

I took a deep breath. I had to remember I scared him, but my anger rose, and I didn't want it to. I exhaled, then asked, "Where are we? What happened while I was out?"

He reached out in his mind and linked it with mine. I saw images of Ledger healed and astonished. Ryker's anger was palpable, but his fear ... His fear was like a vice grip squeezing his heart. He wanted to howl out in agony that I was passed out again, but he refrained to keep me safe. They had words about how I could do such a thing. Ledger sat beside me, prayed, and thanked the Fates for healing him while Ryker silently prayed I'd wake. Time ticked and night fell, and eventually, Ledger left to get the book once they no longer sensed Cain's presence.

Ryker wouldn't leave me. He refused. He was afraid for Ledger but had to trust he would be fine. Ledger eventually returned, and this time with a car. He had a friend a few towns over that he could trust, and they brought me here, where I'd been ever since. That seemed easy enough, but then Ryker showed him by my bedside, pleading with me to wake. Images of him caring for me, talking to me for endless hours, hoping and begging the Fates to return me to him flicked through my mind. He'd do anything if I came back. I felt his pain, and it sliced through me.

Placing my forehead against his, I silently cried. *"I'm sorry I keep hurting you."*

He lifted my chin and kissed where our foreheads had been pressed together. *"We make decisions together. We're mates."*

Then he lifted my chin a tad more, and his lips were back on mine. His beard brushed against my face as his soft lips eased mine open. His tongue darted out and brushed against mine, it was as if in that instant all of my guilt, shame, and regrets were washed away.

He cupped my face, making me feel cherished. My arms slid up his back and over the strong hard ridges. Seriously, I never knew I had a thing for backs until Ryker.

Breaking the kiss, his lips trailed over my jawline and down my neck. His hands moved until the soft pads of his thumbs rubbed against my nipples. He'd slid his hands up the tunic without me even realizing it.

I arched my back at his touch. "Yes." What a simple word. Filled with everything I wanted. I could barely say a thing because my desire ran so hot, but I could get out that simple word. It said it all.

"Yes!" I cried again as he pulled my tunic over my head, and his lips found my hard bud. I needed his clothes off just as badly. I pulled at his shirt, momentarily becoming distracted as he broke free from my breast to pull it overhead. His skin looked flawless.

"Ryker."

"Mmm," he mumbled back between kisses.

I got lost in his touch for another moment, then ran my fingertips over his sculpted abs to his nipple. Something had changed. Something was different. Pulling back caused him to look at me. Even though the room was dark, I could see him perfectly.

"What is it?" he asked.

"Your scar ... It's gone." He'd had a long giant scar run through his chest, and I no longer saw the silver glint. More than that, there used to be an indent where the skin was thinner. It wasn't there any longer, either.

"When you healed me ..." He didn't finish his sentence because he pulled my core against his erection. "Gods, the smell of you. You've no idea what you do to me."

I arched back, forgetting about his scar and needing his jeans gone. His hand left my body and undid his jeans.

Reaching down, I gripped his length.

"Yes!" I pleaded as my finger brushed over the precum on his tip. His fingers glided over mine while his other hand slipped between my folds.

"You're always so ready for me."

"Always," I murmured back as our hands guided him inside.

Closing my eyes momentarily, so relieved by the feel of him, the connection of him, I almost missed the love shining back at me when I reopened them.

It was a sight to see, the way the darks of his eyes mingled with his wolf. It was absolutely one hundred percent love. There wasn't a single shred of doubt that this man loved me. His hips surged forward, and my pussy tightened in response.

We were all hands and mouths and groping and touching. And our connection. It was ... *Yes.* It was everything.

He rolled my clit as he pumped vigorously. I groaned out in pleasure.

He pulled out and ordered. "*I want you on your knees.*"

I was panting as I complied. I barely reached my knees when he gripped my hips and hauled me higher. I wasn't prepared for the change in position and gasped as he entered me in one swift thrust. "*That's it. Take me deep.*"

"*Ryker!*"

His fist tightened in my hair, and I marveled at the bite of pain and how the simple mix of a little pain with pleasure could make tingles shoot through my entire body.

"I'm going to come," I warned.

"I know, love. I know every little thing that drives you wild."

His hand tugged at my hair while his other hand released my hip. He quickly rubbed my clit and then moved his hand to my backside, prodding as he circled my anus and then gently slid it inside. It was at that touch that I went off, exploding around him.

He paused while I spasmed around him, letting me ride the wave of sensation.

Then he went wild.

He surged in and out, making me yell out each time. His thumb continued to play, and our play completely changed when he added another finger, and I was stretched in an entirely new way.

I mewled at the different sensation.

"That's right, purr for me, kitten."

Then he was pulling out of me, and I felt the gentle push as he entered me in a new way. There was a small bite of pain, but as turned on and wet as I was, I was already lost in pleasure. He moved slowly at first, letting me adjust, then glided back and forth. "My gods, you're so tight."

"Mmm," was the only reply I could give because then his fingers rubbed my clit, and just like that, I was set off again, and so was he. It was deliciously beautiful as he surged inside of me, emptying himself.

After he held me, when we both had our breath and our bodies recovered, he cleaned me. It was gentle and sweet, and I was reminded again that my big man wanted to take care of me.

Chapter Thirteen

"Something smells delicious," I said, walking down the hall with Ryker on my heels. A brief crinkle from Ledger's eyes indicated he knew exactly what happened between Ryker and me. The clink of a spoon against a pot had me turning my head and noticing a woman who had to be in her late fifties stirring a pot over a stove. Her raven-black hair with a large section of silver framed her face.

She looked at Ledger with a fondness that made me think they shared a past, and then she smiled at me. It was a smile that welcomed you but also told a tale of years of sadness as it didn't quite reach her eyes.

"Elle, let me introduce you to Farah. We're old friends, and Farah is good people. I trust her."

"Thank you for your hospitality." My cheeks must've been crimson. Ryker and I had been loud. I didn't care about Ledger hearing us, but a stranger? Wait, since when did I consider Ledger more than a stranger?

She nodded, gestured her head to the pot, and motioned toward a small kitchen table. My brows scrunched in confusion. Ryker's hand prodded the small of my back, and I did what she wanted.

"She doesn't speak."

"You two are doing that weird head talk thing again," Ledger accused, then turned to Farah, "It's some silent wolf communication thing."

I gasped, it dawned on me that Farah knew he was a werewolf.

"Ariel, sit down," Ryker urged.

I sat at the table as Farah limped to grab a bowl, spooned some rice in, and then poured the delicious-smelling food over the rice. Ryker and Ledger sat, and Farah served them both a bowl, then finally served her own, sat, and joined us. I was surprised when she grasped Ledger's hand, then my own, and indicated I should do the same with Ryker. Her head tilted towards me.

"You want me to say grace?" I asked.

She nodded.

"But ... I'm not ..." I stopped when her face fell slightly. I wasn't sure why, but I didn't want to disappoint her. I sighed. *What the heck! I could do this.*

Closing my eyes, I began, "Thank you, Father, for this food we are about to receive." I was going to go the traditional route Father Archibald said so many times before. Suddenly, something strange happened, my hands felt warm, and words from my heart poured out freely. "Thank you for your strength and guidance. Thank you for my love and friendships. We give you thanks for this nourishment and the sacrifice the earth has made to feed us. So mote it be."

I squeezed Ryker and Farah's hand one last time and let them go. Everyone was staring at me when my eyes opened, their jaws slightly slack. "What, did I do something weird?"

Farah made the sign of the cross, kissed her fingers, and looked at the ceiling. Ryker looked at me with love and astonishment, and Ledger's jaw was a little slack.

"You talk to God," Ledger accused.

"I mean, I was only praying like she wanted me to."

"No, lLove. It was more than that. It felt divine," Ryker added

"How do you know what divine feels like? Are we talking like a really good feeling, or do you mean divine as in divinity?"

He raised an eyebrow at me telling me I knew exactly what he meant.

I shrugged it off and tried to change the subject.

"She really is ignorant about herself, isn't she?" Ledger asked Ryker.

"Hey!" I snapped, not liking the word ignorant.

"Relax, I didn't mean it like that. I just meant it's like you have no idea how spectacular you are." My cheeks reddened, and I looked at my bowl, taking a bite while keeping my eyes averted.

"She doesn't like attention."

"I see that."

"This is so good!" I declared, changing the subject. It was a spicy curry with fresh vegetables and what I presumed was chicken. Between bites, I looked and saw someone's eyes on me. I didn't like it. So, I looked everywhere but at my friends as I took in the room.

The kitchen was lit by an overhead lamp, and the rest of the living space had a few small lamps lit, giving it a soft glow. The small kitchen with a nook carved out specifically for the table we were sitting at was open to the living room. Rich-colored Persian rugs covered the floors, overlapping in some areas. A window was open and a small circular fan sat on the sill blowing air. The walls were a deep shade of purple. The sofa, a dark velvet green with throw pillows with green, pink, and blue swirling patterns weaved throughout it. The side tables were made of dark wood with knots of chocolate brown throughout them. There were large pillows on the ground for lounging, which made me curious since Farah couldn't talk.

Stopping my perusal of the space, I looked at Farah and how difficult each bite seemed to be. "What happened to you?" I asked, hoping I wasn't being rude. I knew she couldn't respond but asking Ledger made it seem like I wasn't acknowledging her presence seemed more rude.

Ledger cleared his throat. "You share an enemy: the Rosi—well, Cain. He didn't like the truth she was going to share, so he took out her tongue."

I gasped and squeezed Farah's hand. "I'm so very sorry this has happened to you." She gave me a squeeze back.

I looked to Ryker, who watched me curiously.

"*Maybe I can ...*"

"*Absolutely not.*"

"*Oh, you are not going to order me. Why not? Shouldn't I try?*"

"*Every time you do, I think I've lost you. Don't do that to me again,*" he pleaded.

I hated the way that felt. I hated that I continuously passed out from using my gift and the pain it caused him. I also didn't like knowing I could do something to help someone but had to choose between doing what was right and protecting Ryker. It made me feel adrift and like I wasn't being true to myself.

I ate another bite of the delicious curry, then met his eyes. He was torn too. Then an idea struck. "Ledger, you got the book?"

"I did, not that I can tell what any of it says. Are those even words? What language is that?"

I ignored his questions because, frankly, I was afraid I knew the answer and it scared the bejeezus out of me.

"Do you have the satchel that the book was in? There were stones there."

"Ah, you mean the bag of rocks?"

"Yep, that's it. Do you have them?"

He stretched his long arm behind him, grabbed the satchel off the counter, and then handed it to me. Apparently, when I was looking over the room, I did a good job avoiding the space directly around me because if I had, I would've noticed that the satchel was practically right in front of me.

I held it protectively as if something precious had been reunited with me. Odd.

I looked inside, finding the book along with the stones.

"*You mean to use the stones?*" Ryker questioned.

"*What if I can help her? I have to try. Besides, the stones ground me. I may have been tired when I used them before, but it didn't put me out. When I used them, I was also holding an entire village asleep. This would be so much less work than that. I'm sure I could do it. Ryker, you love me, right?*"

"*You know I do.*"

"*Then you need to love all of me. You can't ask me not to try to heal her any more than I could ask you not to be a wolf. It's who you are.*"

He momentarily closed his eyes, accepting my words as truth. You couldn't love someone completely and, yet pick and choose which parts to love. If you loved them, you loved all of them: the easy and difficult parts.

"See, they're doing that thing again. It feels trippy, like someone is slipping me caffeine."

I smiled at Ledger. "Farah, would you be open to me trying something? Something that may or may not work?"

"I didn't bring you here for that," Ledger defended. "I don't want you to hurt any more than your mate does." He looked at Ryker. "Sorry man, I know it's weird, but ever since ..." He let his words trail off. "I can't explain it."

"I know, brother." The two shared an intense moment filled with years and years of friendship.

I placed my hand over his and said gently, "I won't be. You wolves and your protective nature need to learn to let me be who I am." Ledger looked to Ryker for assurance. I wasn't sure if it was when we were linked when he was in wolf form or if it was the fact that I'd healed him, but somehow, I'd gained his allegiance in an overly-protective brotherly way.

Farah studied us and felt the heaviness of the room. I took another bite, trying to make it seem less heavy by doing something as normal as eating.

Ryker and Ledger were studying each other, trying to figure out if it was worth the risk of me trying to heal her, but I already knew the answer.

After seemingly concluding their silent conversation Ledger finally spoke. "Farah, she'd like to try to heal you. It may work, or it may not. She has done some amazing things. I was hurt pretty badly. But you're missing a body part. I'm not sure if she can do all of that, but it's worth a try. Even if it brings you less discomfort, what have you got to lose?"

Ryker sat back, watching her reaction and mine. If there were any hesitation on my part, he would end it. He didn't have to worry about that.

Farah nodded once and closed her eyes briefly as if she, too, was talking with her higher power. I took that second and really looked at her. Her skin was flawless. She had a few small wrinkles at the edge of her eyes, but if anything, it added to her beauty. Her cheekbones were high, and her lips full. If she hadn't been carrying the weight of the world on her shoulders, I would've immediately noticed how incredibly beautiful she was. Burdens can be a blemish, you never know the scars they create or the marks that they leave, but their weight will sit differently on each person's shoulders.

We sat for a few more minutes, and I finished my bowl. I needed all of the energy I could get. Everyone seemed to be on edge, waiting for what I would do next, making me feel a bit like the elephant in the room.

Finally, when I was finished, I looked around again, trying to decide exactly where I would do this and if there was anything I needed. "Is there grass outside?"

"Does she not realize we're in the desert?" Ledger asked Ryker.

Ryker smacked Ledger on his arm. "How about plants? Do you have any houseplants? Would those work?" He first asked Farah and then me.

"If she has them, yes. I think they will."

Farah walked down the hall and into her bedroom, returning with a 10-inch potted plant. Then, she moved to a windowsill with a small succulent. Next, she opened her door and grabbed a plant from her doorstep.

"Let's sit on the living room floor. Can you place them around where we'll be sitting?" She nodded and did as I asked, then I followed her into the living room, and I propped a big comfy pillow behind me. I felt like I needed to be directly on the ground, but that didn't mean I shouldn't have some comfy back support. Farah sat across from me and watched me curiously, with a bit of hope lingering behind her eyes. I really wanted this to work.

The feel of the stones in my hand energized me. One by one, I placed them around us, where I felt their energy would do the most work. I readjusted the plants, and by the time I took my seat in front of Farah, I felt incredibly ready. It felt good and right and I knew something big was going to happen.

Closing my eyes, I grabbed her hands and thought about what had been done to her. Warmth spread between our fingertips, and I thought, "heal" repeatedly. I let a minute pass, then opened my eyes and looked at Farah, hoping something would be different.

It wasn't.

It was absolutely one hundred percent the same.

Closing my eyes again, I prayed.

"Please heal her. Take away her pain. Give her strength. Earth that I love, ground that I walk upon, grant us this and heal her. Give her your strength. Give her your guidance. Give her back her voice.

A rush of energy moved between us. It seeped from the ground and the plants, encompassing us. We held onto it for a beat, then another, and before I knew it, it slowly faded. It wasn't until it was completely gone that I chanced a glance at Farah.

And, this time, when I did, I knew it absolutely one hundred percent worked.

Chapter Fourteen

They say time heals all wounds. In this case, I must be Father Freakin' Time because it worked! She had a tongue! Her body wasn't broken the way it once had been. I couldn't believe it! It actually worked.

That was great and all. It really was. Farah cried and prayed and thanked the heavens, but something else happened to me. Something I had no idea how or why or what I should do.. Something the minute Ryker got to me and inspected me to ensure I was okay, made him immediately pause.

"What is it? What's wrong?"

"It's not that something is wrong ... per se ... It's ..."

"It's what?"

Ledger stood and crossed the room to see what Ryker was looking at. All the while, Farah was crying and thanking God for the miracle in her melodic voice, and if it weren't for the hysterics in it, I would've wanted to pause and listen to the sweet quality in it that I'd rarely heard.

"Whoa, what's that?" Ledger asked.

"What is it? What are you talking about? You're kind of freaking me out here." I stood and found a mirror. Nothing looked off. I looked exactly the same. Okay, maybe my hair could use some serious work, but besides that, I was all good.

Ryker grabbed me by the shoulders and turned me so I could look behind myself. Two things happened. The first was from underneath my dress. it appeared I'd started to sprout wings. *Wings!* And immediately following this, my heart rate increased, and before I knew it, I was out cold.

***

"There she is," Ryker said soothingly.

I looked up at Ryker who was perched over me, cradling my head in his lap. From my vantage point on the ground, relief flashed through his features.

Drats, that's the look he gets after I pass out.

"How long was I out?"

"Seconds."

"I ... shit. I have wings?"

I sprung to my feet and headed toward the bathroom.

"Where's she off to?" Ledger asked. Ryker didn't answer as he was hot on my heels. I made it to the modest bathroom, found the light switch, flicked it on as Ryker closed us in, and then I whipped my dress over my head.

I didn't have wings, but I had the start of what looked like wings jutting from between my shoulder blades. They were exactly where my scars used to be.

"You're seeing this, right? I'm not dreaming this up? These things are coming out of my back."

"They're real. May I?" he asked, reaching out his hand. I nodded, and Ryker rubbed his hand over a wing, making me flinch.

"Shoot, did I hurt you?"

"They're sensitive—almost raw feeling." I reached back to touch one and was surprised at the feel. It was almost like how a baby bird did without any fur. They even had a pink hue, almost iridescent, making bone visible through the nearly translucent skin. They weren't wing-shaped either, just two bone-like structures jutted out several inches. I didn't know what to make of them, but I wouldn't be wearing anything to show them off anytime soon. Years of insecurities from my scars surfaced, and I wanted to cover them. I didn't want Ryker to see them. I turned away from him and quickly put my dress back on, then held my arms to my chest and took a step back.

If he noticed my body language, he didn't say anything.

He watched me curiously, analyzing me, perhaps he was waiting to see what I'd do next. His fingers scratched his beard in deep consternation.

Then, he finally said, "They look like growing baby wings."

"Stop, okay? I don't want to talk about them."

"How can we not talk about them? They're amazing."

"Amazing? Are you kidding me?"

"No, I'm not kidding you. You are amazing. Do you see that woman out there on the floor? You made her talk. You healed her. You. And your body healed you. They took something from you when you were a child that they had no right to, and you know what? You are in the process of healing yourself as well. You're amazing."

My shoulders relaxed, and I melted into him. I let his arms fall around me as he slowly, reassuringly kissed me. After several seconds, he pulled away and assessed my face, his body relaxing when he was satisfied with what he saw. His kiss did what it always did, it gave me peace while simultaneously turning me on.

It wasn't the time to act on that carnal desire. It didn't mean that I didn't need to squeeze my thighs together to try and stop the ache. I totally did. But after a deep breath, I managed to control myself.

Then, suddenly, the emotions of it all hit me. I'd been so strong and held onto the change of it all, but right then, surrounded by Ryker, I couldn't stop myself. I gave in to a rare occurrence for me and cried big fat wet tears. He enveloped me in his arms, holding me to his chest as I let it out.

"Shh, I got you. It's okay. You're going to be all right."

"I have wings. What's happening to me?"

"I think in healing Farah, you healed yourself as well."

"What does that even mean, though? They chopped off my wings, and now I have nubs that replaced them? They aren't even wings. They look like raw chicken wings attached to my back," I blubbered.

"They do not. They look new like they're growing. Even now, they seemed to have changed since they first sprouted."

"Sprouted, huh? Like I'm a flipping plant." I couldn't help it. I was being hysterical. But come on! "I was lured through a portal to the Middle East only to find out my family's long-time friend betrayed me. I learned some crazy Rosi guy thinks I'm prophesied to marry him, which is nuts since I'm clearly in love with you. He kidnaps you. Stabs your friend. Now we're hiding out with a woman whose tongue he cut off, and I magically healed her and sprouted freaking wings! Wings!"

"Calm yourself."

"How can I be calm?"

"Breathe."

I sucked in a huge lungful of air, hoping to do as he said, then it hit me. "They changed?"

"I don't follow."

"My wings. You said, 'even now they changed.'"

"I can only see parts of them through your dress, but they already look less raw, and the fur has gotten a tad fuller. A cub was born too soon once, and its fur wasn't quite developed. It sort of reminds me of that. Or like when a newborn baby has that fur covering its body."

Fascinated by what he described, I tore the dress off again and turned to watch my back in the mirror. He wasn't wrong. It was changing. Where it nearly looked like raw bones, it was now coated in a soft fuzz, and they were even less translucent than mere moments before.

"This is crazy. Werewolves. Vampires. A secret organization. And now I'm what? An angel."

"Calm down."

"I will not calm down!" My voice rose. Taking matters into his own hands, Ryker grabbed each side of my face and kissed me. It wasn't a soft kiss. It was a full-on punishing, forget-the-world around-you kind of kiss. He kissed me to the point that my lips might've bruised, then when he knew my mind was on him (which didn't take long), he yanked himself free and slipped inside of me.

Chapter Fifteen

"There is a great deal to share," Farah spoke, and I still couldn't get over the fact that I healed her and she sounded the way she did. We were in her kitchen. I had my dress back on but cut out the back of it. With Ryker's help, we made a cloak from an old dress to hide my back.

After Ryker and I left the bathroom, it took a while for Farah's "thank you" and "praise be to God" to subside. Ledger protectively held her waist, and it wasn't lost on me from how he murmured in her ear that there was something between them. I couldn't tell if they were former lovers who maintained a fondness or if something was currently happening between them.

Eventually, Ledger calmed her, and we moved to the kitchen to have tea. I was trying to play it cool, despite my back itching, and I could tell my wings were still changing, mostly because as soon as Farah calmed, Ledger had her share what she knew about Cain.

"Go on," Ryker prompted Farah.

"I know."

I lifted my eyebrow in question wondering what she knew when she seemed to collect herself and carried on.

"—I know my behavior seemed like a lot. But you can't imagine what was done to me and how they did it." She shuddered.

I needed to see and felt a bond with her. "Do you mind if we try something?"

Ryker looked at me questioningly.

"Take my hand, and I want you to open your mind to me."

Without hesitation, she reached over the table and grabbed my hands.

"Good. Now clear your mind."

"*Show me what was done to you.*" The images rolled in instantly, and unfortunately, when I witnessed them, I witnessed them as if I were Farah.

***

The room was dark and smelled of urine, vomit, and whatever putrid smells came from torture. And even though I'd only been beaten so far, I knew more was to come.

How long had I been here? Hours? Days? Weeks? Surely it couldn't have been that long. I lay on my side, staring at the wall. How many before me had done the same? How many people did Cain hurt? He is not good. He is not pure like Abbas.

I thought back to what brought me here. I was staying late in the grand hall researching. I'd gotten correspondence from a longtime acquaintance of the Rosi.

His words haunted me.

"I've been having dreams that something big is coming. I always meant to protect the light, but protecting my daughter became my priority. Now, I find that what I'm meant to protect is in jeopardy from the very people I've trusted. You must be careful. As long as there is darkness, the light is unsafe.

So mote it be,

John

I gasped, opening my eyes and breaking the connection.

"What is it?" Ryker asked.

Farah opened her eyes and looked at me. "That is ... how can you do that?"

I shrugged, pretending that I wasn't an evolving anomaly. Ryker squeezed my shoulder wanting me to tell him what I saw, but I needed to see more. Now wasn't the time to acknowledge my dad. Curiosity was killing me, but she had a story to tell, and I needed to see all of it. I shook my head, then silently said, "*Soon, but not yet.*"

He nodded back in acknowledgment.

"Do you mind if we continue?" I asked Farah.

She nodded twice, squeezed my hands, and closed her eyes.

A few seconds passed to get to where she was calm enough for me to slip in, but when she did, I was shocked at what I found.

"Tell me where he is?" Cain's sleeves were rolled up his forearm as he grabbed me by the hair, taking me from the water.

I sputtered and coughed out the water making my lungs burn. "I don't know."

Cain nodded, and a man grabbed my shoulders and forced me under. I was going to die. I knew it. If I didn't tell him something, he'd kill me.

Water burned my chest. Darkness wanted to pull me under.

At the last possible second, I was lifted from the water.

I couldn't do it. I couldn't protect him. I wanted to be stronger. I wanted to hold on, but I was going to die. It hurt so bad. I didn't want to die. I wanted to live.

"Where is he?"

I coughed again, and before I could regain my bearings, Cain slapped me. The slap rattled my jaw, and his ring caught part of my eyes, causing intense pain. "Stop. No more. Please." I begged.

"Tell me what I want to know. Where is he?"

"Seattle." His location barely left my lips, and I wished it hadn't. If I could retract those words and have him put me back under the water, I would have. It was a mistake, and I knew I should've taken death immediately. I should've protected John at all costs. But I didn't. I was weak. And I'd pay.

I gasped again, breaking our link. She gave up my father's location. She told Cain where to find him. She was the reason he was dead. I could no longer hold onto her hands or bare to see when her tongue was taken. I wasn't sure I even cared. Bile raced up my throat. I was going to be sick. I ran from the table and to the bathroom, losing the contents of my stomach.

I barely registered Ryker holding my hair back as I shook. He patiently rubbed my back, and I was grateful he didn't pry. I wasn't ready to admit I healed the woman responsible for giving up my father's location.

Once the entirety of my stomach was emptied and my shaking subsided, I turned my head to Ryker. "We need to go."

"All right, love. We'll go but show me what happened."

I wasn't sure I had the strength to do it, but I needed him to see. I couldn't be alone in what I witnessed. I stood and stuck my mouth under the faucet to rinse my mouth, trying to ignore my reflection and how my cloak moved a little more than before.

Righting myself and reading the look on Ryker's face let me know he, too, noticed my wings. I grabbed his hand and felt how open he was to me, pushing image after image toward him.

What only may have been a second later, he released my hand, and exhaustion pulled at me.

"You need to talk to her. Find out how she knows your dad. Find out what she knows and if she knows why Cain is after you."

"I can't." Anger coursed through me, and I clenched and unclenched my fist in an effort to not throttle her.

"She was being tortured."

"Don't defend her. If it wasn't for her …" My voice trailed off.

"I'm not defending her, it's just that kind of torture, the way it messes with your mind, you have no idea the type of panic that ensues."

"You do?" Curiosity easily took over my rage.

"That is a story for another time. It was long ago." He kissed my temple, and I let out a yawn. "You're dead on your feet. All of this takes its toll on you. You need sleep. I understand you don't want to be near Farah, but she has been nothing but kind to us. I want you to rest. I'll see what else I can find out. I'm sure there is more to the story, and leaving without gaining all the knowledge we can, would be foolish."

I opened my mouth to argue but then snapped it shut again. My body weighed a ton, and with each passing second, I found it harder and harder to stay awake.

Ryker wrapped his arms around me and led me from the bathroom to the bedroom, where he lay next to me. "That's right, love. Sleep." He rubbed the side of my head, pulling my hair behind my ear, and before I knew it, I was fast asleep.

**

"Love, wake up."

My mind was groggy as Ryker's voice pulled me from my slumber.

"We need to go. Wake up." The sharpness in Ryker's tone snapped my eyes open as I sat. Immediately, a weight on my back pulled at me, and I knew if I looked, my wings would be much larger than before.

"What is it?" I asked as Ryker pulled back my cloak to take a look at my back. His stunned face gave it all away.

"They're bigger."

"That they are. They're magnificent. You're magnificent."

I reached back and ran my fingers through the silky feathers that felt unlike anything I'd ever felt before.

"Gods, I wish we had all the time in the world to explore what's happening to you. But something doesn't smell right. Ledger picked up on it first, and I'm unsure how much time we have. We need to hurry."

Once standing, it was clear I had wings under the cloak—either that or a really strange backpack. I'd get looks for sure.

"Ryker, we have to do something about these."

He opened the closet, grabbed a belt, and then wrapped it around my waist, securing the wings to my back. Once secured, they fit closer to my body, almost naturally.

"That will do. I'm ready."

He handed me a pair of Farah's boots, but I didn't care—thinking her name sent a wave of hurt and turmoil through me.

"I learned a lot. Farah's with us. I'll explain more later, but we have to go."

I nodded as Ryker took my hand and rushed us out of the bedroom and down the hall where a waiting Ledger stood holding Farah's hand at the backdoor.

"There's trouble."

I nodded.

"Can you get us out of here, Farah?" Ryker asked.

"I think."

"Don't just think. Know," he responded.

Ledger opened the door, and I halted him. "Stop," I whispered. Something deep inside of me told me we needed to stay put. If we went that way, we would be ambushed.

"We need to go up. Not out. Is there an attic?"

She shook her head.

"A crawl space?"

I received a nod back and we rushed to where she pointed at a small square on the ceiling. Ledger moved it aside.

"We don't have time. I don't know how I know, but we need to get up there now." Ryker lifted me, Ledger lifted Farah, and a second later, both men jumped in as wolves. Farah wasn't shocked by this, which made my curiosity about her grow. I slid the panel back on and then huddled close to my wolf.

The space was cramped, with only a foot or so above my head. I was on my stomach. It was beyond hot, but I didn't care. I instinctively knew we needed to stay there. The glow of the wolven eyes was all I could see, but I felt their intense energy.

It was then we heard it. Glass breaking. Heavy thuds as feet pounded across the floor. Shouts of "clear." Then, as if whoever was below quieted the moment *he* spoke, his voice rose crystal-clear.

"She has to be here. Find her, and find her now. Search the neighbors. Be on the lookout. If he thinks she can take her from me, he has another thing coming. She's mine, and I will not let another have her."

Cain. Why did he think I was his, and what was his fascination? He was going to hunt us forever. Rage poured from Ryker, and I tried to send calming thoughts to his wolf, but he felt challenged, and staying there in wolf form went against his instincts.

Ryker's teeth flashed, and I sent him an overwhelming feeling of calm, hoping to portray what I needed.

There was more shuffling below us, and then the house felt eerily quiet. Cain was gone, but I had no idea how long he would be. I'd trusted my instincts thus far, so there was no reason to stop now. Reaching out, I sensed what Ryker and Ledger sensed. Both were filled with fury. Both were trying to uncover if there was any other threat to us. Their noses wiggled as they sniffed the air and listened intently.

Ryker flashed me an image of us holding steady, and I decided not to argue. Not then, anyway. I didn't know how much time had passed, it could've been an hour, or it could've been two.

I had to pee. My back ached. I was hot. It stunk up here. And—let me repeat—I had to pee. Badly. We were fine to climb out, but I was done. I knew Ryker wanted me to wait, but I felt there was absolutely no reason to stay up here any longer.

Scooching backward toward the opening, I ignored Ryker's disgruntled wolf puffs, Farah's questioning hiss of, "What are you doing?" Ledger's odd indifference, and I pulled the ceiling opening. Ryker was suddenly in front of me, growling.

"Calm, my wolf!"

He continued growling, but I ignored his overbearing wolfy ways, and right before I could jump out of the ceiling, he beat me to it and jumped down, sniffing the air and prowling about. It was easy to forget what a massive creature he was until you saw him in a small space where his entire body seemed to take up the hallway. I moved to follow him but was pushed out of the way by Ledger, who leaped effortlessly behind him.

I harrumphed, crawled on my stomach, and stuck my legs through the opening. Ryker caught my legs and pulled me to him, setting me on my feet.

"If we're ever in a situation like that, you let me go first. Do you hear me?"

Whoa, he was ticked at me. *Me?*

Yelling back was on the top of my tongue when Farah climbed down with Ledger's help, and it only dawned on me right then and there that the men were naked.

"You're naked," I hissed.

"My house!" Farah cried.

I turned noticing the state of things. Leave it to Cain to trash her place. Lamps were knocked over. Tables flipped. Wooden chairs were purposefully broken. Wasn't it enough he tortured her and cut out her tongue, he had to trash her stuff too? I was ticked on her behalf, then remembered what she did, and was torn.

Ignoring the pain that caused me, I stood close to Ryker so his dick wasn't on display. The thought of anyone looking at him made my lip curl.

"You need clothes."

"They're behind the shower curtain."

I followed him into the bathroom. "You can't be naked in front of other women."

"That's what you want to talk about?"

I squinted my eyes at him and was surprised when he grinned back. Then my look changed because his powerful legs were stepping into his jeans, and those thick, corded thighs made other parts of me come alive.

"We have to talk," he said, donning his shirt.

My mouth watered, and despite everything going on, my libido had completely different ideas about what we should be doing, and talking wasn't at the top of that list.

"Stop looking at me like that. We're in too much danger to give in."

He was right. Of course, he was.

I tried to take my mind off Ryker and my overwhelming urge to be connected to him. It wasn't the time, yet still, my body craved him.

He pressed his forehead close to mine. "You're killing me. Your scent is driving me wild, but I need to protect you. We're vulnerable here."

"They won't be back. At least not for a while."

"How do you know that?" he questioned.

"I have no idea. I have no clue why I knew to go up in the attic—I just did."

"Your instincts are strong."

I nodded because what could I say? It was too much.

Someone knocked on the door. "Are you guys almost done in there? As much as I don't mind standing around naked in front of Farah ..." he trailed off as Ryker grabbed his clothes from the tub and stuck them out the door handing them to Ledger.

"We have to talk about what happened with Farah and what she knows," Ryker said after closing the door.

"We do," I admitted, although her giving up my dad sent shivers through me.

"I don't think you should hold her responsible."

My body went rigid when he defended her. He saw what she did.

Before I could respond, Ledger knocked once on the door. "You've got to see this."

Ryker's eyes softened, knowing we needed to talk this out.

"What is it?" he asked, opening the door.

Ledger's head tilted to the side, and we followed him down the hall and into the living room. I winced as I stepped over broken shards of glass. Then I gasped. Over the mantle was a mirror. Written in what appeared to be blood, the mirror read, **You're a traitor. I took your body. I took your tongue. Now, I'll take your life.**

Chapter Sixteen

A wheeze deep in Farah's chest filled the room, followed by a cry as she hit the floor. Her shoulders shook, and her eyes were downcast. My instincts said to comfort her, but I was still so torn. Ledger's lip curled, and his eyebrows furrowed. Anger thundered off him. It was as palpable as the air we breathe. His anger was a tangible thing, so thick we could cut it.

"He raped you!" he thundered.

With his roar, Farah shrunk in on herself even more. "That motherfucker not only tortured you beat you so badly you pissed blood for weeks and cut out your God's damned tongue, but that fucker raped you!"

"Ledger," Ryker warned, seeing Farah close in on herself. "Check yourself, brother, and I mean now."

Ledger was too far gone, though. He either didn't notice, or his rage was too big to stop. He grabbed a cracked lamp, turned on its side, and threw it against the wall.

"I'm going to kill him. I should've done it already. I should've peeled the skin from his body and fed him to the dogs like the vermin he is."

The more he ranted, the more Farah closed down. I was done. I couldn't take it another second.

"Stop!" I commanded in a voice unlike my own. Gone were the insecurities I so often carried, replaced only with determination.

Unbeknownst to me, I walked to Ledger, placed my hand on him, and thought, *"Calm. Pull yourself together for Farah."*

His reaction was immediate, and he stopped, breathing deeply as if my calming thoughts were the balm he needed.

I moved to Farah. This broken woman was no more responsible for Cain's actions than I was. Bending low and as gently as possible, I thought, *Give it to me. Give me all of it. Release the burden you've been carrying. You don't have to go at it alone anymore. I won't blame you. Give me your pain.*

Images flashed through my mind of everything she endured, how she felt, what she'd been through, and how long she tried to hold on.

I dropped to my knees beside her, wanting to scream out at the injustice she endured. It wasn't fair. It wasn't right. No one had the right to do that to someone. Period. And Farah, she was sweet. She was kind. She believed she was part of an organization that sought knowledge for the greater good. It had been that way until it wasn't. Corruption, greed, and pure selfishness took over.

I ached for her, but my job wasn't done. With as much strength as I could muster, I found myself praying, and this time, when I thought the word *"heal,"* it was different. I didn't just want to heal her body; I wanted to heal her soul. It was harder, and the more I tried, the more I learned that I could heal her outer scars and take away her pain, but the way trauma marked her wasn't something I could remove.

Her anguish lessened. Her shame diminished. But it was still there, and somehow I knew that time was what would heal her. No amount of Elle magic could make this one hundred percent right. But if I granted her even a little reprieve, that would be enough. It never would.

I removed my hand from Farah's shoulder and whispered soft, reassuring words about how I didn't blame her, and it wasn't her fault.

Ryker left the room and returned with a wet cloth, wiping Cain's words from existence.

***

We sat in the dark, arguing over whether staying there made us safer or a target.

"We're as unsafe as we can be here. If you try to get me to hide like some coward again, I won't do it," argued Ledger.

"While I agree that was among one of the most unpleasant experiences, it saved our asses, and if Ariel thinks we wait, we wait," Ryker declared, doing it with finality.

My eyes gentled on him. *"Thank you for having my back."*

"Always."

"You really believe in me, don't you?"

"How could I not? You are divine. You create miracles."

When he said that, it didn't feel right.

"I don't create them. I'm merely God's conduit."

He grinned.

"All right, folks. As awesome as it is to watch you two lovestruck puppies, let's not forget we're in danger."

"Not hard to forget since we're hiding in the dark with only a candle so the two of them can see," Ryker bit out.

"I can see," I amended.

"What do you mean?" Ryker questioned.

There had been plenty of times as of late when it was far darker than I should've been able to see, and I did it just fine.

I shrugged, feeling like the freak I was.

"Let's test this, shall we?" Ryker blew out the light, and the room was pitched into darkness.

"How many fingers am I holding up?" he asked.

"Seven."

"Maybe it's because you two are so linked. Try me." Ledger stuck up his middle finger.

"Real nice, Ledger. It's one."

"Who knew you had so many talents, Princess," Ledger joked.

"I knew."

"Your dad knew," Farah admitted. It was the first time she'd spoken since I tried to take away her pain. Her voice stilled Ledger, and he grasped her hand.

I watched the pair, hoping Ledger would handle her with care, at the same time, hoping she would elaborate.

"When you're ready, I want to hear about my dad, how you knew each other, and what you know."

She gave me a thin smile that didn't quite meet her eyes.

"He was a good man. He talked about you. Of course, I didn't know he was speaking about you. We met many years ago. I was new to the Rosi. I'd spent time at the uni, and I could never decide where my passion lay. I'd go from studying architecture to the bible, hoping to uncover secrets. The idea of there being more to uncover from our past is … How shall I say it? Thrilling. One day, I was following a lead about The Knights of Templar. My lead was bad. But I learned other information and met your father, who had followed a similar line.

"He was so smart. Such a wealth of information. He told me about the Rosi and his love of history and how he, too, was a seeker of truth, just like me. My interest peaked. I had to know more. It didn't take long for him to bring me in. He could never stay long because you were so small. He had to leave to be with you, and eventually, he stopped coming altogether. He confided in me that there was something unique about you and your mother—something he worried about. He sought a different truth. A truth that he wanted the Rosi not to know of.

"Cain was younger when I joined the Rosi. It was Abbas who had brought me in and Abbas who encouraged my love of learning. He has blinders on when it comes to his son. But his son whispered in enough ears over the years to gain loyalty from the men. Those men, with the promise of technology and a future outside their old town, have followed Cain."

I avidly listened to every word, nodding as she spoke of Cain. I could see how his men followed him. There had to be some reason why.

"I pieced together that Cain overheard Father Archibald speaking with Abbas about you. Abbas was very hush-hush and dismissive of the Father's concerns. Cain was not. Cain wanted to know more, but even the Father was not inclined to work with Cain. He wouldn't tell him where your father lived, and since Abbas and the Father have long held a friendship, there was nothing Cain could do. If anything happened to the Father, Abbas would know. Me, on the other hand ..."

She trailed off, leaving all the things Cain had done to her unsaid. We didn't need her to go over those. I knew. I saw. I could no longer blame her for giving away my father's location. She'd endured so much.

I placed my hand over hers. "Thank you for telling me."

With her eyes downcast, she nodded. "Thank you for giving me my voice back and trying to lessen the pain. I've held that guilt and shame for a long time. You are a gift, and with everything I've seen you do, I'm certain your father is watching over you. And he would be so proud."

We locked eyes, and I held her stare, our eyes communicating so much with one another.

"What do you know about her mother?" Ryker asked.

I'd been on this journey for what felt like so long, I hadn't really given my mother much thought.

She shook her head. "John must've been wrong."

"What did John tell you?" Ryker asked.

She bit her lip nervously.

"Whatever it is, you can say," I prompted.

"It's just that ... I am not sure it is mine to tell."

"Please. I have no one to ask."

"Very well." She stood and paced as she filled in the blanks about my mother. "Your father loved your mother. Then it destroyed him to learn he was a tool. She's very old and wise, and wanted to conceive for a long time. They were in love, or so he thought. When she became pregnant, he knew there was something different about her. Eventually, he became convinced she was only with him to conceive.

"Her pregnancy went fast. Faster than normal. She didn't want to do the normal pregnancy stuff, ensuring everything was fine, all while she pulled back, and the carefree woman he loved changed into someone else entirely. By the time she was ready to give birth, he was convinced that she wasn't normal. There was something unnatural about her. He noticed fast movements, things he would've normally looked past, but the more he watched her, the more he picked up on subtle nuances. Then you were born.

"First you and then your brother." She watched me, assessing if that was a bombshell or not. Gosh, a short time ago, this would've floored me, but not now. Now, I was getting the answers I so desperately sought.

She nodded. "You know of Gabriel?"

"Only recently, though." I met Ryker's eyes, and they were soft with an underlying sympathy like he could guess where this was going.

"He told me when you and Gabriel were born, Gabriel was placed on her chest while he cleaned you, and to his horror, her fang elongated. She pierced her fingertip and fed your brother. John knew you'd turn if you had her blood, so he hid you from her. He carried the deep burden that he only grabbed you and couldn't take Gabriel. Then, he knew something was different about you—something special—but he had no idea what it was. He didn't think you were like her, but he knew there was something special about you."

I blinked back tears, overcome with emotion. It was a lot of information, and my feelings were all tied up. My father basically kidnapped me from a vampire's arms before she could feed me her blood. Was it because he was angry she lied and didn't love him? Was it because he was horrified by what she was? Was he horrified by me? I thought back to all of the love he showed me and knew that wasn't the case. And Gabriel ... he was left with Lillian. Was she good to him? Had I unjustly been rude to Lillian?

"Come here," Ryker ordered. I stood and went to his warm embrace. "We'll work it all out. Whatever you're feeling, okay? He loved you. This doesn't change that."

"No, I guess it doesn't, but what if she did too?"

"So, let me get this straight. You're not only some crazy cool girl sprouting wings like an angel who can heal people, but your mom is a vampire. How is that even possible?" Ledger asked. I had pretty much forgotten he was even there.

The dream I had and had yet to tell Ryker about flashed through my mind. I opened myself to him and showed him the dream. *I'm both guardian and fallen.*

Ryker's eyes grew large, and we all froze when the back door's glass shattered.

Chapter Seventeen

"Down!" Ryker hissed, then lunged for the door. The back door rattled, then a hand shot through the broken-out panel and attempted to reach for the handle. Ryker was there in a flash, grabbing the wrist of the offending hand, who let out a surprised yelp.

"Ouch! Let me go," a familiar female voice said.

Ryker immediately dropped her wrist. "Pull your hand back out. I'll open the door."

"Shit, yeah, okay."

Her hand was pulled back. Ryker opened the door, and Mindy, followed by Micah, Grey, and Reece, walked through.

"Told you, you should've knocked," Reece said.

"Ryker!" Mindy shouted and threw herself into her brother's arms.

He squeezed her back, whispered something into her ear, and then set her down.

"Elle, you're okay. Thank God. We thought the worst." Mindy wrapped her arms around me before I could stop her. She took a step back, her eyes narrowed after feeling *something* on my back, which was thankfully still hidden by the cloak. I was grateful she didn't ask about them right then and there. It was too much to get into at the moment.

"Brother, it's good to see you," Reece said, clapping Ryker on the back.

"What's he doing here?" Grey sneered, his eyes fixed on Ledger.

Mindy's eyes landed on Ledger, and her body grew rigid.

Micah cleared his throat. "Ledger, you old dog. Was it you who got word to us that our brother was here?" Micah asked.

"It was. Good to see you, Micah, though, I didn't think you'd bring *him*."

"Would you knock it off?" Mindy ordered, then turned to Ryker. "Ryk, what happened?"

"So much, Mins. So much."

"I do not know how much time we have to discuss this," Farah said softly. "What if they come back?"

"She's right," Ledger confirmed. "We need to get to a safe place."

"We're safe right here," I added, feeling that deep in my gut.

"We're targets here," Ledger argued.

"So, this is what we were walking in on, huh?" Reece asked.

"Enough. We don't have time for this." Ryker looked pointedly at the group. "Do you not see the state of Farah's house? How did you even get here this quickly? I sent Ledger to get word to you, what, fifteen hours ago?"

"About that ..." Grey looked contrite. "Just so you know, some of us voted against contacting him."

"Who?" Ryker growled, and its intensity vibrated the air.

"Uh..." Mindy said nervously.

"Well, you see—" Reece began to say.

"I voted against it. Thought it was a terrible idea," Micah said, squaring his shoulders.

"Hey, Sis!" My jaw slacked as Gabe greeted me.

"What did you do?" Ryker bit out.

"See, I knew this idea sucked," Micah said nonchalantly.

"It didn't suck. We're here," Reece argued.

"Only one who sucks is that guy," Micah said, pointing at Gabe and making the corner of my lip tip in an amused half-smile.

Gabe's eyes were locked on me, squinting slightly. "Elle, you've changed."

Grey sniffed the air, "She does smell different."

I wasn't amused. I wanted to slink back into my skin and hope no one noticed what was behind my back. Ryker, sensing my discomfort, moved behind me and wrapped his arms protectively around me, never taking his eyes off Gabe.

"Do you think I'd hurt her?" Gabe asked. "I stole my dad's plane, flew your family halfway around the world to save all of your asses, and by the looks of this place, you need saving. I probably broke seven thousand international laws by flying in without registering my flight plan."

My face gentled, and I had the overwhelming urge to go to him and wrap my arms around him.

"Thank you, Gabe. There's been a lot happening."

Gabe's eyes narrowed slightly. "I can see that."

"Anyone want to tell me who the vamp is?" Ledger irately asked.

"I'm her brother."

"How can that be? She's—"

Farah placed a calming hand on Ledger's shoulder, and the pair locked eyes. I wasn't sure what she was silently communicating, but after a moment, Ledger gave her a slight nod, lifted his chin towards Gabe, and said, "Yo. I'm Ledger. This is Farah."

"All right, introductions are cool and all, but do we want to, I don't know, get the hell out of dodge?" Micah asked.

"There's a lot you need catching up on."

"Ledger filled me in on some, and I briefed the team," Grey replied.

"So, you know I was kidnapped and brought here. Ariel was also being held, found me, and rescued me. She put an entire village to sleep. We left. I was hurt. She healed me. She healed Ledger. She healed Farah. Cain has a lot of men. We've been running from them."

"Why not just rip them to shreds? I've seen you take on armies. How many men could he possibly have that would make you and Ledger combined pause?" Reece asked.

Ryker looked at me from the corner of his eye. It was brief, but there was a small hesitation.

"Ariel is going through something. Something big. Bigger than anything we could've ever imagined, her body becomes tired while changing. I do not—no, I will not risk anything happening to her."

"I fought her. She nearly kicked my ass." Grey said.

"I did? I thought you were just giving me a lesson and letting me get some hits in."

Reece chuckled, "Yeah, right. The day Grey lets anyone get hits in is the day I take a mate, and that shit is never happening."

"Enough!" Ryker snapped, making the entire room look at him. "Ariel is tough. She is amazing and can do things no human could ever do. Nor a wolf. Nor a vamp. She is everything, and I will not risk putting her in danger. Can I show them, love?"

Biting my lip and trusting my mate, I stepped out from his protective hold and faced him. He gave me a quick, chaste kiss.

"Are you sure?"

"I am. You're right. They should know."

"And your brother?"

"He wouldn't hurt me. I don't know how I know, but I do. We can trust everyone in this room."

With his eyes locked on mine, Ryker reached under the cloak, undid the belt holding my wings in place, and swiftly removed the cloak. My wings sprung free, and they gasped, followed by complete silence.

"They're bigger, aren't they?"

I didn't get a response from Ryker. Instead, he dropped to his knee and bowed in front of me. A quick turn of my head showed me the entire room, including Gabe, was kneeling before me. Gabe's eyes shed bloody red tears. And Mindy, my sweet friend Mindy, stared at me with adoration.

"Uh, guys. I'm still me. What are you doing?"

"This must be done, love."

"I pledge myself to you, Ariel, goddess of nature. I pledge myself to you, Ariel Katz, my mate. I pledge my wolves. I pledge my pack. With everything I am, I pledge myself. I will fight and, if needed, die for you. The Fates blessed me when they destined you to me. I vow to honor you. I vow to love you. You have my word as you have my heart."

Tears escaped, and I wanted to go to him. I wanted to throw my arms around him and forget we had an audience. I'm reminded that we did when Reece spoke.

"I pledge myself to you. You're not only my brother's fated mate, but we're honored the Fates have destined you to us. I pledge my life to protect you." His eyes are locked on mine as Mindy spoke.

"I pledge myself to you, sister. I pledge to teach you all I know. I pledge to protect you. I pledge to honor you."

"I pledge myself to you. I vow to protect you. I vow my loyalty." Micah's eyes were also locked on mine.

"I pledge myself to you. I vow to protect you. I give you my loyalty." Grey said, simple and to the point.

I'd hoped we were done.

We were not.

"You gave me my voice. You gave me forgiveness. You gave me comfort. You showed me goodness persists. I may be human and not have the same strengths as your pack, but I vow my loyalty. Thanks be to God, for his grace and for sending you to us. Blessed be," Farah said quietly.

Then, surprising me, Ledger spoke. "Ryker, I pledge myself to your pack. I pledge my loyalty to you, Ariel. You've healed me. You've shown courage and strength. You have shown kindness and forgiveness. I vow to protect you with my life if needed. I vow to do everything in my power to protect you."

I didn't miss Mindy's slight intake of breath; Ledger pledging to join the pack was a big deal.

There. That was everyone.

Except it wasn't.

"Sister of my blood. We shared a womb. Our hearts beat as one. I've lived without you but with the knowledge that you were out there. I knew I'd lived beside purity. I've felt the incredible loss of not having you—my twin. I pledge to you my devotion. I vow my loyalty. I don't know what this makes me, for I am not pure of heart like you, but I vow to try to be. I've not known much love, but I've always loved you."

Tears streamed down my face. Gabe's declaration made a lump form in my throat, and it was hard to talk, but I needed to. After everyone pledged loyalty, something had to be said.

I closed my eyes, felt for my inner strength, and asked for guidance from within. I felt my well of power. I felt the Keeper, the angel, and the other part of me that I'd yet to explore but knew was there. When I opened my eyes, they were blue.

"Rise. All of you." My voice was not my own. "Blood of my blood. Sisters of my heart. Brothers by bond. Mate by soul. I accept your allegiance. I pledge to you to protect you, to guide you, to honor you."

I closed my eyes, and without knowing how I knew to do it, I thought, "*human.*" When I reopened my eyes, they were no longer blue, and somehow, I'd retracted my wings.

Chapter Eighteen

"Do you have a sec?" Gabe asked, sensing Ryker was on alert around him. His distrust was evident in the way he watched his every move. I, on the other hand, felt completely at ease around him. Which may be silly considering I'd only been around him a few times, but he was my twin! He wouldn't hurt me.

"Of course I do." I looked around for somewhere private. "Farah, do you mind if we talk in your room?"

She waved a hand dismissively, caught in rapt attention, by the story Ledger was telling, which by the way, happened to be how he was injured saving us. I winced as he talked about the spear piercing his body.

"Are you sure?" Ryker asked me for the ten-thousandth time.

"Yes. I am."

"We can still feel that, you know." Mindy shot Ryker and me with a look that said how obvious our silent communication was.

"Not hiding the fact that we can do super cool shit." I winked.

Gabe walked down the hall, and I followed, knowing the wall was a pretense to make it seem as though we had privacy.

Closing the door behind us, Gabe sat on the edge of the bed, his head in his hand.

I sat next to him and put my hand on his shoulder.

"What's weighing on you, little bro?"

Calling him little brother made the corner of his lip tilt -up, and I thought not for the first time, that my brother was handsome.

He blew out a large breath. "You don't think all of this is a bit strange? Mom lures you to Ohio, you meet the wolves and are mate with their pack leader. Then you get tricked into coming through a portal that brings you to the middle east, where some psycho thinks you're destined to be together and is trying to kill your wolf. Oh, yeah, and you grew wings."

"You forgot, finding out my brother is a vampire."

"So, what do you think that makes you?"

I sat silently, considering what I wanted to share, then blurted, "Farah told us something."

"What?"

I could relay the entire story of our birth to him, or I could show him. "Here, this might be simpler. Sit next to me and calm your mind. Clear it of any thoughts."

"Is this where we sing Kumbaya?"

I smacked his arm gently. "I'm being serious."

He studied me briefly, then closed his eyes and did as I asked. I attempted to send the images to him, but it was like hitting a brick wall.

"Hmm," I grunted out, then tried again. There was complete darkness when I tried to get in. "That's weird."

"What is the expression on your face? Because sis, I'm not going to lie, it kind of looks like you need to poop."

"Stop it," I giggled. "I'm being serious."

"Tell me what you are trying to do and I'll see if I can help."

"I can sometimes show people stuff, or they can show me stuff."

"What do you mean?"

"Like memories."

"So, you're trying to show me a memory, but it isn't working?"

"Nope. You're locked up tight."

"I got a novel idea. It might be a foreign concept and all, but how about you tell me."

"All right, fine."

He raised an eyebrow, and his carefree demeanor made me laugh.

"I'm waiting."

"Gah, okay. So, Farah told us a story about Mom and Dad. When we were born, Dad didn't know Mom was a vampire. He suspected she was something but not that. Well, then ..." I didn't know how to say this. So, I rushed out, "He saw her give you her blood, freaked out, and took me before she could give me any. You were given her blood at birth, and I was not."

He was silent for a few minutes digesting what I told him. "I'm not sure how I feel about all of this. You're ... you're ..."

"Spit it out."

"You're this amazing creature who grew wings and is part-angel while I'm ..."

"A big scary vampire?" I grinned, attempting to lighten the mood, when his expression turned solemn, and he answered, "Yeah."

"Uh ... sorry to burst your bubble there, but would I feel this at ease with you and joke with you if you were this super scary dude?"

He flashed his fangs

I clapped in glee. I couldn't help it. His incisors extended, then retracted just as quickly.

"Quick. Do it again."

He did, and it took everything in me not to run my fingertip over his tooth. That would be weird, right? Yeah, definitely weird.

"That's so cool."

He shook his head, "You act as though I'm some party trick. It's more than that. Sometimes there's this hunger. You'll want it so bad but don't want to hurt anyone. It's worse than any drug. It's in your veins, calling you. *Feed. Feed. Feed.* It's not this awesome thing, Sis. Sure, I have super speed, my vision is amazing, and I'm way smarter than most people."

I raised an eyebrow.

"No, it's the truth. Mom had me tested. Year after year, she ran every kind of test she could think of. I'm a certified genius. I'm also extremely attractive."

I laughed hard. When I finally contained myself, I asked, "Full of yourself much?"

"I'm serious."

"I bet you are," I joked.

"No, seriously. They did this study where they showed my picture—"

"—You can't be serious."

"I am. I was like her own personal science experiment."

The color drained from my face, and I was no longer laughing. It wasn't funny. I was poked and prodded and asked to give blood as well. I knew what that felt like, and I, quite frankly, wasn't a fan.

My face dropped, "I'm sorry. Not the fun, jovial childhood we all hope for."

"I had my share of fun."

I smiled, but it didn't quite reach my eyes. My mind traveled to surgery when I was a child, which I now knew was Dad removing my wings. "Yeah, I understand that."

He studied my face, and even if our minds couldn't link, it was like our hearts did, and he understood.

His hand reached out for mine, and he squeezed it. "I'll never let anyone do that to us again."

I nodded, and after a few silent seconds, I asked, "It wasn't all bad, was it?"

"I flew here in a plane I learned to fly before I learned to drive. I grew up with a lot of money and privilege, so no, it wasn't all bad."

I pictured a younger Gabe in the cockpit of a plane, and I liked the idea. "That's good," I whispered.

A knock at the door broke the intense moment.

Farah poked her head in, "Hey, the food's ready."

"Thank you," I responded, then asked Gabe, "You do eat real food, don't you?"

"That depends. Are we talking A-positive or O-Negative?"

Farah's face lost color. "I'm joking!" he chuckled, then walked past me, "Gets 'em every time."

***

We were sitting in the living room, most of us with bowls in our hands, eating a delicious rice and vegetable dish, when Mindy asked, "So, Farah, how long have you known Ledger?"

Farah's eyes glinted as she looked at Ledger fondly, "We go back a way."

Mindy glared.

"The games are still in the planning phases," Micah said, changing the subject.

"Who did you leave in charge?" Ryker asked.

"Brogan."

The thought of Brogan made my heart plummet.

"What is it?"

"It's nothing."

"*You know I can feel your emotions.*"

"*I saw your Dad with Father Archibald before I left. He told me not to go.*"

"*He'll understand.*"

Ryker knew me so easily. It felt uncanny. How could he immediately know I felt guilty?

"*Because Love, we are one. My soul is tied to yours. I'm made to protect every part of you. Mind. Body. Soul. All of it. Every inch of you. The Fates gave me you because I am the only man who could.*"

"*Sure of yourself, are you?*"

"*You're getting defensive by throwing walls up. You'll learn it's okay to be vulnerable with me.*"

My eyes flashed to his, and I wanted nothing more than to break eye contact. Sometimes, it felt so big, and beyond us, and maybe that was the point. Love was beyond it all.

Love and tenderness shone back at me in his eyes. I couldn't form another response.

"All right, you two, seriously, this silent puppy dog eyes thing you have going on is cute and all, but it feels like I have so much energy going through my brain I don't know what to do with myself. I either want to fuck it out or fight and seeing as we're in for the night ..." Micah said, eying Farah and receiving a slap on the back of the head from Ledger, which simultaneously made Mindy narrow her eyes again.

"So, Farah," Mindy started again. "You seem settled here. Was there no husband to keep your bed warm, or perhaps ..." she paused, thinking about what she would say, then almost gleefully asked, "Or a wife?"

"Why? Are you interested?" Farah retorted, fluttering her eyes.

Grey coughed. "Sorry, sweetheart, I don't share."

"Then you might want to remind your girlfriend of that," Farah said, causing Grey to squint at Mindy, repeatedly looking between her and Ledger. I wasn't sure how Grey hadn't picked up on the obvious history between the pair.

Reece slapped Grey on the back, causing him to choke on his food. "Grey had an awesome idea about the games. We're hosting it like a county fair and will charge patrons to watch it. We'll have vendors set up along with food.

We haven't had a fair in lord knows how many years. It'll help us make money. If it goes well, it could even be an annual thing."

"Everything will have to be done as men, obviously," Grey added.

My smile didn't quite reach my eyes when I said, "That sounds cool."

"It will be," Mindy added chirpily.

"But ..." Ryker prompted.

"The whole reason you're doing these games is because of my vision of war. I don't want anything to happen to any of you."

"We'll be prepared, and besides, I know this awesome angel that has a ton of really cool party tricks," Micah added.

Reece nudged him in the side. "Cool it."

"Whatever," Micah responded.

The talk continued, giving way to normalcy. It reminded me of when I first moved in, and I had pizza with Mindy, Micah, Reece, and Grey. They all seemed so normal then. But now, knowing what they are, knowing what I am, they still seemed pretty normal.

Chapter Nineteen

"This! This is what you came up with?" Grey laughed, giving Ledger a hard time.

"You asked for a van. I found us a van," he retorted through gritted teeth. "You could've gone out to find something but chose to stay here, where it was *safe*."

"Would the two of you knock it off? The van is fine." Mindy was right. So what? It was a minivan. We'd fit. It would be snug, but with the size of these guys, pretty much anything would.

"Thank you, Ledger," Farah said, placing a hand on Ledger's shoulder. If the hostility between Ledger and Grey over the last several hours wasn't a giveaway that there was a past between Mindy and Ledger, then the way Mindy's eyes squinted on Farah's offending hand certainly was.

"Yes, thank you, Ledger," Mindy replied with a bit of bite behind her words.

I finished throwing away the last bit of broken glass and looked around. Farah's place wasn't perfect. It looked nothing like the beautiful home I woke in days ago, but it was certainly better than Cain and his men's aftermath.

"May I have a word?" Farah asked Ledger, then gave me a subtle nod that she wanted me to listen.

Ledger looked at her questioningly, then glanced at Mindy, whose jaw ticked but remained shut, holding back whatever she was thinking.

We walked to the bedroom. Ryker tracked my movements, so he could also hear whatever was said. I didn't have the heart to remind Farah there was no privacy between wolves, and I had no idea if my brother had "advanced hearing" in his skillset.

With the door closed behind us, she looked from me to Ledger. "I'm not coming."

"What?" I questioned at the same time Ledger muttered, "That's insane. Of course, you're coming."

"I'm not. This is my home. I have friends here. I have a life here. I'll have eyes here and will be able to tell if something is amiss. What good will I be to you from America? I've never even been to America."

"You'll be alive; that is way more than I can say if you stay. If you stay, you'll be dead."

"No, I *was* a dead woman walking, and then an angel touched me with her grace and gave me the courage to fight back and face my demons."

I felt like an intruder in this conversation. She could do whatever she wanted. She pledged to me, but in the scheme of things, if she felt she would be better off staying behind, who was I to argue with her?

"There will be no one here to protect you."

"I'll be fine."

"You'll be dead!" he roared, and *everyone* definitely heard that.

"I'll be smart. I'll be here with eyes on what's happening. I am no good to you in Ohio. I can be useful here."

"And what will you do if he finds you and ..." He couldn't finish his sentence. We all knew what had been done to her, and what Cain was capable of.

She placed her hand on top of his. "What if he hurts someone else? Who will be here to protect them? I know you'll worry. I know you don't want me to be the ears and eyes on the ground. But I'll be careful. I have my voice back. I need to be able to use it."

He stared intently at her, and not for the first time, I wondered how much further their relationship extended. Then I didn't have to wait much longer because he bent his head low and kissed her. It was soft and sweet, which surprised me that Ledger could be gentle. The kiss lacked the urgency of current lovers, though. How long had it been?

I averted my eyes and found a spot on the floor to look at. Then Farah giggled and said, "Now, that's the best way to use my tongue."

Ledger hummed in approval, then he laughed, and I had to look because I'd only heard him laugh once, and watching that man laugh could put a smile on anyone's face.

Farah was pressed closer into him. She stared into his eyes, enjoying his mirth as much as I did.

Then she pulled back, and her eyes connected with mine. "Sorry about that. I hope you are okay with me staying behind."

"It's your choice. You've not always been given one, so who am I to stand in your way?"

"I pledged my loyalty to you, and now I've decided to stay."

"Will you be less loyal here?"

"Of course not!"

"Then don't sweat it. I just want you to be safe. Is there somewhere else you can stay until they stop looking for us?"

"Oh, my friend, I don't think they will ever stop looking for you."

"Then perhaps your presence will be of far greater importance than any of us realize."

"I hate it. But I understand it," Ledger added.

I hugged Farah.

She whispered in my ear, "You'll never know what you did for me. My faith had been wavering. You gave me so much hope. So much to believe in. So much to live for again."

I was speechless as tears burned the back of my throat.

Ryker was at the door as if on cue, sensing my turmoil. "Are you all right?"

I nodded, then went to his open arms. When did I become so needy? It didn't matter. I was so much more at ease there.

"Farah's staying." Ledger explained to Ryker. "And before you give us a thousand reasons why that's a bad idea, I want you to know we've been over them. Her mind is set."

Ryker's jaw ground for a second and I knew he wasn't happy with that either, but instead of arguing, he nodded in acceptance.

"We should go," Ryker prompted.

Ledger nodded, then gave us a look that said, *"Give us a minute."*

Ryker grabbed my hand as we left the room. "For the record, I think that's a shit idea for her to stay here."

"It's giving her back power."

"Fuck power. It means nothing if you're dead."

I couldn't argue with that.

"Everyone ready?" Mindy asked, looking at the doorway Ledger and Farah were still behind.

"Just about," I responded as Reece and Micah piled into the minivan. Grey stood back, watching Mindy watch for Ledger, and I wanted to ask Mindy what the story was, but now wasn't the time.

Then, there was my brother. Gabe stood out with his fair coloring compared to everyone else. He was also built differently, more of a swimmer's body than the behemoth wolf-size men. It didn't mean he wasn't strong, though. He was fit in a way that would put Michael Phelps to shame. He watched everyone as if cataloging each person. His eyes met mine, as if he knew I was watching him and he winked before getting into the van.

Grey cleared his throat. "Are you ready, Mins?"

She jumped in surprise at his presence. "Uh, yeah. I'm ready," she said, averting her eyes from the doorway. Grey got in the driver's seat and slammed the door.

"I'll drive."

"To hell, you will. I'm driving," Ryker ordered.

Grey's nostril flared, but he didn't dare challenge Ryker. Grey got out and got in the back, sitting next to Mindy. His body language was still and stiff when Ryker walked out and sat beside him. I sat in the front and immediately put on my seat belt while my brother squeezed next to Reece and Micah in the back row.

"We look like a clown car," I mumbled.

Farah waved from the open doorway, wistfulness in her eyes as she said, "I'll be in touch."

"Are you certain this is what you want?" Ledger tried one last time.

She nodded, then slowly closed the door as if watching us leave was too much.

***

The car ride was quiet, creepily so. Even though the van windows were blacked out, I had a prickle at the back of my neck. We were far from danger.

"How long until we reach the airstrip?" I asked, breaking the silence.

"It should be about another half an hour," Gabe said.

"We'd be there a lot sooner if it weren't for this traffic," Reece added.

"Yep, there's a reason we don't live in the city," Micah replied.

"And here I thought it was the land," I said.

Ryker responded in my head, *We don't know what your brother knows about the land. Careful.*

"Why? I thought you said all of you beings knew about the land. And why are you acting like I can't trust my brother? He's my brother."

"I said the land helps my kind, not that all beings, as you called us, know why they are where they are. Think about it: when have you questioned why you live in an area? Most people are born and raised in the same area and never question the relationship of the land to them."

"Now you sound like Mins," I joked.

"I think you know better than most that Mindy knows what she's talking about."

I gulped and felt my brother's eyes on us, knowing we were silently communicating again. "I do know what you mean. I was just trying ..."

"To make light of it. You don't think I know that when you feel nervous about something, you tend to make a joke about it?"

"Okay, so you know me."

"That makes you nervous, too."

"Stop. It's like you're reading my mind before I even explore them."

"I don't mean ..."

"Does anyone else think it's funny watching their faces as they do their silent thing? No? Just me? ... Cool," Micah said.

"Would you shut it?" Ledger said, "I got a bad feeling."

Ryker moved the visor and made eye contact with Ledger through the mirror.

"Make a left at the next intersection," Gabe ordered.

Ryker nodded as we stopped in traffic. The turn wasn't far ahead, but it might take us forever at this pace. The van was quiet, and two things dawned on me at once. The first was Mindy and Grey hadn't spoken the entire van ride, and the second was not only did I still have that feeling in the back of my neck, but I was pretty sure everyone else did as well. I felt tied to their emotions.

We slowly moved forward, inch by slow inch.

"We're sitting ducks here," Grey mumbled.

"How much further do you think until we get to the airstrip?" Mindy asked.

"At this rate, it will take hours," Gabe replied.

"We should just leave the van and hoof it," Micah suggested.

"Absolutely not. Ariel will be out in the open," Ryker bit out.

"And we're not sitting ducks right here?" Mindy asked, and I had to admit, they had a point.

"I'll go and look around. I'm faster than all of you. Make sure everything is fine," Gabe said, moving toward the door.

"I don't know if that's a good idea," Ryker said.

I placed my hand on Ryker's thigh. "Let him go. He's fast, and I mean faster than the eye can see kind of fast."

Gabe shot me a look that said, *"How fast I am is none of their business."*

"Fine. Scope it out and come back," Ryker ordered.

Gabe squinted his eyes at Ryker before opening the door and taking off. A minute passed, then another. We inched forward maybe ten feet when I felt his approach.

"He's back. Open the door."

Grey responded to me, "No one is there."

"He will be," I replied.

Grey opened the door, and like I'd said, Gabe was there and closing the door behind him.

"I don't see any danger besides the fact that there is an accident up ahead, and we will never get anywhere if we stay sitting here. The plane looks good. The airfield looks good. There wasn't anything suspicious or out of the ordinary. I think we need to leave on foot."

"I don't like it," Ryker added.

"I don't either," Ledger agreed.

"Elle's fast. Why doesn't she come with me, and we'll meet you there?"

"Over my dead body," Ryker bit out.

Gabe put his hands up placatingly, "Just a suggestion. No need to bite my head off."

"We should all go," I suggested. "Just leave the keys in the van, and let's go."

"Are you sure about this?" Ryker asked.

"No, but what good will it do if we sit here?"

"Fine, but you stay by my side the entire time. Reece, Grey, I want you on our flank."

"Micah and I will stay on Mindy," Ledger said.

"Mindy is a very capable female. She can take care of herself," Grey replied, watching Ledger more closely than he had before.

"Mindy is still a female, and there is no way she is going out there without someone having her back," Ledger bit out.

"Then I'll be at her back," Grey replied tersely.

"Would you two knock it off? Ryker gave you an order, Grey. And Ledger, I don't need you to have my back. I'm very capable, but Micah over here..." She trailed off, pointing at Grey's brother jokingly.

"Are we doing this or what?" Gabe asked, cutting off their banter.

"We are. Let's go," Ryker ordered.

The door to the van opened, and Gabe said, "I'm going to be fast. You won't see me, but I'll be everywhere, ensuring we're good. Don't worry, sis." Gabe took off, and it was like he said, I couldn't see him, but I felt him near.

We all climbed out of the van, and someone yelled, "Hey, you can't leave that here."

Ryker ignored them, and we all moved swiftly toward the intersection. The foot traffic was as dense as the traffic on the road, and you could easily get swept up in the crowded street if you weren't careful. I held onto Ryker's hand as we brushed past person after person.

We turned the corner, revealing the accident that held us up. My heart plummeted as I witnessed a mother bleeding from her head and holding her limp child in her arms. She wailed and screamed in another language, but the pain she carried was heard loud and clear.

My heart lurched, and I couldn't continue if there were some way I could help. I attempted to release Ryker's hand. He shot me a look, then said, "No. We have to carry on."

I stopped moving, annoyed that he ordered me, but more than that, I felt undeterred.

"I have to."

"It puts you and everyone else at risk."

The mother wailed again, and my mind was made up. I twisted out of his hold, freeing my hand. "It's who I am, Ryker. I can't ignore it, no more than I could ignore the pull of you. I have to help."

He gave me a subtle nod and followed me to the woman and child.

The child had to be no more than two years old. The side of his face was bruised, and a cut on his temple was bleeding. A man shouted, raising his hands toward the heavens. I didn't know what he said, but he expressed his grief as anger. I didn't pay much attention to that either.

What mattered was the small boy who needed my help. I stretched my arms toward the mother, and she clung to him even tighter. Mindy was at my side and it grounded me with her beside me. I looked at the mother again, placed my hand on her shoulder, then again stretched my other hand to indicate she should give me the boy. She reluctantly looked between us as the crowd whispered all around.

With Ryker at my back, I instinctually felt the others around as well.

The mother handed me the boy, and I closed my eyes, finding his weak heartbeat. He didn't have much time. Calmness rushed through me as I sensed the Earth beneath me like I'd done each time before. But now I had everyone else here, at my side and back. It filled me with a sense of peace.

My vision had a haze of blue. I placed a hand on his head, one against his heart, and silently prayed, then pushed the calmness and the healing toward the boy.

It felt so natural. This boy had a life left to live. This mother had more love to give. Love surrounded me from all sides, filling me, letting me give what I could to the boy.

The boy coughed and slowly opened his eyes. "Ima," he cried. Somehow, I knew it meant mom.

Joy filled me.

It worked.

I handed the boy back to his mother, and she silently wept.

"It's a miracle," Someone in the crowd yelled.

"She healed him," Another voice rang out. We needed to get out of there. Exhaustion crept in.

"Let's go, love," Ryker said, placing a hand on my shoulder.

The crowd grew thicker. We needed to go, but I was frozen because the sight in front of me was everything. The mother cradled her son's head as she kissed him repeatedly. Her eyes connected with mine. There was a moment of complete gratitude in her eyes, then, just as quickly, they lit in alarm. It was then I realized my vision still had a blue tint to it.

The murmurs in the crowd grew louder and louder.

"We need to go now."

Ryker grabbed my shoulder and helped me to my feet. People reached for me. Some cried out as they did. A few people dropped to their knees and made the sign of the cross.

We all started to move away, but the crowd grew denser.

I was jostled back and forth, and there were hands everywhere. Suddenly, Ryker roared, and I could feel it deep in my bones. "Get out of our way!"

People moved, feeling the force of his anger. Ledger was there, pushing people aside. Then Micah, Reece, and Mindy all surrounded us, helping us make our way through the initial crowd. A hand grabbed me, and I turned. It was an older man whose eye was fogged over. "Help me see," he begged. "Please, help me."

Ryker shuffled me along, through plea after plea, begging me for a miracle.

Fed up with the constant pull, Ryker stopped, swooped me into his arms, and then jogged away from the crowd. I looked back at the crowd, and instead of feeling peace, all I felt was chaos.

Chapter Twenty

"That was insane!" Reece yelled over the hum of the plane.

Gabe appeared in the doorway of the plane, waving rapidly. I was still in Ryker's arms as he nodded to Gabe in greeting. Reece ascended the stairs, then Micah. Ryker set me down, and I was about to board the plane when a thought struck me, making my stomach plummet.

"What is it?"

"I left the book in the van. How could I be so dumb? I can't believe I left it. We have to get it. We can't leave without it."

Gabe noticed my hesitation and descended the stairs. "What's wrong?"

"I left something in the van. It's important."

"I'll go," Mindy offered.

"You're not fast enough. I'll go. What do you need me to get?" Gabe offered.

"There's a satchel with a book and something else from Dad."

His eyes flashed at the mention of our dad, then he nodded, and in a flash, he was gone.

"Do you think that was wise?" Ryker asked me.

I sighed. "You think he can't be trusted because he is a" —I leaned in as if someone might overhear me— "vampire, but he's part of me, too. He wouldn't hurt me."

Ryker ground his jaw and then looked toward the stairs for the plane. "Are we ready to get out of here?"

"I'm ready," Mindy chimed in, reminding me she was here.

Gabe reappeared with the book and the satchel. "What is this?" he asked, lifting it. "I can read it even though I've never seen this language before." Gabe studied me, looking for answers I didn't have.

"Dad left it for me. I haven't had the chance to go through it."

He studied me, and before he could respond, a bullet sped through the air. I didn't know what was happening as Gabe dove for me, attempting to shield me. The bullet nicked Ryker's arm and hit Mindy in the shoulder. She yelped out in pain.

I wanted to go to her, but Gabe was shielding me and pinning me down with a surprising amount of strength.

"Get her on board, now!" Ryker yelled, moving to his sister, who was clutched in pain. Another bullet came flying, and I fought against Gabe to go to Ryker.

"Ah, shit. It got me again!"

Ledger raced down the stairs in wolf form and ran toward the bullets. In the distance, there was a large SUV with men standing around it, holding large guns. A bullet flew toward Ledger. He managed to avoid it, but another came, and he barely missed it.

"Mindy," I cried out. "Are you okay?"

Ryker pushed Gabe from me, who shook his head and yelled, "Stop!"

A red laser light was aimed right at Ryker's heart. My man survived a lot, but could he survive a bullet to the heart? Ledger yelped in pain as he was hit.

"Ledger!" Mindy yelled at the same time I yelled, "Ryker!"

"Fuck!" Ryker yelled because there was a red light on me.

A man screamed, and then, in the distance, Ledger yelped. Grey was at the doorway in wolf form, and I heard Ryker in my head, ordering him to stay.

"We have to surrender. They'll kill us all," I said.

"No, love."

"Your sister is shot. Ledger is shot. We have to. I can't let them hurt your family."

"Our family," Ryker said.

"Stop," I yelled out to the men with guns. "I'll come willingly. Stop."

Cain stepped out of the SUV and yelled, "Order them all to stand down. I'll send a man to you and the wolf. He'll cuff you; no one else needs to get hurt."

In my head, I ordered, *Stand down. We're surrendering.*

"To hell you are," Gabe said.

"Ledger and Mindy have been shot. I can't let them hurt you."

A man approached us, and Gabe's eyes went from him to me and then to Mindy. He was struggling with not fighting, but then his eyes zeroed in on the red dot on Ryker and me, and he nodded.

Ryker held me in his arms. "I love you. We broke out of there once. We'll do it again. I love you."

"I love you."

"Gabe, promise me you'll get them safe, and you'll make sure they live."

"I don't like this."

"Promise!" The man was getting nearer, and I looked at Mindy lying in pain, bleeding, and Ledger in the distance, lying still, not moving. I closed my eyes, concentrated on him, and then felt his strong heartbeat.

"He'll heal," Ryker assured me.

Then the man was there, and he approached with a confidence he wouldn't have had if there wasn't a bullet aimed at the both of us.

"Nice and steady. Let me see your hands."

Ryker growled, and it reverberated through the air. He was close to ripping the guy's head off, but he wanted to protect me.

"I love you," I silently repeated.

"And I you."

And then we were cuffed, and hoods were placed over our heads. The minute the metal cuffs touched my skin, I could tell something was off.

"Ryker."

I got no response. My wings changed, and the belt holding them in place became loose and hung on my shoulders. We'd seriously fucked up. We should've fought. We should've done anything to survive because I knew right then, that I couldn't feel my light.

Chapter Twenty-One

How many kicks did I have to watch him take? How many punches? How many wounds on my precious man's skin did I have to watch open and try to heal, only to be reopened?

It was torture watching him get beat and being powerless to do anything about it.

Ryker and I had been brought to a dungeon bound by the cuffs taking away our powers. I was kept out of his reach and secured to the wall, powerless to stop the beatings he endured. With each hit he took, I felt like I was physically enduring it.

He would pass out, and I couldn't sleep—the worry over whether he would wake haunted me. I wasn't given water. I was starving.

"Love," Ryker whispered into the darkness. His breath sounded labored. "It's going to be all right. Hang on, for me."

"How?" I croaked. "How is it going to be all right?"

"This can't go on forever, we have to find out what he wants. He'll show his cards. He'll drop his guard."

I nodded hoping he was right even though I felt less than confident. "How badly are you hurt?"

"It's just a scratch," he coughed out, lying.

"I'm sorry. None of this would've happened if I hadn't come here."

"You don't know that."

My chest burned, wanted to cry, but I had no more tears left to shed.

"Tell me about your childhood. What was it like?" I asked, changing the subject and wishing I could touch or see him clearly, but he was cloaked in darkness.

"My mom was beautiful. She had this spirit that attracted everyone to her. Sort of like you, come to think of it." I heard the smile in his voice as he spoke. "There is a magnetic pull to you, you know."

No, I didn't know, but I didn't have it in me to argue.

"Anyways, my dad and her were so in love. You could see it in everything they did. I'll never forget—I was a pup, maybe thirteen or so—there was a barn party, but I was too young to go. Live music filled the air, and I can remember sitting outside the barn peering in, hoping I didn't get caught, and what I saw stuck with me for some reason. My mom and dad were dancing—that wasn't unusual, they'd dance all the time ... In the kitchen after a meal, during different town events ... But this time, it stuck with me. They looked at each other like no one else was in the room. Other people stopped to give them space as they moved, staring into each other's eyes. People looked at them with envy and smiles. They saw and felt it too. The lLove between the two of them was something you felt while you watched them dance. I remember my dad whispering something into her ear. I couldn't hear it—I was too far away—but I saw the expression on her face, and she didn't look at him with the same love she looked at me with. It was different. It was so much more. That's when I knew I couldn't settle for anything but what they had. I wanted it." He paused, and I imagined him shaking his head. "Want isn't a big enough word. It was like, from then on, I had to have that. My sweet Ariel, whatever happens next, I'm eternally grateful I waited, and that it was you."

I closed my eyes as a small wave of coughing spread through Ryker's chest. The door creaked open, and I braced for Cain's men to be there, ready to dole out his punishment.

It wasn't.

Malice-filled laughter echoed around the room. Cain had finally graced us with his presence.

"Look at the pair of you. Your mate is weak. Who do you think is the strong one now?"

Cain's boot thudded as he kicked Ryker again.

Ryker coughed, then grunted, "I'm going to kill you."

Cain laughed again. "I bet he thinks somehow he'll get loose and heal, but what you should both know, in case you haven't figured it out already, is the metal chaining you to the wall binds your power. You are just a man, and she is just a woman.

"He's more man than you'll ever be," I rasped out.

Pain shot through my scalp as my hair was pulled, lifting me face to face with Cain. "You'll see. You'll change your mind when he is too weak to move, when every breath is a struggle ... You'll think differently of me, or you'll both die."

He let my hair go, and I slumped forward.

"Why are you doing this to us?" I cried.

Ryker coughed again, and Cain chuckled as if he thought the entire thing was a joke. There was nothing funny about any of this.

"What do you want?" I asked, annunciating my question. My voice was the only power I had, and I needed it to shoot daggers.

"Ah, there is the question. I want you to be my bride."

"Over my dead body!" Ryker growled then received another kick.

"That can be arranged," Cain laughed again.

"The Fates have already chosen my mate. What is it about me that makes you think we should be married?" I tried not to think about my man lying on the floor, broken and in pain. I needed to hear his reasons because once I knew them, then maybe I could figure a way out of this.

"Does your father know what you have planned?"

"My father is a fool, the same as your father. They believe there is a righteousness to the world. They believe *The Book of the King* was not meant to be taken at face value. They believe the book was not another Gospel, as I do, but heresy."

"What is *The Book of the King*?"

"It is the gospel of Lucifer, the King. And like all good gospels, it is to celebrate the birth. In this case, it is prophesied the son of the rose shall marry the daughter of grace, and with the pairing, a child will arise who will unite the two kingdoms."

"So you found a book full of mumbo-jumbo and decided to kidnap me, force me into marriage, shoot my friends, and hurt my mate because you think some book is predicting you and I are meant to be? Do you know how Jim Jones that sounds? Do you even hear yourself? And if it's some powerful forgotten text, what makes you think you are this special person it's about? Talk about ego!"

Knowing Cain, I should've been prepared for it, but I wasn't. His hand moved so swiftly that it connected with my cheek. My face stung, and my body jerked against the chains.

"You'll not disrespect me again, bride."

Ryker shouted, but a ringing in my ears prevented me from hearing what he yelled. Then Cain left, and it was the two of us again.

"Are you all right?" Ryker asked after several minutes of silence.

I was certain my face was swollen and bruised, but I was glad Ryker couldn't see.

"I'm fine," I lied.

"You're lying."

I guess it didn't take superpowers to hear the crack in my voice.

"Why do you goad him?" Ryker asked, coughing again.

"I wanted to know what his reasoning was. Are you hurt badly?" I questioned, fearing the answer.

"I'll admit the fact that he thinks a book about Lucifer is a gospel and that it's about the two of you is disturbing," he replied, ignoring my question.

We were quiet after that. Both of us, presumably, contemplating what Cain said and our next moves. I'm not sure when I fell asleep, but when I came to, Ryker was wheezing. Something was seriously wrong with him.

"Ryker," I called out.

He didn't answer. He was asleep. His body needed rest, so I didn't say his name again.

What if he died? What if he was bleeding internally next to me, and I couldn't get to him? Not for the first time since being here did I attempt to feel for the light and couldn't.

Come on, work, I demanded it in my head, but I didn't get anything. The light had been snuffed out. I couldn't feel my wings either.

I went over everything about Cain and everything I learned. The book from Dad, conveniently left here for me to find, was in an angelic script. I could read it, but so could Gabe. We're twins. I was fast. Faster than a werewolf. Was that the angel in me? God, that sounded so weird.

If he could read the book, did that mean he was also angelic? Could we both have pieces of Mom and Dad? And how was that even possible?

Cain has a different book that proclaims Lucifer (as in the devil) the king. He thinks it's a gospel which talks about us being married. That's not true since I'm with my mate, but does that matter? Does truth matter, or only what someone believes to be true? After all, isn't it the intention that makes the most difference?

Ryker coughed again and mumbled my name.

"Ryker?"

Again, he didn't respond. Was he sleeping, or did a fever have hold of him? What if he was bleeding internally?

Panic seized me. "Ryker?" I called out louder this time. There was no response. "Ryker!" I shouted. "Wake up, baby. Talk to me."

His wheezing continued, and I prayed, unsure what I could do.

His wheezing suddenly quieted, nothing but the thrum of my panicked heartbeat echoing around me.

"Ryker!"

Silence.

"Please be okay. Please," I begged. I sat there with him in silence, not knowing if the man who had somehow so quickly become my everything was alive or dead. I seriously had no idea and tried to control my erratic breathing so I could listen to his. Seconds passed, or were they minutes? I had no idea. But the man I desperately loved and craved like a drug was chained feet from me, and there was nothing I could do to help him. I felt powerless, and pain, unlike anything I'd ever known, burned through my chest. The thought of losing him was a life-altering, debilitating feeling.

Then I heard it, a slight cough, followed by, "Ariel?"

It was whispered, but my name leaving his lips was symphonic to my breaking heart.

"Thank God, I thought you were dead. You scared me so badly. Ryker, you're hurt badly."

"I'll be okay," he whispered, but I didn't believe him. A new crack in his voice scared me more than anything.

"Ryker, I need to go to him. If he promises to help you …"

"No," he barked out. "I'm not dying. I'll live. You need to hang on. Help will come." He coughed again, and I heard the crack in it and hoped he was right. Help would come, right? It had to.

***

There was a speck of light. How had I not noticed the light before? It was a sliver that moved slowly as the sun moved outside. The light was a reminder that life outside of these walls existed. How long had we been here? How many times had Ryker been beaten? How many times had Cain come in to taunt us?

I wasn't sure how long Ryker could hang on.

I had to reach the light. If I could grab ahold of it, there was hope.

Ryker coughed uncontrollably, although I doubted he was awake. Our throats were scratchy the last time we tried to use them. Lack of water would do that.

Ryker coughed again, and this time, I could smell the metallic tang to the air, and I wondered if it was blood.

"Ryker," I rasped out. "It's getting worse." I was certain he knew this, but it had to be acknowledged that I knew it, too.

"I'll live," he said, choking on another cough.

"Promise me that's true," I begged. "Promise you won't give up."

He coughed again, and the sound affirmed the decision I was coming to.

"I can't let you die. I must give in. I have to go to him. I'll do it if it's the only way you live."

"Ariel, don't you dare," Ryker pleaded.

"I can't lose you."

"If you go to him, you'll be lost to me anyway."

"I'd rather be lost to you and have you alive and breathing than live in a world where you're not in it. I love you. Forgive me."

I was about to call for the guards when Ryker rasped out, "Wait, you dreamed this, remember?"

Had I? It felt familiar, but in that déjà vu— barely remember your dream—way.

"You did. We need to think about this." Ryker coughed.

"Even if I did dream about this, it doesn't mean anything different should be done. You're beyond sick and hurt. If I don't go to him, you might die. I can't take that chance."

"And what if his promises to keep me alive are all a lie? How can you trust him? How do you know walking out of here isn't the moment you sign my execution? There must be a reason you dreamed of this moment. There has to be a reason I shared it with you. Do you think the Fates showed us this very moment only for us to do the exact same thing? Ariel, we need to think and you making half-cocked decisions isn't how we do that."

I was about to argue that it wasn't but snapped my mouth shut. He was right. My impromptu decision-making was precisely what got us into this mess.

"What do you suggest we do then?"

"We wait. We endure. We do whatever we must, and we don't give in."

Chapter Twenty-Two

We were going to die. If I thought it was bad before, nothing compared to the shape we were in now. Ryker was asleep more often than not. I wasn't as bad as he was. Occasionally, I was given water, which was more than I could say for Ryker. He didn't want me to go to Cain, but how could I sit here and watch him die?

If someone were going to come for us, they would have. I'd lost count of how many times I'd seen that sliver of light appear and then disappear. It was the only way I knew another day had gone by.

If roles were reversed and someone wanted Ryker, would I be okay with him going? At this point, he'd do anything to save my life, and I had to do the same for him, no matter what he wished. I told him I'd wait, but he was barely hanging on. The window for waiting was closing. If I didn't do something soon, I wouldn't get another opportunity.

"Ariel," Ryker whispered my name.

"I'm here," I replied with a scratchy voice.

He didn't respond.

"Ryker?"

Still no response.

Panic welled in my chest. "Ryk!" My voice broke as I called his name. "Honey, answer me."

There was still no answer.

My heart picked up, and I strained against my restraints. I needed to get to Ryker. I needed him so badly. "Answer me," my voice cracked, and my throat burned. I had no tears left to cry, but my heart was aching. Then I heard the soft inhale and exhale. He was still alive.

I couldn't go on like this. He was going to die.

So, I did what I often found myself doing. I prayed. I prayed for the answer. I prayed for Ryker to live. I prayed for Cain's failure. Mostly, I prayed for this nightmare to end.

My eyes grew heavy as my prayers subsided, and I eventually drifted off.

The sun shone brightly through the window where Ryker sat at his kitchen table. His eyes gentled on me as they took me in. I knew what I looked like. My hair was a frizzy mess. My legs were bare, and I only wore an oversized white t-shirt of Ryker's that I'd thrown on after our lovemaking.

I took a sip of my coffee and asked, "What are you doing today?"

Ryker's smile changed coyly, and I wondered what he was up to.

"Come here," he commanded.

I walked to him, set my coffee cup on the table, and stood directly in front of him. He ran the pads of his fingers up the backs of my legs, causing goosebumps to break out over my skin. His thumbs stroked the curve of my ass.

"Let's go back upstairs once you're caffeinated and fed. Everything else can wait."

"Mmm. I like the sound of that."

All mirth fled from Ryker's face. "Ariel, you have to wake up now. Wake up. Do you hear me? Wake up."

My eyes snapped open. "Ryker?" Again, no answer.

The door creaked, and my eyes snapped up. I braced myself for whatever hell I was about to endure. A man crouched in front of me, and even though it was dark, I knew I'd never seen him before.

"We must be quick. Drink this," he pleaded, placing a flask against my lips. The water I desperately needed filled my mouth. The man set the flask down and got to work on my restraints. "I've been watching the guards. I only have five minutes to free you."

He had two small tools with which he vigorously worked on the lock, and then amazingly, my wrist popped free.

"Who are you?"

"Who I am is not important. You saved my son's life, and I owe you a debt that can never be repaid."

With my hands free, a strange warmth passed through me. My feet were bound, but not by the metal prohibiting me from using my powers. The man worked the knots there.

"No, I'll get these. You have to free him."

"We don't have time."

"I won't leave without him. Free him, please," I pleaded, my voice stronger than it had in days. He gave me a subtle nod, and even though the light had not changed in the room, I could see him more clearly. He was older than me, maybe mid-forties. His skin was bronzed, and dark salt and pepper hair curled around his ears. He was dressed like Cain's guards. Did he work for Cain, or had he borrowed the outfit?

He moved to Ryker and started on his lock. My fingers were sore and fumbled as I tried to undo the knots around my ankles. The rope caught several times as I unwove it, and then, like that, I was free.

I rushed to Ryker, my limbs sluggish. His skin was cold to touch, and as my hand stroked his face, Ryker's eyes flashed open connecting with mine.

"Ariel," he whispered.

The man picked at the lock and said, "I've almost got it.

Ryker's eyes left mine and darted to the man.

"He's here to help us. His son was the little boy I healed."

"Leave me. I'm too injured. Go get help."

"No, you don't! Don't give up on me."

"I'm ..." he coughed, "I'll slow you down. Go."

"I left you once. I won't do it again." I tore my eyes from his and let the guilt and shame slide through me. I got us into this situation.

"Ariel, look at me."

I didn't want to. He was defeated, I could tell. He was also giving up. I looked anyway. They were gentle and kind, filled with every ounce of love we had for each other. "I don't regret a second of it. You are the most spectacular woman I have ever met. I love you. I'd live a thousand lives all over again to lead me to you."

"No," was my simple reply. This wasn't going to be our goodbye. "You wouldn't let me go to him to save you. Now I won't let you give up."

His wrist restraints popped free, clinking to the ground.

"We must hurry. We don't have much time," the man urged.

With Ryker's hands free, I knew what I needed to do. I nodded to the man who began to work on the knots at Ryker's feet. Ryker's pupils grew, giving a glimpse of his wolf behind the surface. I needed his wolf right now.

I placed my hand on the man's shoulder and whispered, "Stop." Next, I closed my eyes and looked for a connection to nature. Any kind of life at all. There were a few drops of water left in the flask. Why didn't I save more for Ryker? I wasn't thinking.

I was thinking now, though, and I knew it would be those last droplets that would save us. I envisioned the droplets growing. I thought about the soil's need for rain and my wolf's need to run in it and drink from the puddles. Then I thought of something I'd done once before to Mindy, and I put every ounce of energy into it.

Change, I commanded, hoping he'd be stronger in his wolf form.

I felt for that light within myself, and I let all my knowledge about who I was pour through me. Then I did what I'd done every time I used my gifts; I prayed. I prayed for an easy escape. I prayed to be free from all of this and for Ryker to be okay. I dug deep, looking for a new strength as words came to me like I'd spoken them a dozen times.

My cup is filled with filth. My gratitude is plentiful. My divinity is unworthy. Water that grants us life, that fills our veins, save us!

A crack of lightning rent the sky as my eyes flashed cerulean blue. My wolf stood before me as the man helping us cowered in the corner.

Chapter Twenty-Three

"It's okay. He won't hurt you."

"What ... What are you? You're the devil, aren't you? God, save me. What have I done?"

We didn't have time for this.

I lowered in front of the man. "Would the devil heal your son? Would he take the time to care? I'm quite the opposite of the devil." I thought about my wings, and they sprang free.

"Holy Mary, mother of God, pray for our sinners ..." He prayed, repeatedly making the sign of the cross.

My wings retreated, and I couldn't believe how much more control I had over them.

Ryker growled beside me, having no patience for the man. I couldn't leave him. If they found him, I did not doubt that they would do unthinkable things to him.

"We have to go."

Ryker growled again.

"Now," I continued, reaching out and pulling the man up.

He came to his senses and blinked as if he had lost himself in prayer. Next, he shook his head and looked around, searching for something. He found the exit, put up a finger while he listened, then we walked out the door. I expected guards everywhere and would need to fight our way out of there.

We moved briskly down a dark, dingy hallway until it ended, only to turn a corner and find ourselves amongst another row of prison cells.

"Help me, please." A familiar, frail voice called out. My eyes darted around the cells, trying to figure out where the voice came from. Ryker sniffed the air and strode to a door.

"Father Archibald," I cried out. "I thought you were dead."

"Careful, he betrayed us."

I wanted to savor Ryker's voice in my head. It had been so long since I heard it. It almost didn't feel real.

I approached the door to his cell and saw he looked worse for wear. His clothes were tattered, and he looked as if he'd lost a considerable amount of weight. How much time had passed since I'd last seen him?

"Elle, is that you? Are you truly here? I'm not imagining you?" His eyes darted to Ryker and widened as he took him in. I then realized it was very dark and saw far better than I should.

"I'm here," I answered. "You betrayed me."

"You don't understand why I did that. I'm so sorry. Please help me."

"We must hurry," the man said.

"Can you take out the door?"

With his sizable strength and speed, Ryker rushed the door, slamming his body into it. The door hinges creaked, and the wood bent as Ryker broke through.

"I don't trust him."

"Don't worry, Ryk, neither do I."

Father Archibald slowed us as we moved through the dark tunnels. He was unsteady on his feet, and without a hand on my shoulder or our guide's, he was clumsy.

"He smells putrid."

"I wonder what they did to him."

"It's not good, love."

"Are you getting stronger?"

"I am. I can feel your energy. How did you know?"

"I don't know."

"Be on the lookout. I find it strange we have not crossed any guards."

Another crack of thunder tore through the sky, making the building shake.

"This is too easy. I don't understand. We should've passed by multiple guards by this point."

"You get to the stables. You secure the prisoners. You make sure Abbas stays far away from here." A man's voice echoes through the hallways, barking orders at men. Chills shot down my spine. Cain's right-hand man. He'd dished out Ryker's punishments. How often had Ryker taken this man's boots to the ribs?

Fury coursed through me again, and the sky rumbled again, shaking the building.

"Not now, love. We need to wait. I'm not strong enough."

Ryker's confession made me even angrier, but I bit it back and waited to see if someone was coming our way.

"This way," the man guiding us said, leading us into a jail cell whose wooden door was slightly open. We waited for a minute, and I sensed Ryker wanting to pounce.

"Patience."

With us secure behind a door, Ryker slid out past us. There was a small grunt, followed by a thud. I wanted to holler at Ryker to come back and stay by my side. He was hurt, and his body was tired, even in wolf form. A moment passed, then another, and my wolf dragged a dying man into the room. Father Archibald released a small gasp, and our guide whispered, "Please, God, let this be your will."

"It's clear. We must go now."

Nodding my head, I directed Father Archibald and our guide out the door.

"This way," our guide ordered as we followed him.

Torches lit the hallway, making my eyes adjust to the light. Our guide ascended a set of stone stairs.

"He must stop. Something doesn't smell right."

I placed my hand on our guide's shoulder and gave him a quick shake of my head. Then, an inch of water flowed down the hallway, cascading down the stairs. It started as a trickle, but in mere seconds, it flowed like a small river, and before we knew what was happening, the tops of my feet were covered in water.

Another roll of thunder shook the building.

"Come. The storm is a distraction. We need to move."

I directed Father and our guide to follow Ryker, who hurried up the stairs. At the top, he paused, sniffing the air, then moved us to a smaller hallway tucked off to the side for servants.

It was dark again, and Father Archibald clutched onto me. I wanted to soothe him, which didn't seem right.

The energy moved throughout my body. "Something is happening to me," I warned. My wolf immediately stopped and stood in front of me, towering above.

"What is—"

He couldn't finish his question as more thunder rattled the building in a way I was sure it had been struck. People screamed in the distance. Shouts of horror rang out.

"We need to put out the fire," another person called.

"The Gods have forsaken us," another shouted.

"Are you good?"

"Well, that's a loaded question."

"Ariel."

"Fine, this is scary. My body feels lit up. I feel energized. I'm stronger by the second. It's exhilarating and exciting, but I don't know what will happen next, and that scares me."

"I feel your power and am stronger by the second. Your energy is healing me. But we need to move. The faster we can put this place behind us, the better."

He was right. Of course, he was.

We moved down the hall, and Father Archibald stumbled to keep up. Our guide had the father put his arm around his shoulders, causing them to walk sideways in the narrow hallway.

We approached the end of the passageway, light filtering through.

"We must find them. They couldn't have gone far!" Relief washed through me; the voice wasn't Cain's. He'd instilled unimaginable fear in me while we were locked up.

"He's just a man, love. We will crush him."

Footsteps thudded as men scampered away while we waited in the passageway. Closing my eyes, I sensed the room's energy. It was empty. Ryker must've also felt what I felt, for as soon as I reopened them, he led us from the passageway into the lecture hall.

"Those doors are the exit."

More thunder and lightning carried on outside.

"We need to go to the library first, though."

My wolf squinted at me, then nodded for me to lead the way.

Our guide, who was no longer guiding us, followed but not before he looked at the exit longingly.

"You've done us a great honor by helping us, and your debt is paid. You can go. Be with your son," I prompted.

"That is not who I am," the man replied. I nodded as we quickly made our way down a corridor, through another door, and into the library, shocking me when we didn't pass anyone else.

The library was quiet as we entered.

"Do you know of this book Cain speaks of?" I asked Father Archibald. "I need to know what it says before we leave this place." I scrambled to remember what Cain had called it. "He called it *The Book of The King*. He believed it to be a lost Gospel."

"No! That's what this has been about? Elle, you have to believe me. I had no idea this is what Cain believed."

"I'm not sure I believe much that comes from your mouth, Father, but that's beside the point. Where would the gospel be kept?

"That's an artifact. It wouldn't be kept here among regular books."

Water sloshed through the library. Shouts echoed from outside the room.

Irritation laced my words, "If it's not here, where would it be?"

"If I had to guess, Abbas's or Cain's personal vault."

I looked into Ryker's eyes, knowing we'd have to leave today without answers.

Ryker's ears perked up as there was a noise at the door. The feeling of getting ready to fight took over. Ryker sniffed and moved toward the closed door. I wanted to stop him but had to trust he knew what he was doing.

The door handle turned, and I shuffled in front of Father Archibald. Our guide, whose name I really needed to learn, stood off to the side, appearing as if he was trying to hide in the shadows.

The wood creaked as the door slowly opened. I braced myself, unsure of what was coming, then broke out in a huge grin.

Micah, Reece, and Gabe strolled through the door. Gabe quickly rushed to me, threw his arms around me, and hugged me.

"Whatever it is you're doing outside, you need to make it stop."

Chapter Twenty-Four

"What do you mean?" I questioned as Gabe released me.

"What's up, Ryker?" Micah asked breezily.

Gabe's eyes widened slightly, only now taking in Ryker's massive form as a wolf.

"He's one big fucker," Reece said, then his eyes grew soft on me. I had to look horrendous. "It's good to see you. Sorry it took us so long to get here."

Micah's eyes landed on Father Archibald, and his body grew stiff. "What's he doing here? I should bite his head off right now and be done with him."

"Enough," Gabe ordered. "While you all say hello, a town is burning outside. The ground, that's never seen water, can't absorb all the rain. The streets are flooding. There are families outside."

"Oh, God." I closed my eyes and thought about the rain slowing, but then I instantly thought about Ryker giving up on life and trying to let me go. Another crack of thunder shook the building, followed by several screams.

Ryker nuzzled close to me, his warmth radiating into me.

"I'm all right. It's going to be okay. Calm yourself, honey. Stay linked with me. I'll help you."

"I'm scared. I never..."

"I know."

Ryker moved around me again, then bent, placing his furry forehead against mine. I closed my eyes and thought about the rain slowing and the sun peeking out. I thought about tranquility with a light breeze and flowers blooming from the earth. I thought about the greenhouse crops greenhouse flourishing and giving an abundance of food to make up for the storm I brewed, and I did all of this with Ryker's forehead pressed to mine, grounding me.

"Someone's coming," Micah said.

We moved down an aisle filled with books. I had no idea who it would be, and I braced myself, ready to fight.

I heard, "The people gather."

Then another voice, "You have to see."

And another, "It's a miracle."

I wanted to roll my eyes at the commotion. It wasn't a miracle, just me. Then I spotted a table in the back of the room that looked as if it was left unattended in a hurry. Distracted, I moved away from the group.

Several book pages were photocopied, so I gathered them and folded them together. Without a place to stick them, I tucked them uncomfortably into my bra, which was incredibly uncomfortable; however, sometimes, a girl had to do what she had to do.

A wave of tiredness overcame me. This was taking more out of me than I expected. But I was in flight or fight mode, and I couldn't let my body give up on me.

Ryker, being Ryker, sensed something off in me.

"We're going to get out of this hell hole. Get on. You need to ride me. You're exhausted, and it won't do us much good if you collapse mid-escape."

"But you're hurt."

"I told you, you make me stronger. Now, hop on before you topple over."

"How do you always know?"

"You know the answer to that."

I knew exactly what he was saying. He bent low for me to mount him. It was one thing to ride on his back in a field and completely different to ride on his back in a library. I was high

"Ask your brother if he can help the father and see that our companion is safe."

"What are you going to do?"

"My brothers are going to shift, and we'll get you out of here."

A thrum ran through my veins as Ryker commanded his pack, *"Wolves be wolves."*

Reece and Micah locked eyes with Ryker, but Reece raised a hand. "Wait! Elle, I have something for you that might come in handy."

Confused, I studied him, unsure what I could need. Then he handed me the satchel. "The dagger is there. Take it out. Use it if you must."

Well, that sounded cryptic.

Glad to have my dad's relics returned to me, I took out the dagger, feeling the cold metal in my hands, and looked at my brother. "They're going to change. Make sure the father and our friend get out of here. Can you do that?"

Gabe smirked at me, like, of course, he could; then, a thought occurred to me. "What if they come at us with bullets again?" I blurted.

"They won't. Cain can't use modern technology in front of his people. Outside the city, they wouldn't know about it. But here? Here, they'd turn against him," Father Archibald said.

Another thought occurred to me, and I had to ask. "If people can't leave, how come our friend over here was in the city with his wife and son but knew his way around here?"

I looked at the man, "What's your name, by the way?"

"Ariel, love, we don't have time for this."

"My name is Simon, I worked here, and witnessed Cain's cruel ways but left when my wife became pregnant."

"Satisfied, sis? We should go."

I nodded at my brother and watched with fascination as Reece and Micah quickly shifted.

I don't know if I'd ever get over how gruesomely cool that is.

"Be safe, everyone."

My brother nodded and then moved to the library door to open it.

I braced, unsure of what we would find, but he nodded that it was safe, and we prowled forward. We moved fast, my brother grabbing a man, running ahead, depositing him somewhere, then coming back for the second man, all while we raced after him.

"Stop!" a guard yelled.

Reece's body slammed into him, flinging him against the wall and knocking him unconscious. Another guard appeared, and Micha took care of him similarly.

Water splashed around us as we ran, finding ourselves at a new exit. Simon and the father were waiting for us, making me marvel at my brother's speed and strength.

He slowly opened the battered door that creaked loudly.

"We're going to make a run for it," Ryker explained.

"Leave me here," Simon said. "I will only slow you down. I know people. People who do not like the way Cain has changed things."

I looked at him, surprised he would leave. Our eyes connected, and he read my thoughts—my thank yous. He nodded in gratitude.

"May you be safe on your journey. And hug that little boy of yours."

"I'm forever in your debt."

I nodded back. Ryker felt my resolve, then took off at high speed.

It was pandemonium.

Buildings burned. Smoke filled the sky. The hazy gray made it hard to see. The roads were filled with water. As Ryker ran, it sloshed up all around us, hitting the soles of my feet.

I expected people to gasp at a woman riding a wolf followed by two equally large wolves, but no one noticed. No one ran to put out the flames of their buildings. No one did much of anything. That was because their attention was aimed at the sky, where a lightning bolt was frozen, piercing the side of a rainbow. It was marvelous and shocking at the same time.

I wanted to stare at it. Could I have done that? As much as I wanted to marvel at the image, I was focussed on Ryker.

We broke through the crowds in the center of town.

Unimpressed by the sky, a man shouted, "Wol—" Before he could get the rest out, Micah rammed into him, and he went flying. A woman screamed and ran in the opposite direction. We moved briskly, and if the wolves could silence someone, they did.

"Don't hurt them." I pleaded, not wanting any actual damage to come to an innocent.

An uneasy feeling formed in my stomach pit, followed by an arrow landing mere inches away from Ryker.

"They're shooting at us"! I yelled in my head, and surprisingly Micah responded.

"I spot him at your six."

"Whoa, this is some weird shit. You guys silently communicate with each other like this all the time?" Gabe replied (also in my freaking head), then added, *"Micah, can you take the old dude?"*

"I got him," Reece added.

They did a quick exchange that I barely saw as Ryker dodged to the right to avoid being impaled by an arrow. I looked behind me, and in a blurry flash, Gabe tossed the shooter out a second-story window.

I felt that funny feeling in the pit of my stomach again and called, "*Gabe. We got another one up ahead. I can't see him, but I can feel it.*"

"*Damn, that's what that feeling is in my stomach! I thought it was indigestion!*"

"*It's a bad time for jokes.*"

"*Who said I was joking?*"

"*Focus. I smell him about half a click due east.*" Ryker admonished.

"*See that. Like, what does a click even mean?*" Gabe questioned, which was an excellent question because who knew how far a click was.

Ryker pushed out a wave of annoyance, and Micah, Reece, and Gabe reacted.

"*Whoa, what was that?*" Gabe asked.

"*The power of the pack leader. Don't worry, Ryker. I got this one. He's close to the ground. I can smell him.*" Micah responded.

Ryker slowed a tad, and Micah passed us. I didn't see what happened, but there was a small scream like he didn't have the time to get it all out.

I felt that feeling again, but my spidey sense must've only lasted so long because almost as soon as I felt it, there was a pop of a gun, followed by immense pain as it tore through my shoulder.

"*Ariel!*" Ryker yelled.

I gritted my teeth. We were almost clear. Another shot ripped off, and fury like I'd never felt before tore through me. I came here looking for answers. I didn't ask for any of this. I didn't want some creepy dude to show me attention, act like he thought we were supposed to be married, and then shoot at us. They shot Mindy. Jesus, he shot me! Warm blood dripped down my arm. This wasn't good. It hurt something fierce, but I was too ticked to comprehend the pain.

I didn't ask for any of this to happen.

I felt them, even though I couldn't see them. There were several, all holding guns. They must've felt like we were far enough away from the city that it was safe to use them. None of that mattered. I wouldn't let them hurt Ryker or the rest of my pack. Feeling where the danger was coming from and sensing they were about to strike, I summoned all the pain and fury and asked the earth to take them.

There was a rumble beneath our feet, and the earth began to move, but all I could think was, "*No more. I'm done with games.*" My vision went blue, and the threat was gone without knowing what had happened to the men.

My vision remained blue as we raced on. "*Nothing will hurt us,*" I told the men.

"*Ariel, my love.*" I barely registered Ryker calling to me. An immense amount of energy flowed through me and my need for safety. We'd been through enough. We were going to get out of here.

"*Ariel.*" Ryker coaxed.

I couldn't respond. Not now. Not after my flesh had been torn apart and *my love* almost gave up. I nearly lost him. I nearly lost everything.

We approached a wall. *Screw that wall.* It wouldn't be the barrier that stood in our way.

I barely thought about it, and the ground rumbled, and the wall cracked. Dust filled the air, and as we approached the wall, it was as if the rumble knew where we were, and the wall fell enough to make our escape seamless.

We raced over the wall, and I looked behind me one final time. No rainbow filled the sky. Nor was there rain or lightning. There was smoke and fire. There was screaming and shouts. But no one chased us. There was no longer a threat.

"*Get us out of here,*" I ordered.

And then, just like that, my energy was completely drained. I did what I typically did in this situation ... I passed the fuck out.

***

"Is this normal? Why isn't she waking?" Gabe was talking, but I couldn't see him. *Why couldn't I open my eyes?*

"It's not the first time this has happened," Ryker responded.

"What do you mean it's not the first time?" Gabe's voice was pitched higher.

"When she expels too much energy, it takes her body a long time to recover, and based on everything she did back there ..."

"She could be out for days," Reece finished Ryker's sentence.

"I cleaned her wound as best as I could, but I'll need more supplies," Farah said.

"What do you want me to do with these?" Micah questioned. I didn't know what he was talking about. "Hey, what's this?" He asked.

"In the library, she stuffed something in her dress," Ryker replied.

"There's blood on it. Do you think we can make out what it says?" Reece asked.

"Who cares about anything! Look at her. She is out cold with a gunshot wound. She toppled walls, made the Earth shake, and flooded a city. People are after her. And you guys are acting casual as fuck. What the hell!" Gabe, having had enough, shouted.

"Do not take my calmness as casual. She tends to feel my energy." Ryker said through gritted teeth. "I know what she did, and we nearly died so many times in the last few weeks. It haunts me that I've been unable to protect her, and she took that bullet, not me. It haunts me that my sister is recovering from her own bullet wound, and a man who is practically my brother is in far worse condition. We don't have any damn answers as to why he's after her in the first place, and I'm ticked. Instead of trying to make everyone else around here panic, why don't you do something useful and study the damn book? If we're going to find answers, the book your dad left is as good a place to start as any."

"You're right. I'm sorry. Me panicking isn't helping anyone."

"Ah, don't be so hard on yourself. It's gotta be weird adjusting to having a sister," Reece added.

"It is, and a twin at that. I always felt like a part of me was missing."

"If this is the part where you say, 'She completes me,' I might barf," Micah replied.

"Enough," Ryker commanded. "Leave us."

"I want to get an IV in her. With everything you've been through, getting her on fluids would be beneficial," Farah explained.

"Please," Ryker replied softer.

"At least the bullet went clear through. She'll scar, but she'll heal Ryker."

"I've done a shit job protecting her, Farah."

"She's alive, isn't she?"

"Her heartbeat is so weak, though."

"She's different, but she's strong. She might need to take her time to heal."

"It's enough Gods-damn time. I can't keep losing her like this."

Ryker was silent after that, and if I could wake and wrap my arms around him, I would. I hated that he took this on as his responsibility. I hated that I kept losing consciousness. I hated that I felt powerless to do anything about it.

It was quiet after that. I was surrounded by darkness, and the silence was deafening. Suddenly, that blue light appeared, and those words that I hadn't heard in ages called to me.

"Keeper. Keeper."

Chapter Twenty-Five

Feeling a little like Alice running after her white bunny, I chased the blue light. It was a beacon calling my name, with nothing but darkness surrounding me.

"Keeper," it whispered in the same layered way.

Then, suddenly, it stopped moving and burst like a firework, bright and blinding. I was no longer in the darkness.

I was in a room that appeared to be in a castle. Large crystal-like pillars rose thirty feet high. Looking up, the ceiling was made of dozens of crystals, sparkling and shining kaleidoscopes of rainbows upon hundreds of people who gathered. I gasped. It wasn't crystals. It was ice.

The room, which was more like a massive ballroom, was filled with people dressed in a way I'd never seen before. Everyone wore shades of white. Some gowns had tints of pink or iridescent purples. One woman I passed wore an off-white avant-garde dress that came up high around her throat and poofed at least three feet from her hips. Some dresses were slim fitting, but each was a work of art. It was a fashion designer's paradise. Men wore white tuxedos, some with bodacious top hats, while others styled their hair in a high bouffant. Everyone's attention was on the front of the room.

"Excuse me," I asked one woman as I passed, trying to get a better look. She ignored me as if I wasn't there. "Well, you don't have to be rude." I marveled at how she didn't even blink in response to me.

Next, I tried a nicely dressed man, slightly less interested in what was going on up front and what brought everyone together. "Hello, sir?" Again, I was met with no response. I waved my hand in front of his face, and it dawned on me that he couldn't see me.

I must be dreaming.

I made my way to an incredible throne where four women sat. Each dressed in a pure white gown. The first woman had curly red hair pinned atop her head. She appeared to be in her late forties or early fifties, with slight wrinkles around the edges of her eyes. Her strapless dress cut across her chest in a straight line, and although she was sitting and I couldn't see the back of the dress, I could see her kick-ass white, heeled leather boots and her cape, which had a collar that framed her face and rose to nearly the top of her head. There, she, and every subsequent woman on the throne, wore a crown.

The next woman's hair was similar to mine—big and blonde. Full curls tumbled over her shoulders. Her nose was narrow, and her lips had a slight peak. Her dress, cut low in the front, showed off her ample bosom. It cinched tight at the waist, and layers of thick tulle cascaded around her, covering the floor.

The next two women made me blink twice because they were identical in their appearance and every move they made even as they spoke. They both had dark brown hair braided back on one side of their head, and the rest had perfect volume as it tumbled in soft waves. They looked younger than the other two women but somehow seemed older in how they carried themselves. Deliberate in the things they said and the way they spoke.

I stilled as I saw a woman kneeling in a bow before them, dressed in armor.

"Holy shit," I whispered. Unfreezing, I moved closer, then bumped into a chair that scraped along the slick marbled floor. The woman kneeling turned her head, and her eyes connected with mine. Holy shit, holy shit, holy ... she looked just like me. It was as if I was staring into a mirror.

I had to get a better look.

I passed by a man with a serving tray carrying small, delicious-smelling mini croissants.

Wait, since when did I smell things while I was dreaming?

I quickly moved past that strange thought because, OMG, there was another me kneeling before four goddess queens with beautiful, over-the-top fashion sense.

"Are you sure this is the sacrifice you're willing to make?" The two brunettes asked the version of me kneeling before them.

Her eyes briefly connected with mine again, and she nodded, then said, "I'm sure."

"Then it is done. Your ancestors will carry your genes. They will protect the light. This will be a burden and a gift. When the time is right, and you are needed once more, we shall call on you, Ariel, Angel of Earth, sand, water, and light. We thank you for your bravery, and we bless you. We ask the Gods to shine upon your future generations. We ask the Gods to guide you as you embark on a long journey."

Oh, my God. I knew what this was. Of course, I didn't remember it, but I knew what I was seeing. This was me, or a version of me, and those four beautiful women were the Fates.

The crowd applauded, and shouts of joy echoed around the room.

A man appeared, dressed in black, a stark contrast to the entire room. No one else was startled by his presence. In fact, he moved around the room the same way I did, nearly invisible.

His eyes connected with mine briefly and took my breath away. I'd seen those eyes. I felt that stare. I'd run from him, or the other me did. I don't know. It was all too confusing. He was the man on the armored horse chasing me in my dreams, visions, or whatever the heck they were. He was the man who threatened me. He wasn't in armor like on the battlefield. He was dressed in a black suit tailored to perfection.

He grabbed a flute of what I guessed was champagne from a passing server's tray. I watched as he sipped it, curled his lip, and tossed it to the ground. Again, no one acknowledged his behavior.

It was as if the two of us were invisible. His eyes found mine, and he raised an eyebrow. I felt a chill go up my spine because I didn't thinkt he could see me. But he *could*.

He approached, and I wanted to run in the opposite direction. Everything about him was all wrong.

He wove through the crowds and stopped beside me, staring at the front. The words spoken between the Fates and that version of me were too low to hear.

"You don't belong here." His voice was melodic as he spoke.

"Yeah? Not sure you do either," I replied bitingly.

"Now, now. Don't be so bitter. This is the part where it gets very interesting."

"How are you here in this dream with me?"

He laughed at my question. "Because I am a part of this just as much as they are."

"No, you're wrong."

He smiled an all-knowing smile, and I felt the urge to smack the smugness right off him. Then I quickly added, "We'll see."

"Watch closely at what happens next. This is the good part."

Black smoke filled the air in a swirling pattern, and the armor-clad version of me stood and unsheathed her sword. A man looking exactly like the man next to me stepped out of the smoke, only this man wore clothes that had seen far better days. His vagabond appearance and the dust on his shoulders starkly contrasted everything else. I then looked at my appearance. I wasn't far from him.

There was a collective gasp, and one man shouted, "Lord save us."

The man laughed as he casually strode forth and stopped in front of the other me.

"This is it. Are you ready?" The man asked in a hushed tone. "I don't want you to miss any of this."

"Look at the four of you. You think you have it all figured out, don't you?" His mirror-version said.

"Now, now, Luce. You have forgotten your place in this world. It certainly isn't here," The red-headed Fate said.

"Oh, on the contrary. I'm precisely where I'm supposed to be, and shouldn't you know this since you're the Fates? Or are the Fates not all-knowing as you would have us all believe? After all, He gave them that thing called free will."

"We knew you would come. You never could resist," the brunette Fates spoke in tandem.

"Oh, I do find your monologues to be rather drab. Why don't you save us all the trouble and get to the point? Then you can be on your way," the blonde Fate added.

"Very well," he chuckled. "I thought it prudent you know I know what you're doing with her. You and the wolves might have won the war this time, but the dark stains on my coat are his. He died at my blade."

In a flash, the armored version of me held a blade remarkably similar to my blade to his throat. "You lie."

"I'm a lot of things, but a liar isn't one of them."

"I'll end you."

"You'll try."

"I promise."

He laughed. "Did you have feelings for the wolf? You, an angel, had feelings for the Lycan? Now, you know, *He* doesn't allow that."

Her blade pressed closer to his throat, and it took every ounce of strength from her not to sink that blade into his flesh. Everything clicked together for me. The dreams I'd been having were, in fact, a real battle. But it wasn't me, it was her, and the wolf was Ryker, but not my Ryker.

"Ariel, you must stop. No blood can be drawn here," the red-headed Fate warned.

"One day, Lucifer, you'll pay for this. I swear it."

"Maybe, maybe not. Maybe I have my own fate. Maybe I'll play my own part, and you'll never see it coming."

"Enough!" Ariel roared. "I will not listen to another word from this liar's mouth. Yes, it's true that without you, I wouldn't have the wolves. But you seemed to have taken that away anyway. So, tell me, Luce, while I'm forbidden to spill blood here, what is stopping me from dragging you off these holy grounds and letting the earth have your blood? Lord knows it deserves every last drop."

The crowd gasped at the insult. There was so much more going on here than I understood. It was as if I had stepped into another world with foreign rules and customs.

"Tsk, tsk. Ariel. You know me better than to come in here without a backup plan."

The doppelganger next to me laughed. "God, I was such a showman."

I stared at him. Was he Lucifer, as in the devil? Could I be standing next to the devil himself? Shouldn't I be afraid?

He laughed again. "You're finally putting pieces together. Yes, if I were you, I'd be afraid. Now, watch the show."

I looked to the other versions of us, needing to hear what was said.

"Say what you came to say," the blonde Fate spoke.

"For someone as old as time, you do lack patience," he mocked. "But if you insist. You're putting a plan in place for her return for me. You're devising a scheme that will take centuries and dozens of lives lived and lost by her. But you should know that I, too, have a plan. A plan that will bring her to me. A plan that will connect us for the rest of eternity. You will not know when or how, but as I stand before you, know so does she." He turned and looked at me. A sinister smile coated his face. People turned to see what he was looking at, but they couldn't see us. Then, the other me's eyes connected with mine, and she briefly closed her eyes, knowing her fate would be long and hard. And how I knew what she knew, I wasn't quite sure, but I did.

"So be it," the red-haired Fate decreed. "She is strong. Her perseverance is unmatched. We believe in her. When the time is right, we, too, will give her a gift. For there to be dark, there will be light."

"You think your offer of gifts scare me? We will just have to see who's more cunning." He laughed as irritation was written all over the Fates' faces. "By order of the Rose, so it shall be." He then threw some type of dust in the air. A cloud of smoke surrounded him, and he disappeared.

"Well, that was melodramatic," I muttered under my breath.

The man beside me laughed, and I realized I was so entranced in the scene before me that I nearly forgot he was there.

"It was. I used to have a flair for the dramatic."

"And you don't anymore?"

"Now I'm one step closer."

"One step closer to what?"

"To having what I want."

"All right, Rumplestiltskin, you can stop speaking in riddles now."

"Who?" he questioned.

"It's not important. The real question is, what is it that you want?"

"That is the real question, isn't it?"

"You're impossible!" I harrumphed.

"Why aren't you afraid of me?" he asked.

Instead of thinking of an answer, I blurted, "Maybe it's you who should be afraid of me."

He lifted his fingers, coyly smiled at me, then snapped. In an instant, we were no longer in the grand ice hall surrounded by opulence. We were somewhere much hotter. Fire blazed around us. The sky was dark but illuminated red from the fires all around us. Screams echoed in the distance.

A man yelled, "No, no, please don't. I'm sorry. I didn't mean it."

"Do you hear that?" A voice mocked, "he's sorry."

More screams followed. I shuddered to think about what was being done to the man.

"Is this where you yell to all your creatures, Daddy's home?"

"This doesn't scare you?"

"It's not real. You're not real."

"No?" he smiled.

Maybe I wasn't in some bad B movie and should watch what I said if this was truly the devil. So instead, I asked, "Why Cain and his obsession with me?"

He smiled then, and it felt more genuine than the previous snide smiles. "Religion is funny, isn't it? The scene you witnessed where my younger self vows to have you returned was witnessed by many. Anytime there has been a witness, man's feeble interpretation is allowed. The Bible, with its truth, also has as many falsehoods. Why? Because *His* most fallible creature wrote it. Man can't help but make himself the center of attention. Do you know how many parts about me were left out? You don't have to answer. I know you have no idea. And before you start and say something about my self-importance, I'll save you the details and tell you it was important."

"*The Book of the King*," I whispered, nearly afraid to say the title in his presence.

"Yes, the book. The book talks about the very moment you witnessed. But the book was a recantation of what people saw, and like all stories, they change. The verbiage led Cain to believe he was chosen. Why in any world would I choose such a man? Nonetheless, besides you being shot, which wasn't my intention, he did aid in my plan to bring us to this very moment."

We strode through the fiery pits of hell as if casually walking on a warm summer's day. Disfigured crows circled overhead. A gruesome spider at least three feet tall approached. Its legs clinked like they were made of glass as it came near. I could deal with a lot of things, but a giant spider? I shivered but managed to maintain my composure. Lucifer reached out and scratched the spider behind its tentacle, and its legs danced back and forth, reminding me of a dog wagging its tail. Then the spider ran off only to spear another giant bug and eat it.

Shouts and screams came from every direction, but there was so much that none felt real. It didn't feel like there was one immediate person in danger that needed help; more like the background soundtrack at a haunted house.

Finally, I asked, "And what of this moment? Why am I here?"

"You really don't remember the past, do you?"

"No, this life is the only life I've lived."

"No, dear, this life is the only life you recall living."

"That may be so, but this life is mine."

He smiled coyly, "So it is. However, the Fates had no idea of my plan to make you part of me. You are my child as much as you are a child of His."

I gasped.

"You have as much dark blood in you as you do light. You are a complete conundrum."

"What of my brother?" I asked.

"Your brother is not angelic."

"Why am I here ... with you? What is it you want?"

"Child, you are here because I wanted to extend an olive branch. I did not intend for Cain to shoot you nor for him to think *The Book of the King* was about him. I wanted you to hear it from me. He is merely a man who has interpreted a book in his own way and believes what he believes."

"He has a following."

"So does the Pope."

"So did Jim Jones."

He smiled. "Jim Jones, now there's a fellow who took the word of God and did what he wanted with it."

The terrain became rocky, and Lucifer offered his hand as we climbed a slight incline. I took it and was shocked at how unafraid I was. A large red snake slithered nearby, and as much as I wanted to recoil, I didn't. Lucifer wouldn't allow anything to hurt me, which was strange. I wasn't even really here, right? I mean, I was shot. I'm sure I'm resting somewhere, and this was all a dream, right?

I'd have to ponder that thought later. It was a lot, and with how much had been happening to me, I could use some R&R. A vacation. Somewhere warm. Warmer than this. A chill passed through me, and my teeth chattered. How could I be so cold with blazing fires all around me?

"Your body is fighting infection," Lucifer shared.

We reached the top of a ridge, and there below me, a battle played out. Warriors on horses fought against one another. We were quite a distance away, but echoes of steel hitting steel as the swords clashed drifted to us. A blonde version of me fought below, and I witnessed the version of Lucifer with his red beady eyes coming for her. The wolves raced forward, and then, Lucifer snapped his fingers again, stilling the moment.

"You've seen this before, haven't you?" he asked.

"I dreamt it," I confirmed.

"So, you're not completely separated from the past."

My eyes sought out Ryker on the battlefield, and my teeth chattered. No, I remembered this, and if I were honest with myself, I'd always felt an unwavering connection to my wolf.

Then I recalled Lucifer's words in the ice castle. "Did you kill him?"

"Several times," Lucifer answered casually.

"Like you, his soul is tethered to Earth, and he keeps coming back. You two are undoubtedly linked, only this is the first time you love him."

I answered immediately, without thinking about my reply, "I've always loved him."

He smirked in amusement.

I'd had enough. "Why am I here?"

"I wanted you to see the moments they kept from you. I wanted you to know time and again you've ended your life for them. If you've loved him, then you should know you've continually lost him. Oh, but the Fates ... they control your destiny, and again and again, they break you ... watch."

He snapped his fingers again, and his mirror-version reared up on his horse. With a fierce downward swipe, he cut into Ryker, driving him to the ground. A gasp left my throat, and I wanted to go to him, but Lucifer put up a hand, halting me.

"Just watch."

"You hurt him," I growled, ready to fight the devil himself.

"Silence," he ordered, glaring at me.

I needed to see what happened next as an unbearable ache lanced through my chest. My vision turned blue, and something told me to draw it back. I closed my eyes, praying it would go away, then opened them, knowing I needed to see what was happening.

The other version of me swung her sword in small circles, playing with Lucifer. She didn't seem devastated. She didn't seem like her soul was being crushed as I did. We were quite a distance off, and I couldn't hear what she said. Then, with one fell swoop, Lucifer's sword sliced, and he took off her head!

Her head! I turned and glared at him, disturbed at seeing a version of me crumpled to the ground.

"What's wrong with you? Why would you show me that?"

"I wanted you to see with your own eyes that we've been down this road. I win. I always win. You die. You come back. It's cumbersome, and I wanted this time to be different."

He snapped his fingers again, bringing me to a room I didn't recognize where Ryker lay with me cradled in his arms.

He wiped the sweat from my brow. "Heal. By the Gods, heal," he whispered.

My heart leaped, recognizing Ryker's pain. This was now, and it was real- me in bed. His love coursed through my body as if it were tangible.

"Why are you showing me this?"

"It's time for us to say goodbye."

"So, you brought me here to show me you've killed other versions of Ryker and me? Are you toying with me?" I quickly asked, not wanting him to leave just yet. So much was still unsaid.

"No, dear. If that's what you think, you weren't paying close enough attention. I thought you'd be a tad smarter after all your lives, but if you need me to spell it out for you, I suppose I will. You are the weapon the Fates choose to destroy me. But you never win. I tire of the game, so I decided long ago a time would come when I would make you a part of me. My blood runs through your veins as your angelic blood does. You are all of us. I gave you a choice, which they've never done. I wanted you to see I could've easily taken your life. I've done it countless times before but I chose a different route."

I sifted through my memories and remembered something the Fates said. *"To give you love, you needed a balance. Without evil, there can be no good. You are here to balance out the good and bad. You are both guardian and fallen. You will choose your destiny and your path. But we have faith that you will choose wisely."*

My eyes became blue, and my vision had never felt so clear, even through the haze. I looked at Ryker holding and whispering to me, then at Lucifer, and snapped my fingers.

"This has been enlightening, but I choose him. I'll always choose him." Then everything went black.

Chapter Twenty-Six

"She's coming to!" I heard Gabe before I saw him. Then Ryker's presence was there.

"Love, I'm here. Stay with me."

My body ached, and as I tried to open my eyes, searing pain shot through me. It reminded me of the pain I felt when I first had sex with Ryker.

"Everyone out!" Ryker ordered, followed by footsteps.

The pain was immense, and felt like I was burning up inside. The covers were pulled back, and Ryker's hot skin fell against mine.

"I feel your pain, Love. I'm here. Don't go anywhere."

I tried to focus on his voice. I wanted to say something back, anything, but I couldn't. His hands roamed my body, and his skin against mine calmed the pain.

This was reality. The feel. The touch. Nothing about anywhere else I'd seen felt real, but this right here with Ryker was a tangible thing.

"My eyes hurt."

He shuffled and moved away from me. I instantly regretted telling him. Any moment without us touching caused me instant pain.

"It's dark now."

"I need your skin."

More shuffling, and I tried not to cry out in pain as Ryker disrobed.

Finally, he pulled the covers back and joined me. His body immediately calmed my pain.

"Is that better?"

"Getting there."

I attempted to open my eyes, and although they were sensitive and took a moment to adjust to the darkness, I smiled when I saw Ryker. He looked exhausted. His features were coated with worry. Dark circles under his eyes indicated he hadn't slept.

His hands roamed over my body, and I felt stronger with him nearby.

"Lay with me. I'm tired, but so are you. You need to rest, Ryker."

"I'll rest when I know you're fine."

"I'm getting better. I can feel it. Now, press your body to mine so I can heal the rest of the way."

His arms circled me and held me close to him. His legs entwined with mine and my breasts pressed against his chest, automatically making my body react, just not enough.

"Damn, I'm tired."

"It's okay, love. You're back. That's all that matters."

"Yeah, going to hell and back will do that to you."

"What?" He questioned irately.

"It's a long story." I yawned, feeling much less pain with his body pressed to mine.

"Ariel."

"Not now. Later. Now I need you to help me heal."

"Anything for you."

"I love you."

"And I you."

Those simple words made me melt into him and feel okay enough to let it all go and rest. Thankfully, these dreams were of Ryker and me. He held me in my dreams, and it felt like a relief to my soul when he finally let go and joined me in sleep.

"There you are." I cooed. We were in the forest he brought me to when he first showed me his wolf.

"What is this place?"

"It's ours."

He looked around and examined it. "It is, but it is different. More vibrant."

"It's how I see it."

"Come to me," he ordered.

I moved to him, only then realizing we were both naked, and he was excited to see me. My body wasn't tired, nor was I bruised. The dark circles under Ryker's eyes were gone, and it was the two of us, completely unharmed by the world.

His hand snaked out, grabbing my hand and pulling me closer to him.

"By the Gods, I've missed you." I smiled coyly at him. "What, no silly remarks?"

"No. I've missed you too much."

He pulled me flush against his massive body, and his hard length pressed against my stomach.

"I'm ravenous for you."

Those words made my heart thump widely in my chest, and my already hardening nipples grew even tighter.

I ran my hands down his biceps, feeling the shared strength he possessed.

A slight breeze blew a strand of my hair across my face, and Ryker noticed immediately, tucking the loose tendril behind my ear. Then he cupped my jaw, bent his head, and kissed me. It was hard, yet soft. Sexy but sweet. It was better than all the kisses before. Then again, each kiss somehow felt that way.

His lips broke from mine, and his tongue darted out, licking the edge of my lips. My hands roamed over his warm flesh while he kissed my jaw, my neck, the top of my breasts, and my nipples—one, then the other. He lowered himself, kissing my stomach as he went.

Then, without much warning, he grabbed the backs of my thighs and pushed his face between my legs. His tongue flicked across my clit. His hands cupped my bottom, and the sensation changed as he spread my cheeks and slid a finger from my backside to the front, circling my slick entrance without fully entering me.

Damn, how he made me crazy.

I whimpered, and he looked up, meeting my eyes.

He knew exactly what he was doing to me. He did it again, not quite entering me.

The torture was exquisite.

He watched my reaction, and his eyes held a wicked gleam as he did it again.

I was close to combusting. He hadn't even entered me yet.

I pushed my hips forward and grabbed his hair, feeling frantic.

"It's been too long, love," he said, releasing my clit. His thumb took its place and rolled in circles. "You taste amazing."

I whimpered again, then begged, "I need you."

He slid a finger inside and curled it. I was on the cusp of my orgasm. Just a little push and I'd fall right over the edge.

He didn't do that.

Instead, he released his finger and stood.

"Take me."

He returned my silent order with a smile, kissed me hard, grabbed me by the ass, and lifted me. My legs automatically encircled his waist, and a second later, my bottom landed on cold stone. He set me against a boulder and lifted my knees, gazing at my wet heat. My vision traveled toward his length, and I licked my lips in anticipation.

He caught my look, and his pupils dilated.

"You like this?" he asked with one deep thrust, pushing into me.

"Yes!" I cried out, my eyes snapping open. We were no longer in the forest but joined together in reality on the bed.

Ryker was beneath me; somehow, I was straddling him and had hopped right on board. Hello, one-way ticket to sexathon!

"Not a terrible way to wake up," he joked, then pushed his hips forward, making me groan. He grabbed my hips and guided my movement. I was thunderstruck momentarily that I woke with him inside me for the second time since I'd known Ryker. Apparently, my sleeping self had no qualms about getting exactly what she wanted.

I moaned loudly as a shock of pleasure coursed through my body.

"That's it," Ryker said in his deep husky tone.

I placed my hands on his chest and ran the pads on my fingertips over Ryker's nipples, and I swear his wolf flashed. Something snapped in me when I saw his wolf below the surface. Gone was my slow pace or my injured self, taking it easy. I ground into him and sped my pace to a superhuman speed. His wolf paced below the surface, wanting to get out. This time I was in control.

I slowed, not wanting to make Ryker lose control.

"Don't," he ordered. "I'm in control."

I bent low and kissed him, not wanting to take him from the moment. Then it felt like he was kissing me, not the other way around. Suddenly, I was on my back, and my leg was hiked high. He pulled out, only to slam back in, making my back arch in pleasure.

"Yes!" I cried again.

He did it again and again.

His sleek skin had tiny beads of sweat trickling down his forearms.

I was so close to combusting. My eyes met his, and I pleaded with him to let me let go.

He didn't listen. Instead, he flipped me over and smacked my ass playfully, asking me to lift it.

"You're the most beautiful being I've ever seen."

I looked back at him, curious by his word choice, and almost did a double take at my wings fully spread behind me. They were so much bigger than when I last saw them. How had I not noticed them? I guess it was like any appendage. You didn't think about it. It was just there, a part of you.

He kneeled behind me with one foot planted in the bed and the other bent at the knee. This made him able to practically mount me. He flicked his cock over my opening, and I pushed back, telling him what I wanted. He backed up a little teasing me. Then with another hard thrust, he entered me. The new sensation made me moan loudly.

He pushed in and pulled out slowly, making me feel on the brink of something huge.

I reached out mentally and could feel his emotions. His raw need. The way he was excited but more so enthralled. Then I felt his love and worried that I wasn't strong enough. Worried he'd hurt me. He was waging war within himself over giving in to his carnal desires and taking it easy on me to protect me.

"I'm good, my Wolf. Let go. You won't hurt me."

When he didn't move, I did what any woman would do—I reached behind me and cupped his balls, gently stroking the soft skin behind them. That earned me a growl as he slammed forward again, and this time, he lost all control.

Nothing held him back as he fucked me. Bent over me, his hands cupped my breast, and I felt his teeth at my back, only they were sharper than they should be. I had a piece of the wolf. He pierced my skin, setting me off.

"Yessss!" I moaned.

"Fuck," he grunted back, close himself.

I pushed back into him and squeezed my muscles tight. It made my orgasm spasm like crazy and made Ryker finally let go.

He held me there momentarily until our heartbeats slowed, and my wings retracted.

"They're gone," he said in amazement.

"What are?"

"Your wings. It looks like regular skin."

"Don't sound so amazed. I mean, you shift to a werewolf."

He rolled next to me and gathered me in his arms.

"You're truly okay?"

"Yeah. How long was I out?"

His eyes met mine and then looked away.

"Tell me," I pleaded.

"You were out for almost a week."

I sat up and looked at him with my mouth slightly open. "A week? How is that even possible?"

"I wish it weren't so. I can't tell you how much this scares the hell out of me every single time it happens. I've been going out of my mind."

"I'm sorry. You have no idea where I've been."

His head tilted to the side the way a confused puppy would. "Explain."

It was at that moment that my stomach growled loudly.

"She needs food," Ryker snapped loud enough that whoever else was in the house would hear us.

My face flamed when I recalled how loud I was being, and my eyes grew wide. "Who's here?"

"Everyone."

"What do you mean 'everyone'? And where is here?" I looked at my nakedness. "Where are my clothes? I need clothes."

Ryker chuckled at my panic, then stood from the bed. I couldn't help the spark of desire coursing through me as I watched his beautiful ass walk to the other side of the room and grab an oversized t-shirt. He tossed it to me, then ruffled through a bag, grabbing a package of cotton underwear and tearing them open. They looked like they would ride, but something was better than nothing.

He riffled through another bag and found a comfy-looking pair of black loose cargo pants, then brought those to me.

"Stop looking at me like that, love, or I'll never let you leave this bed. In fact, that sounds like a good idea."

There was a knock at the door, and my stomach made another loud noise.

"Give us a few, and we'll be out." Ryker bent low and snagged his pants off the floor. I winced as I lifted my arm to put my shirt on. I guess I was still a little sore from being shot. Next, I stood for the first time in a week, but my legs wanted to give out.

"Whoa," Ryker said, steadying me. He led me to the bathroom, and after I did my thing, we moved down a dark hallway, then another, until finally, we walked into a large room that reminded me of a war room. There were oversized bulletin boards with maps and several low-hanging lights over tables. The tables were long and metal. It wasn't a war room but an industrial kitchen with twelve stools around the large metal island.

"What is this place?" I asked in astonishment.

"It's a war bunker."

"That's what I thought it was!"

"Alright, not really," Ryker said, smirking. "It's a safe house that used to be a school. It closed years ago because the population dwindled as people moved to larger cities."

I nodded and abruptly stopped thinking about the interesting room because Mindy excitedly rushed in.

"You're up!" she exclaimed, setting a tray down and rushing me for a tight hug.

Tears sprang to my eyes as I remembered her being shot. "You're okay?"

"We heal, silly."

I looked at Ryker, then at Mindy, and I was relieved they were both okay. "What about Ledger? Is he okay?"

Ledger strode into the room, eating an apple. "I am," he said, followed by a loud crunch as he took another bite.

"I was waiting in the hall," Mindy explained, nodding towards the food. "I didn't know how Ryker would react to us, and I wanted to give him a second."

"Where's everyone else?"

"Gabe, Reece, and Micah took off on a scouting mission the moment they heard your sex noises," Mindy explained.

My eyes popped out of my head from embarrassment.

"It's fine. Over the years, do you know how many times I've heard my brothers—" Mindy stopped talking as Ryker gave her a death glare. Then she froze. "Your aura's all off. Where have you been?"

Grey walked in with Farah behind him, an immediate scowl on his face at the proximity of Mindy and Ledger. He quickly inhaled and schooled his features.

"How about we let her eat first?" Ryker asked, pulling out a stool for me to sit on and sliding the tray of food in front of me. He took the lid off the pasta, and steam billowed from the sauce, making a sweet aroma of garlic and tomatoes fill the air.

"This smells delicious."

"It is. It was my turn to cook," Ledger said arrogantly.

I took a bite, and all eyes fell on me as I chewed. "It's delicious," I said once I finished chewing. "Ryker, why don't you eat something so I don't feel like I'm being completely ogled."

Ryker nodded to Mindy, "Why don't you get me a plate?"

"Sure!" she said, then left the room.

I looked at Ledger like we were old friends, "You're going to fill me in on the story there."

"There's nothing to tell. She made her choice years ago, and it is what it is."

Something about that felt utterly wrong to me. My face scrunched up in disbelief. He didn't seem like the type of man to accept the outcome and move on.

Mindy returned with a plate of food for Ryker, and he sat beside me and began eating.

"So, what's been happening while I've been out?" I asked between mouthfuls.

"You say that like you went to Disney or something."

"It was something, and I'm not sure if you'd believe me if I told you."

"Of course, we would. You're a walking contradiction. Anything is possible with you," Ledger replied.

"I'm a walking contradiction?" I asked, squinting at the man.

"You know what I mean."

I was about to argue, but Ryker put his hand on my knee. "He means you're an angel with a vampire for a mom, yet you seem completely human at times. None of those things should go together, yet you do perfectly."

"Thank you."

He winked at me and then took another bite of pasta.

"So, where did you go, then?" Mindy asked. "Because it seemed like you were right in the other room the whole time, but now, sensing your aura, I'm not so sure."

I thought about my dreams and tried to make sense of them, but it felt like a bunch of jumbled bazaar things, and trying to explain it felt off.

"So first, I was in this winter palace or crystal palace, I'm not sure, but the Fates were there, and Lucifer, too. There were two versions of us. My other self made an agreement with the Fates, and then the other version of Lucifer showed up and caused a stink. Then, Lucifer and I went to hell, and we took a walk and kind of talked, and now here I am."

You could've heard a pin drop from the ensuing silence.

I felt the rumble in Ryker's chest before I heard it. My eyes connected with his, and the roar he emitted shook the glasses on the table and made the pack freeze and flinch in pain.

"Ryker." I tried to calm him by placing my hand on his shoulder. He jerked from my touch and left.

I attempted to go after him, but Mindy stopped me. "Let him go," she said, looking at me strangely.

Ledger went after Ryker instead, and I stood there in shock, unsure what to make of Ryker's behavior. Beyond the room, there were several crashes, then a thump, followed by muffled shouting.

"What's going on?" I asked Mindy.

She looked at me incredulously. "You told him you were literally in hell with the devil. Do you know how dangerous that is? He is wired to protect you and knowing he can't in your dreams fucks with his head. You need to let him deal."

"All due respect, Mins, I know he's your brother, but he doesn't have to deal with this alone. We're a pair." I pushed past her and followed the commotion until I reached Ryker, where he was having a man-trum.

His eyes locked on mine, and he puffed out a large breath while Ledger put his hands on his shoulders and ordered, "Breathe."

"Stop it! You don't get to close yourself off."

"I can't protect you, and it's driving me fucking mad!"

"I was fine."

"You went to hell! How could you possibly be fine?"

"I'm right here. Look at me. Don't I look fine?"

He slumped his head, and Ledger looked at him, then looked at me, nodded once, silently telling me I had this, then left the room.

"I can't protect you. I don't know how to protect you, Ariel." Even in my head, his voice sounded so defeated.

"Don't you see? Your love keeps guiding me back here."

I went to him, wrapped my arms around his neck, and placed my forehead against his.

"I'm going to show you what happened. We can figure it out together, but this man-trum you're having isn't getting us anywhere. Do you want to see it or not?"

He gripped my hips and looked into my eyes. "*Show me.*"

Chapter Twenty-Seven

"First things first. We have to do something about Cain. He's unstable, and his obsession with Ariel will only end up hurting her," Ryker told the room.

Everyone was back in the kitchen. Since I showed him my dreams, Ryker had changed. He went from freaking out to calm and in-control boss mode. My brother, Farah, Micah, Reece, Mindy, Grey, and Ledger were all here, and Father Archibald, but he was being kept in another area. We had all of the information laid out before us. I'd translated the book and had the pages I'd taken. Between those items and recounting my dreams, we'd been working together to decide what to do next.

"He beat us, shot us, and nearly killed us several times over. I'm with you on stopping him," I replied.

"We need intel," Ledger said.

"The father is healing, and I'm sure I can make him give me what he wants," Gabe added.

I didn't want Father Archibald tortured, but then again, his deceit was why we were here.

"So be it," Ryker ordered.

"Reece, Micah, Grey, I want you to call in connections and gain as much intel as possible. If you need to be a wolf to hear what gossip the wind carries, then do it."

"And me? What would you have me do?" Mindy asked.

"I need you to work with Ariel. She's come so far in such a short amount of time. If she has your guidance, she'll move further quickly."

"Then that's what I'll do." Mindy squeezed my hand in reassurance.

Ryker nodded to the room, silently dismissing them.

My brother approached me, looking nervous. "Elle, do you have a second?"

"Of course."

I nodded, hoping he would continue, but he looked around sheepishly. I tilted my head to the side, leading him away. Ryker began to follow, and I shook my head quickly. Whatever Gabe had to say to me, he didn't want an audience.

We walked down a hallway and then another until we came upon a room used to store school books. Gabe flicked on a light and sat on the edge of a desk. I leaned against the back of a bookshelf.

He sighed.

Not knowing what he was thinking but taking a stab at it, I guessed. "It's been a lot, right?"

"I've hardly had a chance to get to know you, yet you keep nearly dying."

"I didn't almost die," I defended.

"Twice now, the sister who I've dreamed about my entire life ..." his voice trailed off as if he was at a loss for words.

I wanted to comfort him and tell him I was fine, but it seemed like more was on his mind, and I needed to let him get there on his own.

Finally, after several long pauses, he spoke, "You know, I've been taught my entire life that wolves are the enemy. They'd come after us and try to kill us when we weren't looking. I was taught they hated us for what we are, and in turn, I've hated them."

Suddenly, I was on edge. Did he hate Ryker and my family? How could I pick between the two? Would I be asked to choose?

"But your pack isn't like that. They're a family. You should know, although Lillian and Bronson are difficult to read, they're family too. I've spoken to them. They're worried and want to help."

I shook my head. "No. Ryker will never go for that."

"They have resources."

I shook my head again, knowing deep in my soul it wasn't the right move. "I'm sorry, but I don't trust her. I've known Father Archibald my entire life, and look at how he betrayed us. There's something about that woman."

"That woman is your mother."

I shook my head again, feeling deep-rooted anger toward Lillian. "She was never a mother to me."

Gabe let out a deep breath. "Maybe not, but if you—"

"—No," I cut him off. "I don't need help from *her*."

He lifted a hand placatingly. "All of this is a mystery to both of us. I'm not trying to set you off, but I needed to suggest it. They're not all bad."

"Did you ever wonder about Dad?" I asked, changing the subject.

He shrugged, "I guess I always thought of Bronson as my dad. I'm still unsure how we're twins, and I'm the vamp, and you're ... I don't even know what you are. Half-angel with the speed of a vamp."

I didn't even want to mention the Seeker and the light. That seemed like an entirely different thing, but what did I know?

As if reading my mind, Gabe answered, "You know, you have all the answers pretty much in front of you. Take all your dreams, your visions, the books you've found, and your relics, and let all those things be true. I don't understand why you're running from this Cain guy and allowing yourself to be shot, yet you could also freeze people. You're not singular. None of us are. Instead of trying to be so many different things, just be. Accept you are whatever you are and that you are exceptional, and just be. This whole trying to figure things out is exhausting. Your body will tell you. You need to trust yourself more."

After that, Gabe left, and I stood against the bookshelf, thinking about all he said and what it meant.

***

Lying in Ryker's arms after making love, Ryker drew small circles on my back while I lay half on his chest. Our legs entangled with one another's.

"We *can* handle this, you know? We were caught off guard before, but I won't let that happen again."

"I know."

"I want you to consider staying here or letting me sneak you out of this country before they know you're gone."

I propped myself on an elbow to see Ryker's eyes. "Are you serious?"

"Don't get mad."

"How can I not get mad?"

"Because I'm asking you to consider it, is all. I'm not demanding it, even though every part of me wants to."

I blew out a large breath. He was right. My feelings were quick to trigger, and I always acted on impulse.

"When I spoke with Gabe earlier, he suggested I'm not accepting of who I am, and I'm fighting against it."

"I heard him."

"You were listening?"

"You know I hear better than most. I wanted to let you process what he said and come to me when ready. Just because I can hear better than most doesn't mean I need to put my two cents in on everything I hear."

"I don't know how I feel about everything he said."

"And that's okay. Parental relationships can be tricky."

"Yes, and you've met mine. She's not winning any mom of the year awards."

"I think you're right for not bringing them in on this."

"It would be too much and distracting. I'll figure out how to proceed with them when we get home."

"Home ..."

"Yeah, that sounds nice, doesn't it?"

"It does, love." He rubbed my stomach, then lifted me up so that his lips met mine. His kiss was sweet and filled with the promise of our future.

I pulled back and looked into his eyes and saw the depth of love he had for me shining brightly. "I love you."

"And I you."

A knock on the door broke our connection. "Are you guys up? I want to show you something," Grey said through the door.

"Give us a few, and we'll be out," Ryker replied, then pulled me on top of him. "I don't want to leave this bed. I could stay here with you all day."

"I know what you mean." I bent low, gave him a quick kiss, and was about to climb off him when he grabbed my hips, halting me.

"Think about what I said. You don't have to be here. We can take care of Cain, and I'll have the satisfaction of knowing you're safe."

"I couldn't do that. It's not who I am."

He nodded, and we eventually got dressed, but those words played through my mind. I'd been acting like I needed to learn things. I'd been struggling to figure out who I was, but the truth was I knew who I was.

I was Ariel Katz. I was John Katz's daughter. I was part angel, and somewhere deep inside, my mother's blood ran through my veins. I was loyal to my friends, a terrible cook, adventurous, but mostly, I was just me. There'd been other versions of me, but all I could be was the me I was meant to be, and I needed to start believing in that and trusting in my abilities.

Chapter Twenty-Eight

The mood was somber. We'd been preparing for our attack for weeks. We gave ourselves time to review all the texts I'd acquired. I'd spent days working with Mindy to make my wings protrude and tap into my natural talent and affinity toward nature. I could now call upon powers within myself as if it were second nature, so Ryker's concern was unwarranted. I'd also seen the plans. Our first goal was to get to Cain and take him hostage. I needed to expose him to his father. From what we learned, there was no way his dad knew everything he's done. Abbas was a lot of things, a misogynist being at the top of his list, but he also cared about his town's way of life. If he knew his son took men from the town to run errands at his whim, including using them to fight a self-prophesied fight, he would ally with us.

When I left Ohio, I did so because I wanted to know who I was and be in control of my abilities. I didn't want to hurt anyone the way I hurt Mindy accidentally. If the last few weeks taught me anything, it taught me I had control over my body and that what I could do was amazing. The more I practiced small things, the easier it became, and the less it took from me.

"I still think we should have Elle use her powers, knock everyone out, then go in and kill that fucker," Gabe said.

"Me too," Grey replied.

"I'm not risking her being knocked out for another week."

"We should just go home," I argued.

"And have them come after you at home?"

"It would be on your turf. Don't you think we'd have the advantage there?"

"And what if we're attacked at the airport again? I'm not risking anything happening to you."

"We've been hiding out here for two weeks, and they haven't found us," Mindy added, making eye contact with me. We'd talked about this for a while, and she agreed, but I could see why Ryker wanted it done. He feared what bringing a battle home would mean for his small town.

"The moment we make it to an airfield, I guarantee they will be waiting for us," Gabe reminded the room of what we'd been over again and again.

"This is useless. We're talking in circles and not getting anywhere. I'm sick of sitting around. Let's move on them. The longer we wait, the longer we give them a chance at having the upper hand. They have a network of people."

"He's right," Micah added.

"Yeah, and I'm ready to get out of this shithole," Reece replied.

"I trust you," I told Ryker. I needed everyone to hear me say it because arguing in front of everyone only caused contention. "If you truly think this is best, then I'm on board, but I'm coming with you."

He let out a puff of air. "I know you feel like you must do this, and I have to accept that. I just want you safe, is all."

"I don't get it," Mindy said. "This guy worked with your dad and was supposed to be in some secret sect searching for the truth. He twisted this verse to think his truth is you're intended to marry him and he will rule some ancient kingdom."

"You're not telling us something we don't already know," Reece replied.

"She was hurt, though. What kind of man would put his bride at risk?" Grey asked.

Ryker shot out of his chair and got in Grey's face. "Never suggest she is another's bride. She's mine."

I calmly walked over and placed my hand on Ryker's shoulder. Every now and then, Ryker would have these possessive flairs that he struggled to control.

"I'm sorry, man. I didn't mean anything by it," Grey apologized.

"Ryker, it's okay," I soothed.

Ryker turned and looked at me, coming to his senses. He stepped back from Grey and looked at the room. The others had also become accustomed to his outbursts. His eyes held remorse.

"You're a wolf, Brother. No worries," Ledger added. "It's normal for you to be protective. We get it. Every single one of us is envious."

I wanted to hug Ledger. That was precisely what Ryker needed to hear.

Ryker took another step back and leaned against the wall. I attempted to move back to where I was, but his hand darted out, pulled me to him, and wrapped his arms around me. His chin settled on my shoulder, and I felt a tickle from his goatee. Then he silently asked, *"Are you mad?"*

"I can't fault you for being you. No more than you can fault me for being me."

Oh, how the Gods bless me.

"It's me who is blessed."

"It's cute, you think so."

I nuzzled into him as his hand possessively gripped my waist.

"If we're doing this today, we need to go before those two end up in the bedroom again," Grey said.

My face flushed as I noticed all eyes were on us. We'd been having a lot of sex, and I mean a lot! In some ways, even though we were here and plotting an attack, it was also a peaceful time for me. We'd had two weeks of spending every night together and waking in each other's arms. I hadn't had a dream. In fact, I'd been sleeping better than I had in years.

I felt refreshed when I woke and had an energy that boosted everyone else's. It was uncanny. They all knew how much sex we'd been having, and slowly, I was becoming used to the fact that wolves heard all.

"You're mad because you haven't been getting any," Micah said, earning himself an elbow to the ribs from Reece.

Mindy squinted her eyes and left the room in a huff. Something had happened between Grey and Mindy, but it didn't need to be aired out in the open. If they weren't talking about it, it wasn't our business.

"I'm going to go after her. Let me know when we're ready."

"Take good care of her."

"You know I will."

"By the gods, I love you."

I grinned at him and left the room but not before I noticed Grey and Ledger exchanging death glares.

***

Mindy was sitting in an old soundproof musicroom, staring at a chalkboard on wheels. "It's not getting any easier," she whispered.

"You've been pretty tight-lipped about what the deal is between the three of you. Do you want to talk about it?"

"I don't even know where I'd start."

"How about at the beginning?" I encouraged.

"Grey and I are happy."

"I know."

"But there's history."

"I can see that too."

"Is it that obvious to everyone?"

I sighed, unsure how she'd take my words. "Sometimes, I catch you looking at him, and you look almost wistful. And Ledger looks at Grey like he wants to kill him, who looks at you like he's hurt."

She put her head back and stared at the ceiling.

"Counting tiles isn't going to solve anything. Did you love him?"

"You know how it is with wolves. They can have their fated mate. Neither of them is mine, but Ledger, when we were together, it was like he didn't even want to try to be part of the pack. It's one thing to care for a man who knows he isn't what the Gods intended for me, but it's another thing to care for a man that doesn't even want to stick around. We've been over for decades. But seeing him again ... I never expected this longing. And I'm happy with Grey. He cares about me. We have our music. Life is good."

"But?" I questioned.

"But what you've seen—so has Grey. He knows about our past. Now that Ledger pledged himself to you and is returning with us, I have no idea how to handle that. I wish I could flip a switch and erase the past. I can't come to terms with the pain of knowing he was shot trying to protect me. Plus, I hate what I'm doing to Grey and feel like shit for it."

"Don't beat yourself up. You're human."

She looked at me and raised an eyebrow.

"Okay, not totally human, but you know what I mean. You're allowed to feel things."

"Is it strange?" she asked, catching me off guard.

"Is what strange?"

"Knowing there is one perfect match for you and having him?"

I laughed. "I haven't had more than two seconds to consider it. But I guess it isn't really. Once I accepted my identity, it was much easier to accept Ryker's love. That was the biggest shocker for me. Trying to understand how someone I had just met could love me as much as he does felt surreal. But strange? No ... More like grateful."

She covered her face with her hands. "What am I going to do?"

"I hate to be Yoko Ono here, but if you're looking at Ledger, then Grey isn't totally keeping your heart."

She nodded like she knew what I meant, then ran her hands through her hair. "It's hard."

"I know it is."

"Thank you for coming after me."

"Of course."

"I always wanted a sister. The Fates definitely blessed me when they gave me you."

My heart melted at the sentiment. I felt the same way, but before I could say anything, footsteps echoed in the hall. We both looked toward the doorway when Micah appeared.

"Mins, you got a sec?"

"Of course."

"I'm sorry," he blurted. "I didn't mean—"

"—it's okay," she replied.

I wanted to give them time to talk, so I started to leave the room, but Micah stopped me. "We're leaving soon. Ryker wanted me to let you know."

I nodded, then took a moment to use the restroom and collect myself before joining the others. I was nervous and didn't want it to show. I splashed water on my face and told myself it would be okay. Then I silently prayed, feeling strength deep within myself every time I did.

Once I joined the others, I felt more at ease about what was coming. Ryker was a good strong leader. He'd strategized every possible scenario and thought of every detail. I was confident we would go in and expose Cain for who he was. The Rosi weren't an evil group. Mostly, they helped protect sacred knowledge, but under Cain's beliefs, the group had seriously strayed.

Ryker cleared his throat and focused the entire room's attention on him.

"You got this," I silently said.

"I know."

"God, every time they do that, it's like a high," Reece muttered.

Micah nodded in response, then Ryker shot him a glare and straightened his shoulders.

"They shot us. They nearly killed Ariel and me. They tortured us. They conspired to take my mate. For these reasons, they must be stopped. He's relentless and won't stop coming for her. She has a destiny that's clear to each one of us. We've all pledged to protect her, and it's time to end that man's tyranny."

"Here, here," Ledger shouted.

I grinned, thinking it was a totally good speech.

Grey stood, scraping his chair along the floor as he did. "Let's do this."

I nodded to Ryker as Reece came over and clapped me on the back, only it brushed the tip of my wing. "Ouch!"

"Shit, sorry! It's easy to forget they're there."

I shrugged.

Micah placed his hand on my shoulder, "Are you nervous?"

"I trust Ryker knows what he is doing. Also, I have some pretty kick-ass abilities."

"Yeah, you do, Elle," he responded.

"You ready?" Ryker asked, tucking me close to his side.

"Yeah," I responded.

Gabe strode towards me. "Take care of yourself. I only just found you. No more getting shot or anything else crazy, okay?"

"I haven't done anything crazy!"

He looked at me incredulously.

"Okay, fine, maybe a little."

His face changed with a softness I wasn't sure many men could recreate. He was both beautiful and handsome, and the soft look in his eyes and bow lips gave him a model-like quality. "I'm serious, Elle," he said softly, then continued, "You've never seen me angry, but if something happens to you, I'll destroy all of them." A dark undercurrent coated his words, like my brother had seen carnage.

It was a threat against the Rosi, not against my wolves. I nodded once, left Ryker's side, and moved into an embrace with my brother.

His hug was tight, like he hadn't hugged someone in years. What kind of love had Lillian provided him?

After our embrace, there was a flurry of movement. Everyone had jobs to do, including myself. Working with Mindy, we figured out I did best with elements nearby, so we made necklaces filled with things like earth and water. I also wore my father's ring and had his medallion safely secured. His dagger was sheathed on my thigh, and I had to admit, I felt like a badass.

I was like a blonde Tomb Raider. All right, that might've been a stretch, but I felt like it! As for Ryker, he was doing the opposite of me. He was undressing. My mouth watered the way it always did when he was shirtless.

Farah cleared her throat, no doubt being as affected by the shirtless testosterone in the room as I was. "The water is at the stops we discussed, and your change of clothes and weapons are at the drop-off point."

Ryker, Ledger, Reece, Micah, Grey, and I were all headed to Zoar. Gabe, Mindy, and Farah were going to ensure the plane was ready. The rest of us were headed to Zoar. Gabe didn't like this plan, wanting to be close to me. He reiterated he didn't think this was a good idea, but we'd be stuck here if something happened to Gabe.

"Elle, turn around," Reece mumbled.

I looked at him curiously.

"I'm about to shift, and I don't want your big bad wolf to eat me when you see how hung I am."

Grey smacked Reece upside the back of his head.

Laughing, I turned around.

"You better stay turned around because if you're afraid of his little prick, then you definitely don't want to see mine," Micah joked, earning a growl from Ryker.

Ryker pulled me close and kissed me. He poured so much love into the room I forgot all about the boys. When he stopped kissing me, Grey, Reece, Micah, and Ledger had all shifted.

"You ready?"

I nodded. *"I love you."*

"You are my heart."

Then with practiced ease, Ryker shifted. I was still amazed at the sheer sight of him.

We said a final goodbye to Farah, Gabe, and Mindy, then I climbed on Ryker's back, and the rest of us took off into the sunset, heading to Zoar.

Chapter Twenty-Nine

A warm breeze tousled my hair back as we rode through the night. We stopped at our designated stops for the wolves to drink and rest. I could've tried to run with them, but they had far more stamina than I did.

Running with the pack and working with them over the last several weeks honed our ability to communicate as a pack.

"Left flank," Ryker ordered, and Reece and Micah split off. Ryker, Grey, Ledger, and I approached a large olive tree with a massive twisty tree trunk. Ryker bent low, and I dismounted. The wolves drank while I reached into the tree's nook and took out bundles of clothing. I set them on the ground and moved to the other side of the tree while the wolves returned to men.

I sat in front of the tree and felt the energy thrumming through it, then I placed my hands and forehead against it like Mindy, and I had practiced. Behind me, bones cracked. A warm breeze brushed against my skin, and the faint smell of licorice lingered from the wilting flowers on the tree that olives would soon replace. Those beautiful flowers had to wilt away to become something more. Maybe I wasn't so different. It was still hard to wrap my head around the fact that I'd lived multiple lives. Yet, here I was, someone completely different and new, with abilities unlike any version of myself.

With my head against the tree, I prayed for our safety. I asked the tree for strength, immediately invigorated as I did. Once I was "boosted," as Mindy would say, I turned to the men dressed similarly in plain clothes that looked like they were dressed as peasants at a medieval festival.

"I look ridiculous," Grey mumbled under his breath.

"It could be worse," Ryker replied.

"Don't worry, your girl isn't here to see you like that," Ledger said harshly.

We made the rest of the journey on foot as it wasn't far. Reece and Micah stayed in wolf form to sniff out any danger since they were more finely attuned than Ryker was as a man. They stayed in the shadows, watching out for us.

Ryker had sent scout teams several times and found a secret entrance into the city. The wolves went before us to ensure the coast was clear, and we approached once it was.

"I'm going first. I want Ariel behind me," Ryker ordered, going over the plan we already knew.

"Relax, we got this."

"I won't relax until we can put this behind us and move on with our lives."

We walked in far too easily. There weren't nearly as many people out as I expected. There was usually an abundance of activity. I stayed close to Ryker, but Ledger and Grey tried to blend in behind us, pretending to be interested in various things.

A boy ran towards the center of the town, followed by another. I grabbed one as they ran by, "Excuse me," I said, startling the dark-haired boy. "What's going on?"

"It's judgment day, of course," he replied and ran on.

Grey strode up to us, "Something's wrong."

"No shit," Ledger replied.

"The boy said it was judgment day. Anyone else getting weird Terminator vibes? No? Just me, then?"

"Let's find out what's happening," Ryker ordered, ignoring my awkward movie reference, then added, speaking to Grey and Ledger, "Keep our flank."

"We didn't plan on this. I don't like it. Keep your guard up."

"I will."

"I love you and won't let anything happen to you. You're everything to me."

We shared a look, pouring our love into one another.

Ledger muttered, "Damn, it's like a zap every time."

"Every damn time," Grey replied.

I smiled at Ryker, and we let that pass between us for a moment. Ryker nodded his head, and we moved toward the commotion.

It was easy to blend in. Most of the town appeared to be crowding around large steps leading to the Rosi temple. I weaved in and out of people, trying to get a closer look. The crowd was dense, and everyone was trying to get a look.

The thunder of hooves surrounded us as horses neared and parted the crowd. My skin prickled as I peered through the crowd, trying to get a glimpse. That's when I saw him—Cain. The man strolled up the stairs with an air of arrogance. My hand twitched, aching to smack the smugness from his face.

People shouted, then cheered as Cain ascended the stairs and turned to address the crowd.

"People of Zoar, we have all felt the loss of my father."

My eyes immediately darted to Ryker's. If his dad was dead, our entire plan was shot. We'd been counting on his father to assist us and were betting he would put his people first. But if he died, it would explain how Cain imprisoned us, and not once did his father come.

I listened intently as Cain continued. "It is an incomprehensible tragedy. One we will all feel for years to come. To think one of our own was behind his demise ... It sickens me. But rest assured, my people, justice will be done today. I will rule Zoar the way my father did, with an open heart and an open mind. We are a place of truth seekers, and I will rule in hopes of being half the man my father was."

"He's lying. Every single word he said was a lie."

"Men, bring the traitors," Cain ordered.

The crowd threw fruit and bread at the feeble men wearing brown sacks over their heads and rags for clothing. These men were no murderers. From how they dressed and carried themselves, they had been imprisoned in Cain's dungeon. Cain was behind his father's death, just as I knew I couldn't stand here and let these men befall whatever was going to happen next.

"We have to help them," I silently said to Ryker.

"We can't help them. We have a plan."

"Ryk, our plan is already shot."

"It isn't."

A rock sailed through the air, pelting the man. I needed to do something drastic.

Ryker's eyes connected with mine, and he quickly made a look that said no.

"He's hurting them, and he needs to be exposed. Call the men closer. If there is one thing I learned about Cain's people, it's that their belief is what drives them. I'll give them something to believe in. Something that isn't Cain."

"Ariel, I swear to Gods, don't do anything foolish. Stop."

But it was too late. I watched with horror as a rock and then another sailed toward the prisoners, and on instinct to protect, I yelled with a force I was sure everyone felt, "Stop."

Eyes darted toward me in confusion, but I straightened my shoulders. I would give them all something to see. People were curious, but Cain signaled his guards. Cain stood on the stairs while the prisoners were below him, as was I. I had only moments to make a huge decision and needed to make it fast.

I tore off my cloak and willed my wings to pop free. People gasped, and everyone, including Cain, looked awestruck.

"Ariel!" Ryker yelled in my head, hating my deviation from our plan, but it didn't matter because I knew these men were innocent.

I sent him an overwhelming feeling of love and then silently begged him to trust me.

The focus was no longer on the prisoners.

Cain began to call for his guards, but I spoke loudly for everyone to hear.

"You will not cast another stone. I am the angel of nature, and I ask you all to stop. It is not these men who killed Abbas. They're pawns in Cain's foolish games. Cain has deceived you all. He's not a truth seeker. He leaves this place freely and goes after people with guns. He is not a man who lives by the laws of this place. He has been touched by the devil and had a hand in his father's death, not these men."

"She's lying," Cain shouted.

"I am here as an extension of your God, and I ask you all to make a choice and follow light and goodness. If you cast another stone at these men, I ask you cast one upon me as well. This is not the lord's way. This is not the way of the light. You are being deceived. I ask you to see Cain for what he is and trust in God. Trust your soul will be guided more fruitfully to his heavenly Father if you live in lightness. This is not the way."

I spread my wings to their fullest height, strolled toward the prisoners, and ordered the guards to release them.

One guard had tears running down his cheeks as he pleaded, "Forgive me."

"Keep your eyes on Cain."

"You never cease to amaze me."

The prisoners were unshackled, and Cain yelled, "I did not command you to release him!"

I stopped in my tracks, stared straight into Cain's beady eyes, and then spoke tersely. "You are no ruler. You are no truth seeker. I am intended for one man alone. You've misinterpreted the scrolls in your arrogance. You thought they spoke of you because you believed yourself worthy. However, they could never speak of you. You are not worthy. People of Zoar, if you truly seek the truth, you must remove him from his throne."

Cain quickly darted his eyes to a man on his left, then back to me. He hoped I wouldn't see, but I easily saw the threat. Ledger snuck behind him and incapacitated him.

Jomana, the girl from the lecture hall, stepped in front of me and yelled to the crowd, "She is who she says she is. I've seen with my own eyes her make the tree of knowledge grow and bloom. We would be foolish and would condemn ourselves to an untrustworthy man when the heavenly father sent an angel here to guide us."

"I second that. I saw it, too," another boy from the class shouted.

"Seize Cain!" a man shouted.

"We can't argue with the Gods," came another voice.

I didn't have much time before things got out of hand. I steeled my shoulders and commanded, "Bring me the prisoners."

Ryker was by my side, watching the crowd intently.

"That was a huge risk."

"*Their faith is strong. They couldn't deny what they witnessed with their own eyes.*"

I pulled my wings back in, hoping my point was made. I was met with gasps as people were awestruck by what they witnessed.

Ryker nodded toward Cain, where several of his guards turned on him and backed him into a corner.

"*Ledger, Grey, Reece, Micah, we have new cargo to take, then we're out,*" Ryker ordered. Grey casually strode up with a few horses while the men holding the prisoners unlocked their heavy chains. I could see the weight on their frail bodies. How long had they been held prisoner?

The prisoners were brought before us, and Ryker pulled off the first man's burlap bag. I recognized the man who had set aside my father's book for me, causing shock to register on my face. His face was black and blue, and he looked close to losing consciousness.

Ryker then pulled the burlap from the second man. His hair was long and straggly covering his gaunt face. I noticed a blood-soaked rag tied around his face and preventing him from talking, not that he would even be able to. He barely had the energy to stand. Lacerations marred his skin from being whipped. Enraged, my eyes darted to Cain.

Ryker removed the gag from the man's mouth, and he lifted his head to meet my eyes.

Suddenly, my entire world shifted and simultaneously fell apart.

"Ariel," he croaked.

My knees buckled, and it felt like my entire world was shifting. I managed to say one word—one word that would shift my entire being.

"Daddy?" Then, I immediately passed out.

Chapter Thirty

I groggily came to, surprised and confused as to why I was sitting on a horse galloping out of Zoar with Ryker behind me.

It all came rushing back to me. My dad was with us. I looked around frantically, spotting him sitting behind Ledger. Relief rushed through me. My dad was here, and he was alive. How could that be? They told me ... and therein lay the problem.

Truth-seekers lied.

Rage, unlike anything I'd ever felt, brewed below the surface.

"Ya!" Ryker yelled, trying to get the horse to move faster.

"Why are we running?"

"When you fainted, Cain broke away. It was pandemonium. The guards that were loyal to him started fighting the townspeople. Then people began grabbing you. It was unfolding badly. We needed to get out of there."

"My father," I croaked out loud.

"I know. No one was as shocked as you, but I was a close second."

"I blew up your plan. Are you mad?"

"How could I be mad when you were only being you. I could no more be angry at the sun for shining than I could be mad at you for being exactly who you are."

My heart fluttered. I made a rash decision to come out as an angel hoping their faith would be enough reason for Cain to fail. We didn't need to go to war when their belief would be enough to stop him. Then again, more wars were fought over beliefs than anything else.

We made it to the secret entrance of the wall where Micah and Reece waited for us in wolven form. Ryker and I dismounted the horse then Ledger helped my dad. I spotted Grey riding up at a fast gallop with the other man behind him.

I rushed to my dad and threw my arms around him. His body felt so frail. How was he even standing?

"I can't believe it's you," he whispered as if talking was taking his remaining strength from him.

"I thought—" my voice cracked.

"I know what you thought," he replied.

"He needs water," I said, hoping someone had some.

Ledger grabbed what reminded me of a bota bag from the horse's side. It was a leather pouch and usually filled with water or wine. He tasted it first, then nodded. I took the bag and placed it against my father's lips.

"Drink, Dad," I coaxed.

He was slow at first, the simple act taking more energy than he had to expend. He had newly healed scars. He was bruised and emaciated. He was filthy and smelled of rot and decay.

"Guys, we gotta go!" Grey said, looking around us. My gaze followed his to a crowd coming our way.

"There she is!" Someone yelled.

"Our savior!" Another voice yelled.

"Can you walk?" I asked Dad.

"Not well, I'm afraid." The frailty of his voice made me want to cry out in rage, but getting him out of here was more important.

"Do you think you can hold on?"

His eyes found the horse we had dismounted, and I shook my head, "No, Dad, not the horse, my mate."

He looked confused then his eyes widened as Ryker shifted from man to wolf.

The other man, who I'd all but forgotten about, gasped. As Ledger quickly changed, I tilted my head toward the other man. "Ledger, do you have him?"

Several people shouted as they approached, and I couldn't let them come after us.

"Go," I said to Ledger and Ryker.

"I'd never leave you."

"I need you to take care of my dad, please. I will get the townspeople off our backs."

"Ariel."

"Ryk."

His black nostrils flared, letting out a large puff of air.

"Dad, you need to climb on Ledger's back. Hang on around his neck. He'll take care of you."

My dad looked at me wearily but did as I asked, and the other man followed suit.

"Go!" I shouted as they slipped through the passageway as a townsperson approached.

They were hysterically crying and begging. For what? I wasn't sure. A man who appeared slightly older than my father reached for me. "Please, don't go."

I put my hand up and ordered, "Stop."

Several people halted in confusion while others further away continued in my direction.

"Stop," I said again. "Do not come after me. Protect your city from the man who has told you lies. If his father is truly gone, I do not doubt he had something to do with it. Protect your city and leave me be."

"But you're an angel ... You can heal my cancer."

"I've lost my job. You can give me wealth!" cried out another man.

"My wife ... she's barren," called out a younger man who looked desperate, like a man in love searching for a miracle.

"My husband died three months ago. Can you tell me how he is? Is he in heaven?" An older woman shouted.

"Tell us about heaven, please," another woman shouted.

"Stop," I called out again, feeling overwhelmed by their need.

I hoped my words would be enough to make them see reason. Then again, if I was searching for a miracle and an angel presented herself, I'm not sure reason would be at the forefront of my mind.

I spotted a small weed growing into the wall. I touched the tiny green leaves and felt the energy hum from where my fingers met the grass. *Grow. Protect me. Protect them. Grow.*

From that weed, twisty branches with small thorns grew outward. People gasped, and a few called out in prayer as a wall of dense prickly bushes, unlike anything I'd ever seen, came between the townspeople and myself. It smelled of the earth with a hint of pine mixed with jasmine. Spiky pink flowers blossomed, and I needed to leave before I was sandwiched between my creation and the wall.

Grey sat by the exit, surprising me. We quickly left, finding Micah and Reece waiting for me.

Then we ran.

It wasn't long before we caught up to Ryker. He was stopped at a water stop, lapping at the water while my dad sat against the tree, drinking. The other captive man was nowhere near as bad as my dad and wasn't interested in water. In fact, he seemed indifferent to all of it. My eyes squinted, and I silently communicated with Ryker. "*I don't trust him.*"

"*I picked up on that. I'll keep my eyes on him.*"

"*I can't believe my dad's alive.*" Tears filled my eyes.

"*I know. It's unbelievable, but we need to stay strong for now.*"

I blinked away my tears. "*I love you.*"

"*I'm so incredibly proud of you. I love you so fucking much.*"

I turned to my frail dad. "Were you able to ride okay?" I asked.

"It was challenging, but I'll make do. I can't believe it's truly you."

I hugged my dad again, wanting to weep. It was a relief to have him back. In some ways, it left me with more questions than answers.

"How are you alive?"

"It's a long story, my dear." His voice shook as he spoke.

The wolves drank, and I could see how much strain this put on my dad. He didn't have much energy. We needed to leave, but I needed to do something for him. I poured a small amount of water onto the earth and placed a hand on dad's shoulder.

Earth that I love, which grounds us and brings us peace, give my father strength.

A soft glow emanated from my hand and moved to my father.

"Ariel, what are you doing?" Dad asked.

It dawned on me that his head was covered with the sack when I exposed my wings.

"I'm healing you," I replied.

Color returned to his face, and the dark circles and nearly translucent skin from malnourishment faded.

"Ariel, this is ... What is this?" He looked at his skin as he opened and closed his hand.

"We'll talk later," I assured. "Gabe is waiting on the plane for us." Then it hit me, Gabe would meet Dad for the first time.

"Gabriel?" Dad questioned.

"My brother," I confirmed.

Dad clasped his hand over his heart, briefly closed his eyes, reopened them, and asked, "he's okay?"

"Yeah, Dad. He's good."

"We have to go," Ryker silently said gently.

"Dad, we have to go."

My father nodded and mounted Ryker's back. The other man climbed back on Ledger's, and we moved out as a pack, with me running beside them. I felt more invigorated now like a burden that had been weighing on me was finally lifted.

***

It was an understatement to say I was surprised we made it back to the plane without a problem. Could the people's faith really have been enough to stop Cain? If anything, I hoped my stunt had usurped him.

None of that mattered now. All that mattered was we had my dad, everyone was safe, and we were going to go home to put this place behind us.

Mindy waited at the doorway; her eyes were wide when she saw the two newcomers.

"Everyone okay?" she asked, looking over us all.

"We're all good, Mins," Ryker responded.

She quickly pressed a button, lifted the door, and then spoke into an intercom on the wall. "Captain, we are clear for takeoff." Then she winked at me. "I'm living my best pretend-stewardess life." Then her face broke out in a grin, and she said, "Ladies and gentlemen, prepare for takeoff. Please fasten your safety belts and remain seated until the seatbelt light disengages."

Her smile was infectious, and I immediately smiled back. That was until I saw Grey and Ledger each had a seat open for her. With one glance, I could tell they wanted her to choose them. She saw it, too, and sat across the aisle from me next to the other man accompanying us.

My dad sat on one side, and Ryker sat on the other. Dad looked at me questioningly. His thoughts were evident without him voicing his question. "Gabe is flying the plane. Hopefully, he can put this thing on autopilot once we're in the air."

The plane began to move and pick up speed. Before long, the tires lifted from the tarmac, and we were pushed back into our seats, flying far away from this place. I waited until we stopped ascending and let out a loud breath.

"I'm relieved too," Ryker commented.

"All right, you guys are killing me. Who are the old dudes? What happened, and why are you back so soon?" Mindy asked.

"Reece and I were on the perimeter, and our plan was shot nearly as soon as we got there," Micah responded.

"People were running toward the center of the town, and that dipshit was on the stairs rambling on," Micah added before Reece chimed back in. "Then Elle went all angel goddess and saved the men who were about to get seriously dead from Cain's men. These old dudes were hooded, so naturally, Elle took off their hoods, and voila, the old dude next to her is her dad!"

"No way," Mindy muttered.

"No clue about the other old dude."

Gabe suddenly appeared in that fast vampire way he sometimes moved. My dad gripped my arm. "He's beautiful," he whispered, and his chin wobbled. Gabe stood before us, and I couldn't read the expression on his face.

I looked at our dad and then at Gabe. Both men seemed shell-shocked, staring at one another until finally, Dad spoke. "Leaving you with her was the hardest thing I've ever done. Not a single day has gone by where I haven't thought of you. Oh, my son. Just look at you. You're perfect."

Gabe stared back, unsure of what to say. The plane jerked, and Gabe muttered, "Autopilot is only good for so long. We'll talk, okay?"

Dad squeezed my hand again as tears filled his eyes.

"It'll be okay, dad."

"I never thought I'd see him," his voice cracked as he spoke. "It was as if this empty space was in my chest." The tears filling his eyes spilled over. He released my hand, placed his head in his hands, and silently cried. It broke my heart to see my dad so upset.

I placed my hand on his shoulder, attempting to comfort him. "When this day began, I thought it would be my last, and now here you are, and my son—he's here with you. How can this be? Am I still in that dungeon dreaming?"

"Oh, Daddy. I want to know everything. What happened with the Rosi? Why did you keep so much from me?" I suddenly thought about my wings and the scars that were no longer there, and I wanted to ask how he did what he did with Father Archibald, but I couldn't. Not now. Not when I only now got him back. "I have so many questions."

"As do I, sweet child. But I'm exhausted. Do you mind if I close my eyes for a little while?"

Guilt coursed through me. He had been through lord only knew what kind of hell, and here I was on him like beans on rice.

"Go ahead and rest. I'll be right here when you open your eyes."

Dad closed his eyes and wasn't asleep at first. I almost felt his thoughts as the pain and anguish mixed with relief. Eventually, the soft inhale and exhale of breath came as he slumbered.

Ryker's eyes met mine. "*I can't believe we found him.*"

"*Maybe the Fates had something else in mind for you.*"

"*I feel like they keep blessing me over and over again. First, they brought me to you, and then they brought me to another world where I eventually found my dad.*"

My eyes dropped from his, and guilt coursed through me. He had to endure so much abuse for us to be where we were. Was it wrong of me to be happy about it?

His fingers gripped my chin, and he tilted my chin up to meet his eyes.

"*Don't do that. Don't ever carry shame for what we went through. I'd endure torture all over again if the outcome was you happy by my side. We're all safe. And we have your dad.*"

I nodded, trying to let his words sink in, but failed to feel absolved. I had a part in my friends being shot and Ryker being tortured, and although I wasn't the perpetrator, I was the flame igniting it all.

"*We're safe.*" He reassured me.

"*I know. I can't help but feel like we're at the start of something big. It all felt so confusing between my dreams and Lucifer and the Fates. We've barely even touched on my mom being a vampire.*"

"*Your father will have answers.*"

"*You're right. He will.*"

"*Why do I get this sense from you that you are unhappy?*"

"No, you mistake my fear for unhappiness. The unknown is scary."

"You will have answers soon enough. Let him rest. It's a long flight."

He pressed his lips to mine, and warmth rushed through me. This man could make me feel electric with only a kiss.

He didn't need to say how much he loved me. Words were unnecessary as his love penetrated every inch of my heart. Gone went my guilt. Gone went my fear. All I was filled with was love.

He wrapped an arm around me and provided comfort. Before I knew it, I, too, drifted off to sleep, this time, thankfully, without any dreams.

Chapter Thirty-One

"Ariel, the plane is getting ready for landing. Wake up, love."

Panic gripped my chest as I spotted my dad's empty seat.

"He woke hours ago and has been sitting with Gabe in the cockpit."

Relief flooded through me. Hopefully, Gabe had cooled off. Blaming Gabe for his initial reaction to meeting Dad for the first time seemed pointless. I wasn't all sunshine and roses when I met Lillian. She was so cold—which reminded me to ask Dad what he saw in her when I got a chance.

"How long have I been sleeping?" I asked, stretching my arms over my head and feeling less magical than before. My shoulder blades rotated normally, not like my wings would pop out at any given moment.

"Maybe ten hours? I'm not sure. I'm afraid I fell asleep too. This little adventure finally caught up to me."

"Adventure? You've got to be kidding me. If it weren't for finding my dad, this entire journey of mine would've been pointless."

"For starters, yeah, *you found your dad*. You have that angel book. And, let's see, you sprouted wings while we were there. I'd say it wasn't all that pointless. I'm certain the Fates had their reasons."

"My wings don't feel like they're there," I blurted.

"I've also been a little discombobulated. It's because we're in the air. Once we land and are in a power zone again, you'll feel them."

"Ladies and gentlemen, we will be descending shortly. Please stay in your seat and fasten your seatbelt. Arriving in Ohio today, it's a balmy, humid as fuck, hot summer day. We hope you have enjoyed this trip with me as your flight attendant and Gabe as your hot vampy pilot. Thank you for flying Paranormal Air."

Shaking my head at Mindy's antics, the pressure changed in the cabin as we slowly descended.

I had no idea what would happen when we returned home, but I was grateful to be there.

Like a kid in a candy store, I reached over Ryker and peered out the window. We didn't seem to be anywhere close to a big city.

"Where are we landing?"

"A private airfield owned by the Valderes," he said with a bite to his tone.

I gulped at a loss for words. Our return would mean more than just coming home. Unease filled the pit of my stomach, followed by a tight pinch in my shoulder blades, indicating we'd re-entered a zone where my power would be strongest. I squeezed Ryker's hand, receiving the outpouring of love through our bond.

***

The door to the plane opened. I squinted at the sun as we descended the stairs and onto the tarmac. We were on a private runway strip surrounded by lush grass fields. The sun's warmth immediately hit my skin. I inhaled freshly cut grass as I stood next to Ryker and Mindy. Everyone else followed us. My heart swelled as Dad, and then Gabe appeared. We were home, and we made it!

Ryker's head snapped to the side, and I followed his line of sight as two large black SUVs raced toward us.

Gabe groaned. "I'll handle this," he said with apprehension.

"Are you okay?" I asked Dad as Gabe walked ahead to greet the approaching SUVs.

Dad gulped, "That's her, isn't it?"

"I'm guessing it is."

"So, you've met her? You met your mother?" His voice quivered as he spoke, and I couldn't quite read his emotions.

Bronson and Lillian stepped out of the car, followed by several bodyguards who wore the classic Men in Black garb.

Lillian did something I was so completely shocked by. She ran to Gabe, threw her arms around his neck, and held him. "I was so worried about you. I told you we would help, but we didn't hear from you. What if something happened to you?"

This wasn't the stone-cold Lillian I'd met. This was a mother worried for her son. Witnessing that she could be a warm, caring mother when she needed to stung. Thickly layered emotions balled inside, and I hadn't a chance to unwind them. They burned in the back of my throat, but I'd be damned if I would let her see them.

"I'm fine."

"But you've never flown for so long before. You could've been hurt."

"He's safe, Lillian," Bronson tried to calm her.

"I'm totally safe. Besides, I had Elle with me, and she is one serious badass."

It was as if she had forgotten she had an audience, and her eyes snapped to mine. Her guard was down, and her features showed her remorse and pain.

"Ariel," she said my name as if her prayers were answered.

At the sound of her voice, my father and Ryker moved forward slightly as if to shield me. Witnessing that she could be a mother and she had warmth when she needed to stung. Thickly layered emotions balled inside, and I hadn't had a chance to unwind them. They burned in the back of my throat, but I'd be damned if I would let her see thWith the movement of my men, her eyes darted from me to Ryker and then widened as they landed on my dad.

It happened so fast. Her eyes turned red with deep veins stemming from her sockets, and she lunged for my dad, grabbing his throat. She squeezed, and for once, I took Gabe's advice. I didn't think about anything. I let my feelings take over, and a surge of power from within me came out in a ball of blue energy, slamming into her chest and knocking her back.

Gabe rushed to her side, looking shocked.

"You don't touch him," I ordered.

Lillian's eyes were wide as she lay on the ground, seemingly in pain.

Bronson eyed me warily, trying to assess the situation, then said to Ryker, "We allowed you onto our property, but this is going against the treaty. It's time for you and your dogs to run along now. Ariel, you're welcome to stay as long as you promise to behave, and John, we will be having words."

He helped Lillian stand, and Ryker quickly nodded to his pack as they all rapidly shifted. Lillian squared her shoulders and tried to act unaffected, but she was shaken.

"Gabe," I didn't know what I was going to say, but he looked between his mother and me. Then his eyes moved to Dad, and he, too, was feeling all the conflicted emotions.

"We'll talk soon. You'll always be welcome wherever I am," I assured my brother.

Dad rubbed his throat where Lillian grabbed it, and I saw bruising starting to form. If I hadn't tossed her aside, the damage she could've done would've been permanent.

Lillian squared her shoulders and looked like she was trying to act unaffected, but I could tell she was shaken.

Farah held our belongings as she mounted Ledger's back. Micah nudged the guy I didn't know much about and silently told him to get on, then Reece approached my dad. I could run with the wolves, but I needed to make a statement. I needed to show Lillian it was Ryker and me. I placed my hand atop his back. He bent, reading me perfectly, and without another glance back, we ran.

Chapter Thirty-Two

Wolves from his pack joined us on our run. First, it was a few, then little by little, wolves ran with us. Eventually, Brogan, Ryker's dad, ran beside us, too.

We approached Ryker's road, and people who hadn't shifted yet, stood on the side, watching our return. Ryker stopped in front of our house. I dismounted, as did the others riding wolves. Ryker tilted his head to the sky and howled. The other wolves followed suit.

A rush of power slammed into my chest, followed by the overwhelming desire to pounce on my man. He caught my scent and tilted his head to the side, indicating I should get inside. He didn't have to ask me twice.

I opened the door to the house, and Ryker instantly shifted. His naked form with his well-defined muscles added to my desire. His mouth was on mine, and I felt the tight pinch between my shoulder blades as my wings sprang free.

Ryker kicked the door closed behind us, and I had no idea how much of a show we gave the outside world. I didn't care, though, it was him and me, and I craved him.

His lips pulled away from mine briefly as he murmured, "Finally, I have you back in our bed."

"I don't see any beds around," I panted as his head descended, taking my nipple into his mouth.

He grinned at me. "Then I'll fuck you against the wall first."

My hands roamed his broad shoulders when my eyes caught sight of his glorious cock. I didn't want to wait. I wanted him inside of me. The need almost felt as strong as the first time we'd been together, only now it was different.

Now, it was so much more because this man drove me insane with lust and held my heart. I didn't fully understand my past lives, but I understood my love for him held me to the present, wanting to soak up every moment.

He flipped me around, my wings to his chest and my breasts pressed against the wall.

"Spread your legs," he ordered. I happily complied, his warm breath against my neck. "I don't think I could hold back if I wanted to."

"Take me," I breathed heavily. The want in my voice was evident. His hands skimmed my sides, gripped my hips tightly, and tilted my hips. His cock gently nudged then he thrust in.

"Yes!" I cried out.

His hands stayed on my hips as he dove in and out of me. With my body pressed against the wall, I could hardly move, driving me even more wild. I tried to push back and meet his thrusts, but his body closed in on mine. There was barely any space between us. He was sending me a message that he was in control and was the one who was fucking me. A hand left my hip as his fingertips trailed up my arm, gripping my wrist, pinning me in place.

"There's nowhere to run, now," he breathed. "I have you right where I want you." He thrust deep inside me, and I couldn't help but feel like the big bad wolf had caught me.

"No ... where ... else ... I'd rather be," I rasped out.

"Good," he said, sliding his thick cock deep inside me, groaning as I clenched my muscles, squeezing his shaft.

It was enough to tip him over and take him from a place of being the one in control to being frantic with need.

His pace sped up, and I moaned in delight. My breast pressed into the wall, and I felt as that tight coil built inside me, ready to snap at any moment. Over and over again, his hard length slid into me, building me to a crescendo of bliss.

"Gods, you make me feel like a king. Like I could conquer anything while buried between your thighs."

The deep rasp of his voice set me off. Still pinned in place, my orgasm blasted through me. "Ride it out with me," he murmured.

With the last of my spasms, he used his foot to nudge my feet wider apart. Ryker released my wrist and grabbed my hips, jutting my ass out as I quickly braced my hands against the wall to keep my balance. Then he rode me.

In and out, he pumped so vigorously that it was only seconds until I climaxed again. He gave two hard thrusts, then followed suit, spilling his seed inside me.

He waited for a moment, resting his head against my shoulder. His chin brushed my feathers, and they moved in an involuntary response. Then he pulled out. I turned toward him. Tiny beads of sweat glistened against his skin, and I couldn't help but lick my lips in anticipation of licking that delicious body.

His nostrils flared slightly, and his dark eyes appeared darker, somehow more intense. We would go again and again tonight. We'd made it back here. We'd made it through hell. Now it was time for us to get lost in each other.

"Our cum drips down your leg, and our combined smell makes me wild."

It took everything in me not to look but keep eye contact. I'd take dark and bossy anytime.

"Come here," he commanded. I didn't think I could get much closer, but I took the small step between us, and because he was right there and his lips looked so delicious, I stretched on my toes and kissed him. It wasn't sweet. It was a hot and heavy kiss filled with all my passion for my mate.

He lifted both of my thighs, and I hooked them around his waist. He didn't break our kiss as he carried me to our bedroom. Once there, he laid me on the bed, breaking our kiss.

His fingers trailed feather-soft up my arm contrasting the wicked way he had just fucked me.

Goosebumps broke out against my skin. I ran my hand up his chest, feeling the tight muscles beneath my fingertips. I bent and licked his nipple, causing a slight growl, so I did the other one. His fingers slipped between my folds, and one lazily circled my clit.

My hand brushed the tip of his cock, and I ached to take him in my mouth. "I want your cock in my mouth. I want to taste what we taste like."

"By all means, love."

He rolled to his back, his giant cock lying against his stomach. I took him in my hand, pumped a few times, then moved to my knees to take him in my mouth. I swirled my tongue around the tip, opened my mouth, and took him in. His silky skin, mixed with our essence, drove me wild and made my pussy clench as he hit the back of my throat. He raised his hips and fucked my mouth as I relaxed my throat to take more of him. He moved deep again, and my pussy trembled.

"Move that beautiful ass toward me."

He popped free as I stroked him while angling myself so I was on display. Then, I bent forward and took him in my mouth again. He soared up, hitting the back of my throat, and simultaneously slid two fingers inside me. I moaned and could instantly tell by how his body tightened that it felt good to him. One hand stroked him while the other cupped his balls, and then his fingers entered me—first one and then another. As I bobbed, they slid out and massaged my tight, puckered flesh rubbing my asshole, causing me to moan again.

"Gods, I want to play, but I need to be inside of you even more," Ryker said, popping free and silently ordering, *"Ride my cock."*

"Bossy. Bossy." I tsked back, crawling on my hands and knees a short distance and swinging my leg over his hips. I rocked along his shaft for several moments, shuttering from the sensation of him hitting my clit. After a moment, I slid him inside of me.

Reverse cowgirl hit all the right places. I squeezed my muscles and rode him. His hands found my hips, then played with my ass cheeks, spreading them so he could watch.

He surged as I moaned so loud I was sure everyone heard it.

"You look amazing riding me."

Over my shoulder, lust burned in his eyes. His wolf was below the surface. His eyes darkened, then the space between his eyes elongated a little as the bone over his eyes morphed too. He was still a man, but his wolf was merging.

His speed quickened, and he reached around, rubbing my clit. I looked away from his face and to his fingers, drawing circles.

"My wolf wants you as bad as I do."

"Of course, he does. You are the same, are you not?"

"Fuck, Ariel, but I feel like I'm losing control."

"Let go. You won't hurt me."

"What if it's too much?"

"Then I'll put you to sleep or something."

A growl rumbled in his throat.

"Too soon?"

He surged forward again, making me shut up because another moan escaped my lips. He grunted in return, still holding back.

"Let go." I urged again. *"Let your beast free."*

"Fuck," he roared, then with an arm around my waist, he moved me forward and shifted behind me. I looked back at him again, and the shape of his eyes changed, looking more wolf-like than man. I wasn't bothered by it in the slightest. I loved every part of my man.

He grabbed my hips more forcefully as his wolf took control. I swear his dick hardened and grew larger, and I cried out from the fullness.

"Take it." His voice sounded deeper, giving me an order I felt compelled to obey. I arched my back and tried to open myself more to him. His hand left my hip, moved up my front, slid over a breast, then rested on my throat. He held it firm but not to hurt me. He rose to his knees behind me, and I braced for something.

I moaned again and clenched my muscles as he slid in and out of me.

"Yes!" I was getting close to that sweet place.

"Not yet, you don't." He pulled out and buried his face between my legs, licking my sensitive flesh from one side to the other. I whimpered in response. He repeated his actions several times without warning, so quickly I was sure it was his wolf's speed and not the human's. He slammed back into me, his erection shocking me. That shock was quickly replaced by pleasure and awe as he savagely fucked me. It was fierce and raw. He placed his hand against my throat again and raised me so my back was to his chest.

My moans were loud, followed by his deep grunts. Our bodies were slick with sweat, and the room smelled of sex.

"You're mine—my mate. You'll bear my cubs. You were made for me as I was for you."

"I am yours."

Then his teeth sank into my shoulder, and an orgasm so intense shattered through me. Just when it seemed like it would end, it picked up again. The intensity was so strong I felt it in every inch of my body. He grunted as he came, and then he let out a roar shaking the house.

As we relaxed, our bodies were spent. He held me in his arms. *"I'd go through hell all over again. It brought us right here with my father alive. I've never known this much happiness."*

"I'll spend my life ensuring every day is filled with the same love and happiness."

"I know you will."

"I love you," I whispered into the night.
"And I, you."

Chapter Thirty-Three

We pulled up in front of Brogan's house. Micah and Reece had brought Dad here, and we thought it prudent to drive instead of run. First, because after last night's sexathon, I was a tad bit sore, and second, we weren't sure how Dad would react to having to ride a wolf again. Perhaps a car was best.

Dad was sitting outside, watching the sunset over the cornfield. In the distance, you could just make out the colorful tents for the tournament the wolves were planning.

I walked briskly toward my dad, he stood, and I immediately hugged him. Brogan walked from the house.

"There you are. I thought you'd never let each other up for air," Brogan said, winking at me, causing my face to flush.

Ryker greeted my dad, "Hey, John. How are you?" he asked as he reached his hand out for my dad to shake.

My dad wearily took Ryker's hand, and I got a good look at his face. He looked tired in a way I'd never seen him. Our time apart had aged him.

"I'm grateful to be alive," Dad answered.

I swallowed all the hurt and angry feelings believing my dad was dead gave me. I looked at Brogan because it was easier than dealing with the knot of emotions inside me. "Hey, Brogan. Sorry about ..."

Brogan waived off my apology. "Not me who it affected. Besides, I think it all worked out. Anyone hungry?"

"I'm good," I said.

"Thanks, Pop, but we ate before we got here. How've things been around here? Has anything happened since we've been gone?"

Brogan scratched his chin momentarily as if in deep thought. "Let's see. I was visited by a set of bloodsuckers looking for their kids' whereabouts."

"They came to you? On your land?" Ryker seethed. Lillian and Bronson had a role in Ryker's mom's death, but now that we were linked, his anger, rolling off him in waves, caused me to flinch. I returned his fury with a feeling of love, hoping that would help.

"That's ... What is that?" Dad asked.

"Incredible, isn't it?" Brogan responded. "It's their bond. They're fated mates, which are extremely rare. Their match is more powerful than any match I've ever felt. It's not usually like this. It's a physical feeling, but I am surprised you feel it."

"Why is that?" Dad questioned.

"Because you're human. Unless," Brogan paused, sniffing the air, then looked at John, "You're human, but you're something more."

My eyes darted to Brogan and then toward my dad. The Keeper bloodline was from my dad, even though I'd yet to explore what that meant.

I summoned my courage and asked, "Dad, tell me what happened to you. Tell me about the Rosi, and your role, and how come I believed you died. Tell me about the Keepers, my mom, and my wings. I have so many unanswered questions. So many things I've had to piece together. I need to know who and what I am."

My dad looked at me with a slight tremor in his chin like he wanted to cry but was holding back. "I'll tell you everything, but by the looks of it, you've already figured a lot out."

"I need to hear it from you, Dad. I need to hear your version. Not some version I've dreamed about or put together."

"Very well, but I think I might need a drink first. Anyone?"

"Do you like a good scotch or bourbon, John?" Brogan asked.

My father looked at him pleadingly and replied, "Bourbon."

***

We were cuddled into each other. Seemingly knowing I needed his touch, Ryker pulled me onto his lap on Brogan's couch. Brogan's kitty purred against my legs until it finally became bold enough to sit on my lap. I lightly stroked her soft fur as she purred against my hand.

My dad sat across from us, sipping bourbon while Brogan leaned against the wall. We all waited for my dad to be ready to tell us what was happening.

Finally, after several long seconds and a large sip of his bourbon, he began.

"I don't know what you know, so I will start at the beginning. You were born to an ancient bloodline. Our bloodline has been responsible for keeping many things, secrets being the most important. Our ancestors led the Knights of Templar in protecting the holy grail. We've done our best to keep paranormal creatures like your mate from the rest of the world. We've sought out life's greatest mysteries and helped honor and protect them. They call our line the Keepers."

I nodded. "I've had dreams or visions with the Fates telling me I was the Keeper," I shared.

"Truly?" my dad asked in awe.

He looked away, "They have not spoken to me in some time."

For a moment, he looked lost in thought.

"John," Ryker said, bringing him back from wherever his thoughts had taken him.

"Oh, yes. The Rosi is a division of truth seekers who have worked alongside the Keepers for many years. It has always been an organic relationship and mutually beneficial as the magic cloaking the village from everyday view has been a great area of study for me. I've not worked for them but alongside them. For many years, this worked.

"When I met Lillian, I was enraptured with her. She took my breath away. I wasn't even sure she was a vampire. She acted so human and so soft. Every vampire I'd met had been anything but soft. I felt more alive with her than I had my entire life. When she became pregnant, I was over the moon. I loved her. She had secrets, but I loved her anyway. Who was I, after all, to judge someone for their secrets? I was a damn secret keeper!

"Her pregnancy happened faster than any human pregnancy, and something was different. There'd been something secretive about her lately, too. She'd take calls in other rooms and purposefully shut me out. I felt like I was losing her and wondered if I ever had her. She changed. Gone was the woman I fell for. She was sharper in her tone, more direct. I made excuses for her. Blamed it on the pregnancy. But as time passed, we became more distant, and then I questioned everything she did and her motives.

"I never told her about the Rosi. And I certainly never told her about my bloodline. It has been a secret I'd carried closely. Then one day, while Lillian was sleeping, I got curious. I went looking, and what I found shocked me. She had pages from some ancient book. It spoke of us and how a child born of a vampire and Keeper could unite the kingdoms and bring peace between the Fates and hell."

"You know, for everything being so secret, there sure are a lot of books ..." I mumbled.

"What books do you speak of?" My dad's face lit up.

"Let's see. I have pages I took from Cain. I have the book you left for me, *The Angels of Light*. I also know about *The Book of the King*."

He looked at me remarkably. "You found out so much in such a short time."

Ryker cleared his throat. "The story ..."

"Oh, yes. Sorry."

My eyes darted to Ryker, who held little patience. I should've been more astute. Hearing about Lillian might bring up a lot of emotions. I sent him a feeling of love, hoping to calm him.

He squeezed my thigh and looked at my dad pointedly, prompting him to continue.

"I didn't want you to be used. Some books have been written to manipulate, like *The Book of the King*. Words have power. There might be parts to that book that have truth behind it, but that book is dangerous."

"Don't I know it," I thought, sending that thought to Ryker.

"I put pieces together and saw what I'd been too blinded by Lillian's beauty to see before. She sought me out to get pregnant. She used me. It all started to make sense. When I confronted her about it, at first, she denied it. But then her callousness showed, and she told me she tried for years to have a baby to no avail. That's when she came across *The Book of the King*, knowing it would be her ticket. A vampire baby mixed with my blood would be everything to her and Bronson." He spat out Bronson's name like it tasted foul.

"She delivered you both earlier than expected. Bronson wasn't there, thank God, not that he hadn't been coming around more and more." He shook his head as if remembering the betrayal was too much for him. "Your brother was born ... and as I cleaned you and cradled you, I returned to the room and found her feeding him her blood. I had to flee with you. Once he had her blood, he became dependent. But you ... you were pure, and I had to take you. She was so caught up in him that we were gone before she noticed.

I ran. I didn't want you to turn out like her. It wasn't until you grew that we knew you were different." My father closed his eyes, pained to talk about this.

"How could you leave Gabriel?" I asked, my voice barely above a whisper.

He sighed, "I was too late with him. What was done was done, but you hadn't had her blood yet."

My chest filled with immense pain deep for Gabriel. I couldn't imagine how he felt knowing Dad had walked away from him. I also felt a bit angry. Dad could've figured out how to bring Gabriel with us, and besides, he's not a bad person. He's different, just like me.

Ryker rubbed my back, and my wings tingled, reminding me how different I truly was. It also reminded me of the atrocity my father did to me.

"I grew wings, and you cut them off?"

He looked shocked at my outburst. "Well ... you see ... It was—" He couldn't make a coherent sentence as he stumbled over his words.

It dawned on me that I still hadn't shown him my wings, only my abilities.

"Dad, look at me," I interrupted.

Relief that I wasn't expecting an answer washed over dad's features. I was but now wasn't the time.

Stretching and knowing what I needed to do, I was grateful to be wearing a dress with my shoulders exposed as my wings popped free. Brogan and Dad gasped.

"Every time you get faster and faster at that."

"I know. It's cool, right?"

Ryker grinned at me and silently asked, *"Are you doing okay?"*

"It's a lot. Some of it I pieced together already."

We were so caught up in our silent dialogue that I missed their reaction until a slight hiccup caught in my dad's throat as he silently cried and made the sign of the cross while Brogan sat looking awestruck.

"They grew back, " I said quietly.

"I'm so sorry, my dear. I'm so very sorry. I was trying to protect you. Look at you. You're magnificent!" Dad cried out.

"By the Gods, son," Brogan said.

"I need to tell you everything that has happened. From my dreams to my changing, to what Lucifer said."

Ryker emitted a slight growl at the mention of Lucifer, but they needed to know.

Brogan looked at Dad and said, "I'll get more Bourbon."

***

We talked for hours. Things came to me that I had forgotten to share with Ryker even. By the time we were finished going over every detail, it was late into the evening, and I was exhausted. Ryker, of course, noticed and called it a night. I felt dead on my feet, and the idea of lying in bed with Ryker was enough to have me practically running for the door when Ryker suggested it.

Brogan stood to escort us. "You've been through so much. Why don't you take the next few days for yourselves? I'll help with the pack. John and I will talk and see what our years of knowledge can come up with to help you. But don't worry about the pack right now. I'll run with them tonight."

Ryker clapped his dad on the back while I went back to my dad, who sat looking shocked by everything he heard. I bent low to hug him and whispered in his ear. "I forgive you, Dad. I love you, and I'm so grateful you're alive."

Emotion poured from him like a thick wave of heat hitting me in the face.

"Elle, are you alright?" Dad asked, drawing Brogan and Ryker's attention.

Ryker rushed to my side and put his hand against my head. Okay, so maybe it wasn't dad's emotions that felt like heat.

"Ariel, your skin feels warm," Ryker announced with panic lacing his voice.

"Would you like some water?" Brogan asked, heading toward the kitchen.

"I'm fine. Really." The whoosh of a heat wave came over me again.

Brogan rushed to me with a glass of cold water which I took a sip and then another. It cooled me momentarily.

"I'm taking her home. Dad, call Doc. Tell him to meet me at the farmhouse."

"I should come," Dad said.

"John, I'll call you if anything changes. I want to get her home."

"I'm fine," I protested again as my face flushed.

"Don't argue with me. Let's go," Ryker said firmly.

For once, I didn't argue. He was scared. I felt it.

I nodded, and Ryker practically carried me out of the house, ushering me to the truck as quickly as possible.

We arrived at his place at record speed.

"*Relax.*" I tried to calm Ryker, but I suppose throughout our relationship, I'd passed out too many times for him to feel relaxed.

"I'll relax when I know everything is fine. I want time with you where life is somewhat normal," he snapped.

"Hey," I said, placing my hand on his arm, trying to calm him. "I'm fine."

"You keep saying that, but your skin is burning up."

We weren't even to the front door when a set of headlights followed by another approached.

"*It's Doc,*" Ryker explained before I could ask. "*And Mindy.*" I was about to ask why Mindy was here when he answered again. "*I'm guessing Brogan called her.*"

Ryker opened the door and directed me to the couch. "Lay down. I'm going to talk to them. I'll be right back."

I obliged, feeling not necessarily unwell, just strange. With everything I'd been through, I wouldn't be surprised by any change at this point.

Ryker stayed outside, talking with Doc and Mindy, surprising me that they were out there for as long as they were. My impatience grew thin, and I was about to go out when suddenly, a huge wave of heat passed over me, and my stomach roiled. Leaping from the couch, I ran to the bathroom just in time.

Ryker rushed into the house and pulled my hair back, rubbing my back. I hated puking. Always had. I always cried whenever I did.

Mindy's presence was palpable as she peeked her head into the bathroom. "I think I know ..." she singsonged. Literally, I'm puking, and she's finding joy. *W.T.F.*

"I'd like to run some tests," Doc said.

I puked until nothing else was in my stomach, and I wanted to yell at everyone to get out. Who wanted to go through this with an audience?

"Mins," Ryker said, and when I lifted my head, she was gone.

Ryker was grinning at me. Do I have a massive glob of something gross on me?

I looked in the mirror. Everything was fine, then I quickly grabbed my toothbrush and rinsed my mouth. Ryker's hands gripped my hips and pressed his pelvis into me, showing me he was more than a little hard.

I turned back and gave him a death look. "Ew, do not tell me puke does it for you."

"Nope, not that," he grinned.

"As much as I love your sexy body, we're not having sex. I feel gross."

"I know."

"Then, dude, get that monster dick away from me."

He chuckled, then said, "I can't help it. When I'm around you, my body goes wild. Especially now."

"What do you mean, especially now?" It was safe to say he was officially freaking me out.

"Mindy is in tune with things."

"I know."

"She has a way with healing and life."

"I know," I said again, annoyed and watching Ryker's eyes in the mirror as they blazed with delight.

"She senses you're with child. Our child. Doc wants to run tests. But sweetheart, it looks like we might be having a baby." I looked at his fingers splayed over my stomach. Ryker seemed so hopeful, but all I felt was panic. We've been through hell. I'm Lord only knows what. Ryker is a werewolf. Then there's a touch of vampire.

"She could be wrong," I blurted. "I mean, how does she know?"

Ryker's brow furrowed. "You're right. Let's not celebrate until we know for sure."

He kissed the side of my neck. Instead of passion from his kisses or joy from this news, I was filled with fear.

Chapter Thirty-Four

It turns out Doc's tests were inconclusive, which made me feel somewhat better. Still, we'd been having unprotected sex since the beginning, and I wasn't ready to be a parent.

Even though the tests weren't conclusive, I still had bouts of hot flashes and vomiting spells. Ryker was more protective than ever, and if he sensed my fear, he didn't say anything about it. I figured it was because he was letting me figure out my feelings. Excitement was written all over his face, though.

He was hoping for a baby. He, as well as Brogan, thought there was no way Mindy was wrong.

Spending time with my dad became a daily occurrence, helping me heal from our recent trauma. It also kept my mind off what the future held.

Tonight, we were all going to the festival. While we were gone, the wolves planned their games along with a huge carnival for the town. During the day, there would be a huge carnival, and the wolves would have their private games in the evening.

I had to admit; if it wasn't for the lingering fears and doubts I held onto, I was excited about today. Being with the pack was beyond fun. There were so many different personalities and an overall sense of camaraderie and family.

Despite the games, Ryker had the wolves training, which didn't make much sense to me. Cain was behind us. We'd dethroned him. Why did everyone have this air to them as if they should be preparing for war?

The games consisted of speed, strength, and battle games. Most were set to take place in the forest, which was still as vibrant as the day I left it. Some of the games in human form were being held right out in the open, such as their version of MMA. Outsiders didn't even attempt to join the games, and that seemed strange, but I didn't question it.

Being back had its own set of challenges. Ryker always wanted me with him, but he had other things to do: a bar to run, a pack to lead, and he was overseeing the games.

Word on the street was Ryker might also be challenged for his pack role. So, as much as I enjoyed his company, I urged him to do what he needed.

Reluctantly, he eventually gave in, but not without leaving me a bodyguard. I was back to having a family member with me at all times.

I stepped onto the porch and felt the warm sun, then smiled at my dad as he immediately greeted me.

"Are you ready for a day of fun?" I asked.

"Always ready for anything my little girl has in mind," Dad said, his face alight with glee.

"Are we going to get this done, or what?" Brogan asked, moodier than usual.

"You don't have to babysit me. I'm sure everything will be all right."

"And if your mother shows up?"

I groaned. I hadn't thought about that.

Lillian had been trying to get me to see her, but I couldn't. I wasn't ready, and I didn't trust her. However, I missed Gabe. I hadn't seen him since I returned. Did he have the same feelings toward our dad as I had toward our mom?

Shaking my head, I shrugged off thoughts of Lillian.

"What will be, will be," I said.

"That's so zen of you," Mindy interjected, looping her arm through the crook of her dad's arm.

"Where'd you come from?" I asked.

"I thought you could use a girl."

I smiled. We hadn't been able to spend as much time together. With Mindy helping prepare for the games and her need to avoid Ledger, who had become my number one guardian, she'd been a little MIA.

"Is that what you're wearing?"

I glanced at my jean shorts and light blue tank and shrugged. "What's wrong with what I'm wearing?"

"Oh, nothing at all. It's just the entire pack is going to be there, and you're his mate. People will be taking notice of you in a way that I'm guessing you'll want to be a little more dressed up."

My face fell. I hadn't thought about that.

"No worries. I got you covered." She smiled, then let her dad's arm go, giving him a quick wink, then moved to the porch where a box was sitting. *How did I miss that?*

She handed me the box, and I opened it to reveal a beautiful white sundress. It was a simple design with small, white stitched flowers along the bodice. I held the dress to me. It was long enough to wear comfortably. I was excited to wear it because most sundresses were too short.

"It's beautiful."

"He'll be glad you like it," she responded, letting me know it was Ryker's thoughtfulness, not hers.

"I'll go change."

Inside the house, butterflies floated through my stomach, and I wasn't quite sure why. It was a nervous anticipation without any real reason.

I changed in the bedroom amid another wave of dizziness. Sitting on the bed for a moment to collect myself, my vision suddenly turned blue.

"Keeper," the voice singsonged.

"Keeper."

The blue tunneled, and I laid back on the bed, afraid I would fall.

"Keeper," the voice said again.

Closing my eyes, I let the voice wash over me. A moment later, I reopened my eyes only to be in utter blackness with nothing but blue light and that voice layered upon other voices.

"Your worlds are colliding. Did you know that Keeper? You have a choice that will be presented to you, and it will change everything. We can no longer see what your future holds. If you say yes, the future will be unknown. Do you understand?"

I shrugged. It probably wasn't the most stoic response. *"As always, I understand everything and nothing at the same time."*

"You will understand, Keeper. Very soon, a question will be presented to you."

"Copy that."

"We cannot predict what will happen to you. Free will is a gift."

"Thank you, Jesus," I said with a bit of snark.

"Guiding you has been our duty, and it has also been our greatest blessing. You will no longer have our guidance if you choose what we believe you will. Do you understand?"

Since I didn't remember my past lives with the Fates guiding me, well, I suppose I did, but also I didn't. I nodded even though everything felt like a riddle.

"It has been an honor, Keeper. Be well."

My vision cleared, and I came to with Mindy hovering over me on the bed. I was slightly disoriented and felt a little off, like something was changing inside me.

"Elle," Mindy called. "Elle, are you okay?"

Sitting, I looked at the bedside clock. It was after two. I swear the clock said twelve-thirty minutes before.

"I must've fallen asleep," I surmised.

Mindy gave me an all-knowing look, and the corner of her mouth turned up while, at the same time, joy twinkled in her eyes.

"Dad, she's up," she called. "You should fix your hair. Your power nap must've made it crazy."

I went to the bathroom, and sure enough, my make-up was a bit smudged, and my hair was a mess. Gah, this Ohio humidity did nothing for my hair.

"Where's your flat iron? I'll help you straighten your hair while you get the makeup from under your eyes."

"Straightening this will take forever. I have products in the drawer." She reached into the drawer and sifted through several products until she came across one that worked for curls.

"That's the one," I said, wiping the makeup away from under my eyes.

I ran the product through my hair and flipped my head, working with my curls instead of against them. They were slightly more manageable than usual. I grabbed a white scarf and tied it around my hair to pull it back like a headband. Next, I quickly touched up my makeup. I didn't do much, knowing we would be in the hot sun and not wanting it to melt off my face.

Mindy stood behind me in the mirror, examining me. "You're glowing."

I held in my groan, knowing she was convinced I was pregnant.

"Would it be that bad?" she asked.

I sighed, then gave her the truth I'd been holding back. "It's not that. It's just we're brand new. I'm changing and learning so many things. Everything has been one whirlwind after another. I wish we could just be without feeling like the other shoe will drop at any moment. I didn't think it was even likely I could have his baby. Brogan said it was rare for two different species to mate. What would a baby of ours even be? It's scary. If it turns out I am pregnant, we'll deal, and I'll love this baby like crazy. The thought of him or her scares the bejesus out of me. Does that make me a bad person? Because I feel like it does. People think I should be throwing glitter or some shit, but not even two months ago, I was driving to this town thinking my life was shit and I'd give this place a try, and now ... now I'm ... I don't know what I am."

I wanted to cry. I The back of my throat burned.

"Darling, are you ready?" Dad called from the hallway, quickly approaching.

I plastered on a smile. Fake it till you make it, right?

"Yeah, Dad. I think I am."

Mindy was still watching me in the mirror. "John, can you give us another moment?" she called back.

"Sure thing. Brogan and I will be waiting in the car's AC."

I didn't want to talk to Mindy. I wanted to rush out to the waiting car and pretend I didn't lay out all my emotions.

Panic was written all over my face and she released an exasperated breath of air. "Look, you're young. We forget that sometimes. Couples often wait years before the Gods reward them with a child. This has been a lot. Whenever you need to let it out, I'm here, okay? You don't have to bottle it up. No one thinks you're a bad person. You're allowed to feel however you feel." She rubbed my arm comfortingly, and I stared at her reflection, searching for any judgment. She met my eyes and held them unwavering.

"It's been a lot. You found out your mother is the she-devil. Your dad, who you thought was gone forever, was being held captive, and your instinct to seek out the truth brought you to him. You and Ryker almost died. You've evolved. It's not that you're afraid of being a parent. It's all the change. Most people would crack under these circumstances. So, I get it. There is no judgment from me. You can always talk to me and tell me exactly how you feel. Ryker has been giving you space to deal with your feelings. He doesn't want to push you. He wants to give you the time to process. I respect that, I really do, but maybe you two deal better together. We love you, Elle. All of us. Not a single family member would ever judge you, okay?" She searched my eyes to ascertain whether her words penetrated.

They did. I heard what she said, but it was more than that. I felt it. Her love through the pack was like a blanket cocooning around me.

I flashed a genuine smile. "I'm good. Thank you for being here. I'm fortunate to have you in my life."

"What are sisters for?" she grinned.

Sisters. I liked the sound of that.

***

The fair was packed. The town had more people than I could've ever imagined. Sweet-smelling cotton candy wafted through the air mixed with buttery popcorn. Surprisingly, there was a Ferris wheel and carousel, but beyond that, the rides mainly consisted of fun blow-ups.

We walked past two pre-teens jousting, and I caught sight of a mom and daughter going down a blow-up slide at least thirty feet in the air. Vendors had unique shops set up, and I was excited to look at all the wares. Huge white tents were set up for families to eat under.

Multiple tables were scattered about with signs for free face painting. There was a row of typical carnival games, and I smiled, catching young Ashton throwing a ball at a stack of pins, ready to knock them down.

"You got this!" Mindy shouted, causing Ashton to look our way, grin, then turn back and let the ball loose. He knocked down all the pins and jumped excitedly as the carnie asked him which prize he wanted. He settled on a small gray wolf, causing me to smile because it sort of seemed like the equivalent of a kid getting a baby doll.

Mindy ruffled his hair, and I noticed his mom sitting nearby with a baby to her breast. She didn't have a care in the world about breastfeeding out in the open, and honestly, it was beautiful. I rubbed my stomach. Could it be true? Could I have a tiny baby in my womb? For the first time, watching Caroline nurse her baby, I wasn't as afraid.

Mindy said hello to Caroline, and she quickly introduced my dad. Brogan seemed less like himself, there were too many people for his liking.

"Do you want to play?" Ashton asked so sweetly I had to accept. I attempted to hand the carnie money, but he declined and handed me the ball. "You can do it, Elle!" he cheered.

I let the ball fly and completely missed. Laughing, the carnie handed me the ball again. This time I hit the side of the pins, causing a little wobble but not much.

"Don't throw it so hard," Dad said as the carnie handed me a ball for the third time. I went lighter and missed again. "I guess I'm not a good shot," I said, laughing and handing the ball back to the carnie.

"Do you want to go again?" he asked.

I looked at a little girl waiting patiently behind us and shook my head, indicating it was her turn.

"Are you hungry? Because I am," Brogan announced.

"I could eat," Mindy said, rejoining after talking with her cousin.

I stopped at a booth and ordered a cheese steak. My dad grabbed pizza, and Brogan and Mindy went sweet with elephant ears. The carnies wouldn't accept my money for food either. "What did Ryker do? Show my picture to everyone working here and tell them the fair was free for me?"

"Something like that," Brogan muttered.

"I was kidding."

Brogan deadpanned.

"Seriously?" I questioned and was met with a quirk of Brogan's eyebrow.

"Do you not get that man would literally do anything to ensure your happiness?"

A group of women, who appeared to be in their early twenties, approached us.

"Mindy, is this her?" one of them asked.

"Yup."

"Oh, my God! I'm Angela," a cute redhead said, sticking out her hand.

"I'm Erin," a thin blonde introduced herself.

"Shana," another called out.

I shook Angela's hand. "Elle," I offered.

"Your hair is so pretty," Erin remarked.

"And look at that dress! It fits you so well," Shana added.

All right. I was not used to this type of attention.

Sensing my unease, Brogan stepped forward. "Ladies," he said.

Erin blushed. "Hi, Brogan," she breathed heavily.

He sighed as if he was used to this response but wanted no part. "This is John, Elle's father," he introduced.

My dad said hello, and it was clear he didn't elicit the same reaction as Brogan.

Over a loudspeaker, Micah's voice boomed. "Ladies and gentlemen, the junior category will show off their horse-wrangling skills in ten minutes. Please join us in the main arena."

"Oh, that sounds fun," I said. "Do you want to go?" I asked the group. I only intended to ask my group, but Shana immediately answered. "Yes! My little sister is showing her horse. I'd never hear the end of it if I didn't go."

The large group of us made our way to the arena, but not before picking up a few extra people headed that way. I felt popular, and it was odd. I was never a popular girl, and suddenly everyone wanted to be with us.

It made me think how when I first went to the watering hole with Mindy and Ryker, before I knew the things that went bump in the night were real, and how I'd received looks from so many people. Maybe it was because I was an outsider, and they didn't know me. I remember women's eyes on me who seemed jealous of Ryker's attention. Now I had everyone's attention. It made me feel uneasy, and I was glad for the dress Ryker gave me. Maybe he knew I would have this kind of attention.

Once we walked into the arena, I immediately spotted Micah. I waved at him a little over-enthusiastically. He waved back then nodded at an usher, who showed our group to the front of the arena. Shana, Erin, Angela, and the rest of their posse took their seats a few rows behind us, saying they would catch us later.

"This is weird," I whispered to Mindy.

"What do you mean?" she asked.

I shook my head, "I'm not used to all the attention."

"Comes with the territory," she replied.

My dad sat on the other side of me, and I studied his profile for a moment, thinking he looked like he had a little more pep in his step.

Reece popped by and checked in on us. Staying for only a few short minutes. It was clear everyone was extremely busy. Ryker was preparing for the games tonight, but I missed him.

Jesus, Elle. It's only been since this morning. Get a grip. I told myself while leaning into Dad.

"What was that, dear?" Dad asked.

"Sorry, my thoughts tend to wander sometimes."

"She's not wrong," Mindy added, picking up on the fact that my dad had heard my thoughts. "It's worse when those two are bumping uglies. It's like the entire pack can feel it."

My face flamed red, and embarrassment coursed through me. This was my dad. We didn't talk about this.

"Relax. It's not like John hasn't taken a bite from the forbidden fruit."

"Stop embarrassing the girl," Brogan chided.

"I can't help it. She makes it easy."

"I'm so mentally rolling my eyes."

"She's having fun with you."

My eyes grew wide as I heard Dad's voice in my head for the first time.

"This is pretty neat."

"Yeah. It has its moments."

Kids brought out their horses with pride written all over their faces. I was shocked when Asher came out with the mare who had reacted badly to me. Each child strutted their horse around the arena, and when Asher approached me, his mare gave him a bit of a hard time until she got what she undoubtedly wanted. She stood before us, and I kid you not, she bowed. Yes, the horse bowed. How strange was that?

"Are you seeing what I'm seeing?" Mindy asked Brogan.

"Indeed," he answered.

That was beyond weird to me, and I had about as much of that as I could take, so I did what any rational person would do. I ignored it.

"That kind of thing happen often?" Dad asked.

"Everything weird happens often," I responded.

"Where is that man of yours anyway?" Dad asked.

"He's busy with all of this." I waved my hand, indicating this fair was a much bigger deal than I would've ever imagined. "We'll meet up later," I assured Dad.

I couldn't help but notice an odd look on Mindy's face that was quickly masked.

Over the next several hours, we ate, played more games, and socialized. I was having a good enough time, but I wanted to be around Ryker.

Where exactly was he?

Chapter Thirty-Five
Ryker Hours earlier

"If they're any tricks to this, you're done. Got it?" Ledger pulled the squirrely man who'd traveled back from Israel with us to his feet.

"I saw the father do it. I know how it works. I can take you there and get you back, I promise. As long as you hold your end of the bargain."

"You have my word," I responded, having little patience left for this man. I needed him, though, and he knew it. "We leave in five minutes," I declared.

Ledger nodded for me to follow him, and we took several steps into the woods and out of earshot.

"You're sure about this?"

"Of course I am. She has our child in her womb. Whether she wants to admit it or not, a baby grows. I can feel it. I can't let that man walk this Earth knowing his brand of psycho might come after us at any moment."

"Yeah, but if she finds out …" Ledger's voice trailed, saying what we both knew to be true. Ariel would lose her mind if she found out I was going after that weasel Cain. She would want to protect me, but she doesn't get that I've had centuries of far greater opponents than him.

"She'll never know because you'll never tell her," I ordered.

"I think it's a mistake."

"Maybe, but I won't have her looking over her shoulder. When we were in Zoar, I was so out of my mind with worry for Ariel that I was sloppy. I let myself get captured. I need to rectify that, knowing she's safe while I do so."

Ledger was quiet in thought. "Do you think this time is different?"

"I know it is. I've died protecting her in every life, but never once did she love me the way she does now. It's different. She's different."

"Have you told her that you've loved her before?"

"No. The Fates forbid it; you know this. Just like they forbid you."

"I know … It's just … if we pull this off, then you'll go into this with secrets. Not sure that's a good look, man."

My irritation rose, partly because he was right and partly because there wasn't dick all I could do about it. "What would you have me do exactly? Go against the Fates?"

"No," he said, looking defeated. "You can't tell her any more than I can tell your sister what she is to me," Ledger said, looking defeated.

"Let's get on with this. The sooner we leave, the sooner we'll be back."

We walked back to the man with the father's cross in the palm of his hand. He whispered unintelligible words, and the cross rose. A portal appeared, and the man, Ledger, and I walked through it.

***

The sun beat on us, making me irritated. It was hard to find this place; if I wasn't a wolf, I wouldn't have found it again.

We received several looks as we walked through the town. But nothing put me on edge or made me feel like we were in danger. We ascended the stairs to the palace, and bitterness coated my tongue, a reminder of everything he put Ariel and me through.

"Halt!" A guard shouted, greeting us at the gate.

"Who's in charge?" I asked.

"We have a council that's been appointed until we decide what to do," the guard responded, shocking me that he gave that information so freely.

"We'd like to request an audience," Ledger requested.

"Come," the guard said, motioning for us to follow him.

Ledger made eye contact with me, silently saying he wasn't sure about this, but my intuition told me this was the way to go. We needed to trust not all Rosi were bad.

He led us to a room and knocked twice before entering.

Several men and women sat around a table, and an older woman with long, flowing white hair immediately stood as we entered.

The rest followed suit, but it was easy to see who was in charge.

"We know who you are," she said. "Please join us."

Ledger and I walked into the room, taking into the diverse group.

"We want to start this by apologizing for everything you and your mate have been through. Abbas and his son ... made choices that do not reflect us. We were never meant to be a group born of hate or greed. We collectively know power can lead to both things, which is not who we are. Our mission and values have always been to protect the world's truth and secrets. The world slowly becomes ready for some secrets, but with others, like yourself, we are far from wide acceptance. It has never been our intention to allow a single ruler. We apologize."

"What Cain did to us cannot stand," I demanded.

"It won't—it's not," A younger man replied.

"How can we know?"

"We'll show you," another said, then added, "and if it's not enough, you can have him."

I nodded in agreeance.

"Show us," Ledger ordered.

***

"That's him," Ledger said, looking at a defeated Cain working the fields. Guards stood nearby, watching over several men. One whiff of them and I instantly knew the other men were loyal to Cain, so loyal that they'd assisted in our torture. The urge to shift and bite their heads off was real.

Cain's head slumped forward, nearly passing out from exhaustion. The guard approached him, and Cain's tear-stricken face begged to be left alone. The guard didn't speak, he shook his head once, and Cain cried harder.

"He's pathetic," I admitted.

At my admission, Cain's eyes connected to mine. I was too far away for a human to hear me, and I never sensed him as anything more than a man.

"You—" he barely got out before a guard stood over him and whipped him with a cat o' nine tails.

Cain cried out in pain.

I looked him dead in the eyes and smiled.

His face paled even more.

He knew I wasn't going to kill him.

"What do you want to do?" Ledger asked.

"Nothing. Death would be too easy. He's living his own worst nightmare."

I took one last look at Cain. His lips mouthed, "Please."

Ignoring Cain, I turned my back on him and focused on Ledger.

"You sure? I saw what he did to you."

I looked around at how pathetic Cain and his men were. The moment they were stripped of power was the moment they gave up. Weak.

"I'm sure," I said, not looking back, then looked to the man who brought us here, "Let's go home."

"What?" he questioned.

"That is not a man. That is a broken coward. I came to seek revenge, but the Fates have their own revenge in mind. We're done here."

***

"Is everything ready?" I asked Reece.

"We're all set," he replied with a huge grin. "Micah said she has no idea."

"Good. How long until she gets here?"

"I don't know why you're asking. You said nine. She'll be here at nine."

"And Gabe?"

"Still no response."

"Dammit. She would've wanted him here," I growled in frustration.

"Are the games set for later?" I turned to Grey, who ensured everything went off without a hitch.

"Yeah, the wolves are amped."

"Good."

Thirty long minutes later, I sensed a car. She was here. She was a beaming presence that I felt to my core, and this time she was mine. I wasn't going to waste this life with her. I would do everything I could to make the most of it. I finally had her, and I was damn well going to do whatever it took to keep her.

Every single life we had together ended in tragedy. She loved me in her own way, but we'd never been together, not like this.

Whatever Lillian did to mix her bloodline finally gave her to me, and for that, I was grateful.

But they had a plan.

There was always a fucking plan.

Today it didn't matter, though. Today, I was going to claim my mate in front of our people. When Ariel arrived at my house, I knew the Fates had again decided to intervene, and of course, I was angry. She didn't remember me. She never fucking did. I had to pretend I had no fucking clue who she was when we'd spent lifetimes knowing and losing each other.

Not this time, though.

This time she bared our child.

This time I saw her soul.

This time I've had her body.

Not only is she mine, but she's a force to reckon with this time.

I'm certain Lucifer isn't done toying with us. I'm sure Lillian has her hand in it somehow or other, but I'm not wasting a second of this life. I'm going to love her to the fullest.

I stood in a clearing in the woods, overlooking the watering hole. We were on the opposite side of the small lake, and I wasn't certain we'd ever run this way. The air was warm, but the gentle breeze had a sweetness to it. Many of my brethren were in wolf form. But many stood by, gazing at me with huge grins.

I loved my people. And they loved me. Many of the women took shifts today to make sure this was set up how I wanted it. It was worth it when Ariel finally approached. She looked stunned but also more beautiful than I'd ever seen her. Her blonde curls were everywhere, wild and without abandon, sort of like her. The white sundress hit her hips and flared out, and her ample bosom couldn't be missed. She looked beyond perfect.

An aisle of red rose petals, surrounded by flickering candles, led the way to me. Her face lit up as she took it all in, and I swear my heart missed a beat. She was that stunning.

A small drum, accompanied by a rhythm only our eldest in the pack knew how to perform, thrummed through the forest. The sound bounced off the trees adding to the already electric feeling.

Anne, the best singer in our pack, began to sing in her melodic voice. The song wasn't in a language spoken today, but it spoke of emergence and love. It didn't matter if you knew the words or not. You couldn't help but get swept into it.

Ariel took a step and then another. My fate was about to change forever. I was going to have the life I dreamed of finally.

Chapter Thirty-Six

"What's going on?" I questioned. We pulled up to the woods where the first games were meant to be, but something was off. The woods were eerily quiet, and soft flickering candles lit a path.

My father was beside me. "Ryker asked for your hand earlier today. Even though you're mates, he wanted to give you a wedding. Can I walk you down the aisle?" he asked almost sheepishly, as if I would ever say no.

Tears filled my eyes. After thinking my father was lost to me, and now having him walk me down the aisle, my heart leaped.

I nodded, unable to speak.

I looped my arm with Dad's as Mindy and Brogan disappeared. Then a small smile quirked my lips. It was their job to keep me occupied today.

"Are you ready to meet your mate?" Dad asked.

"So ready," I replied with a smile, even though my voice cracked with emotion as I did.

I stepped on a layer of rose petals. Before we took another step, I closed my eyes, took in the scent of earth and roses, and let nature pour through me. I reached out my senses and felt Ryker waiting for me. I felt everything, including the gentle breeze on my skin and the steam from the nearby swimming hole. I sensed his pack and their energetic hum, my dad's warmth and comfort beside me, and sent an outpouring of love back into the forest.

Opening my eyes, I was surprised—but shouldn't have been—when roses bloomed around me. The reds so red and vibrant that they nearly looked fake.

Dad's eyes widened. "You're incredible, daughter of mine. I couldn't be happier walking you to this future."

Then, we took a step and another. Music, unlike anything I'd ever heard before, played. There was a steady drum beat as voices layered in a hum to create a symphonic melody. A woman's voice sang in an unfamiliar language, filling me with peace and happiness.

Glowing wolf eyes stepped forward from the darkness, lining the path. Then I spotted him—my mate. Ryker.

He wore black dress pants and a white linen shirt. I could make out enough details to know it was made by the same person who made my dress. His hair appeared recently trimmed, and that five o'clock shadow he woke with this morning was long gone. His eyes met mine, and I felt all his love shining through.

More roses popped free behind Ryker, and several surprised onlookers gasped. Brogan stood by Ryker's side, followed by Ledger, Micah, Reece, and Grey. On his other side stood Mindy and Farah, then other wolves I'd met recently. Some people elected to be in human form, while many stood by as wolves.

The singing stopped as I reached Ryker. Dad shook his hand and then found his place next to Farah.

Ryker clasped my hands and brought them to his lips, kissing my knuckles. His eyes were trained on mine when he spoke. He looked to the sky and then back to me. "It's a full moon tonight, love."

I looked up; he wasn't wrong. "Yes, it is."

"You know full moons are when wolves come out to play." His eyes glinted in the moonlight as he spoke. "This isn't a wolf tradition, but I wanted you to have it. I wanted to give this to you. Be my wife as well as my mate. Declare it in front of my pack, your family," he ordered.

"Are you asking me to marry you?" I asked with a smile.

"No, I'm telling you."

"So bossy," I whispered, then in a more serious tone, I replied, "You're my heart, and I wouldn't have this any other way."

Brogan stepped behind us. "Shall we begin?" he asked.

"You're marrying us?" I asked in awe.

"It would be my honor."

"Thank you."

"You're beautiful," Ryker said, eyes fixed on me. "Every day, I wake beside you and know what a lucky man I am."

Tears welled in my eyes.

"Don't make her cry," Brogan muttered, then addressed us so his voice would carry. "When I met your mother, I was so much like you. I was in love and wouldn't trade a second of it. Finding your mate is what we all dream of.

Even if losing her has made me lose myself. She was everything to me, and there's not a day that goes by that I take it for granted."

My eyes softened on Brogan. He was a proud man, and exposing his heart to everyone couldn't be easy.

"Son, you said to Ariel you are a lucky man. I agree, but at the same time, I don't. Today, we are here to witness two mates wed. Not only showing their union to the pack but taking the culture Ariel was raised with and sharing their joy with everyone. The Fates blessed the two of you, and although it may have taken a lifetime to get here, you are blessed. There is no luck. Only two souls that destiny finally decided to let settle. Praise be that you live a long life together filled with all the happiness and joy your mother and I had."

"Praise be," voices murmured back from the crowd.

Ryker's eyes held mine as he spoke. "My whole life, I've waited for you to be mine. I promise to love you always. I promise to be patient. I promise to wake every morning with you in my arms and go to bed each night with gratitude. My heart never knew beauty or peace until it knew you. I'm lost in you. To my people, my father is right. This is a blessing. One I hope for all of you to have one day. Praise be."

My chin quivered. I was going to cry but didn't want to. Mindy sniffled to my right, but my eyes were locked on Ryker's, my hands clasped in his.

"When I first met you, I didn't understand this pull to you. I didn't understand anything, really. This whole place seemed so foreign to me. Honestly, I felt a bit like I was in the twilight zone. I mean, something was a bit different here. I remember hearing wolves in the field." Ryker smirked as I babbled. "Anyway, I've been through many changes and made many mistakes along the way. But through it all, you've stood by my side. You've guided me and held my hand. You hold my heart and soul. I don't know how to explain everything I've been through, but it feels as if I've always known you and every step of this life brought me here with you. Whatever changes are to come, I'm grateful to have you by my side. I love you and the world you opened my eyes to."

"Praise be," the crowd whispered. Mindy hiccupped as she full-on cried at this point.

The rest of the ceremony was a blur of excitement. Several elder wolves brought forth gifts. A young girl brought a crown of flowers and placed them on my head. Several people had things to say, praising the Fates for our union.

Then finally, Brogan grasped our hands, "Son, do you take this bride and promise to give her the life of a wolf's mate, love her always and give me grand-pups?"

There were a few chuckles from the crowd, but Ryker held my gaze, "For all of eternity."

"And Ariel, do you take my son as he is? Do you promise to love him, embrace the pack, and cherish this love?"

"For all of eternity," I responded.

"Then son, daughter ... I now pronounce you fated mates and husband and wife."

People cheered. Wolves howled.

I barely registered them because Ryker was kissing me. It was a hard and demanding kiss that my body instantly responded to. Then I felt something else entirely—something I couldn't quite discern.

My vision turned blue, but not like it had in the past. This was abrupt, beginning at the edges and working toward the center. It drew into me and rushed down my throat, landing in my abdomen.

No, that wasn't quite right—it stopped in my womb.

Chapter Thirty-Seven

I was running.

The moon reflected off the water, giving the night sky a soft glow. My heart hammered in my chest as I leaped over a boulder. Wolves howled nearby.

He was close.

I could feel him.

I veered into the woods away from the water, moving at an unnatural speed, even for me. A large green rock, at least twenty feet in height, appeared. Suddenly, I knew exactly where I was. The cave entrance was ahead.

Butterflies took flight in my belly.

He would find me here.

Slowing and doing my best not to make a sound, I made it through the dark opening. My eyes adjusted from the darkness to the moon-coated clearing. Everything looked sharp and crisp like I'd never seen before. But I had been here.

He took me for the first time here.

I climbed atop the boulder he first pinned me against and froze as I spotted glowing eyes mirroring the moonlight. A massive black wolf prowled toward me.

I should be afraid.

Instead, I was breathing rapidly. The anticipation of what was to come was overwhelming.

The wolf stalked me as if I was prey.

Maybe I was.

"*Undress,*" a deeper voice than Ryker usually used said. It was huskier, more demanding.

Adrenaline coursed through me. I'd never had the wolf boss me, and I didn't know what to expect.

"*Now, Ariel.*"

"Um..." What else could I say? My mate, who was a wolf, but was also a man, was telling me to get naked.

He approached, towering over me.

"Do you fear me?"

"I don't know."

"We're separate but the same."

I closed my eyes, feeling Ryker's soul connect with mine. His cold nose pressed against my neck, connecting me to Ryker. I ran my hands through the thick black fur when my eyes flew open as he nipped my neck. The wolf then lapped it and ordered, *"Get undressed."*

I did as my wolf demanded, my wings springing free once I was nude.

"You glow under the moonlight. Your skin is perfection."

My wolf rubbed against my naked body, then took several steps away from me and transformed into Ryker.

He was naked. Every muscle was on display.

"Did my wolf frighten you?"

"Maybe a little."

"You never have to fear the beast within me. He might be more possessive of you than me."

"It's not that," I replied shyly. "He looked at me the way you look at me."

"How was that? Like he wanted to taste every inch of you? Like he could lap at your sweet body for days and never tire? Or like you are the most precious being to walk this Earth?"

"Yes."

"To which part?"

"All of it."

"That's right, Ariel, because we are the same. He doesn't get to have you the way I do, but he can admire you. I let him taste your skin. You weren't in any danger, but we liked your fear."

"Does it excite you?"

"Very."

"Then come here," I ordered.

Ryker took two steps forward so we were practically touching.

"Did you like your wedding?"

"Very, very much."

"The roses that bloomed were beautiful, but they pale in comparison to all that is you."

"You're beautiful," I told him. "Your wolf is, too. But your heart, your words, and your loyalty are truly something. Thank you for tonight. I loved it, and I love you."

"I love you."

I ran my hands up his chest. One hand settled over his heart while the other hand cupped his jaw. "I choose you." I don't know why those words came out, but they felt important and were exactly what I needed to say.

"With all my heart, I choose you."

Then he kissed me. My lips parted as the tip of his tongue licked the seam. His hands roamed my back and pulled me flush against him. He brushed a spot in between my wings that caused me to moan.

Breaking our kiss so he could trail his lips over where his wolf nipped me, he mumbled, "I think I found a sensitive spot." Then he ran his fingers over that same spot, and I nearly came undone.

"Shall I fuck you against the rock like our first time? Or lay down on the ground and have you ride me?"

Oh, how I wanted all of that.

But what I really wanted was to make love.

"I just want you," I said simply.

"Oh, you'll have me," he replied, his voice thick with an undercurrent of lust.

My nipples hardened.

His cock twitched.

His fingers splayed over the spot between my wings.

I kissed him, moaning into his mouth. With the feel of him so close, my body was on fire with desire.

He hitched my leg around his hip, pressing close.

He guided his cock through my folds. "Always so wet for me."

"Always," I murmured back, too caught up in everything Ryker to form a coherent sentence.

Then with one quick thrust, he was inside me. More intense than ever before.

"Yes!" I cried out.

His eyes connected with mine as he slowly guided himself in and out.

The stone was cold behind my back as he grabbed my other leg and lifted me completely, impaling me on his beautiful dick.

"Gods, you feel amazing."

His hand brushed the spot again, and I instantly came. It was fast, and it was hard, and then it turned his slow into powerful thrusts. Then he was coming, and my entire body felt more alive than ever.

As he finished, I started to move my leg and disconnect.

"No, honey, I'm just getting started."

He laid with me, still connected, and kissed me slowly. His shaft which had never truly gotten soft, grow hard again. He was back to soft and sweet, and it was everything.

This time we took our time. We worshipped each other's bodies.

We connected wordlessly, letting our bodies speak for us, saying everything we meant to one another. When we were both spent and exhausted from multiple orgasms, we held each other under the moonlight and drifted off to sleep.

I did this knowing this was the life I chose with the man I loved, and I felt complete in a way I never had before. I was his, and he was mine. I'd lived lives and lost him. The Fates never quite aligned for us. But they were now, and I vowed to do everything in my power to hold onto that love.

Epilogue

"We should give it to them. Look at how happy they are. They deserve to know everything."

"Sister, you know that we cannot."

The Fates spoke to one another, arguing about what should be done with young Ariel and her mate, Ryker.

"What if we gave them an inkling about what was to come?" Both sisters spoke in unison as they always did.

"She made her choice and chose her man. She chose her future."

"But not the future of their unborn child."

"No, definitely not," both sisters singsonged again.

"When do you think she will realize her baby is the new Keeper?" The blonde Fate asked.

"We will have to see, won't we?" The Fates snickered.

"Oh, sister. Even though this is a deviation of what was supposed to happen, we know there will be a similar outcome—"

"—Lucifer will fail."

"He must fail."

"He always fails."

"And the truth—"

"—It will be protected."

As the twins declared the truth's protection, the red-headed sister threw her head back. Her eyes whitened as they often did when she received a vision.

Moments later, her head came down, and her eyes cleared.

" Ariel and Ryker's story is not over. Far from it."

Thank you

Thank you for taking the time to read this story. It's been a different and unique experience writing these characters. No book is ever created individually. It truly takes a team. Thank you to my ever-talented cover designer, Hang Le. Thank you to Kyleigh Poultney for editing. Thank you to Melissa and Katie for reading and being awesome sisters. Thank you, Jo Annette, you did an awesome job beta reading! Thank you, Louisa Brandenburger. I just love you. Thank you, Mary Tatar. Thank you, Mindy, Shana, Jessica, and Misty. You are my homies. I love you.

About the Author

Abby McCarthy has published both contemporary romance and motorcycle club romances. This is the first in a brand-new paranormal romance series.

She resides in Northeast Ohio with her husband, three kids, and three dogs. In her spare time, she enjoys a fabulous happy hour, good times with friends, camping, reading, and writing.

Read more at https://www.abbymccarthyauthor.com.

Printed in Great Britain
by Amazon